LONE HORSE
— •IN THE• —
HINTERLAND

LYN SHEA

To order additional copies of this book, contact:
Xlibris Corporation
0-800-644-6988
www.xlibrispublishing.co.uk
Orders@xlibrispublishing.co.uk
303749

PART ONE

ONE

The brewery offices were homed in an impressive glass building next to the tax offices in the epicentre of the city. In his grandfather's day they were situated next to the main distillery on the outskirts. Back then a woman sat typing furiously at a front desk, catering to everyone who made demands, from the draymen to the directors.

Mounting the steps he trod slowly to give himself time to prepare and be in command of the situation. In truth he was not in command at all, he was very much the opposite.

The place was deserted, except for an elderly man in a fancy purple jacket with lapels and braiding, sitting behind a desk to the right hand side of the foyer.

Charlie Roberts avoided the man and looked at the floating staircase along which he saw descending a tall woman with exquisite bone structure.

She was wearing tight grey silk-finish pants and a long sleeved garment in a pale blue colour—a design he thought he had seen in an ad for Armani jackets in one of Heather's magazines. The woman's hair was glossy blue black and tied into a long tail which swayed behind her with the same elegance as her figure.

He walked purposely forward and held out his hand.

"Mrs Gordon? . . . I'm Charlie Roberts . . . I think we have a twelve thirty appointment!"

A quizzical expression appeared on her features and she met his hand with two of her slender fingers, not quite sure if she should return the gesture. She smiled widely, her dark brows arching above her perfectly formed face with its flawless skin.

"Have I got the time wrong?" he asked.

She turned towards the desk to catch the eye of the man in uniform and Charlie Roberts felt his confidence ebb away under this unexpected abreaction. It threw him off balance.

Then from another direction came a female voice.

"Mr Roberts? . . . I believe it's myself you want today. I'm Petra Gordon!"

He turned to see a different woman, different in every aspect and sense.

The dark haired beauty laughed and with her slender fingers removed an aerosol spray from the pocket of her jacket.

A dull thud in the pit of his stomach as he realized he had been talking to the cleaner.

"Come this way Mr Roberts!" instructed Petra Gordon, a manufactured cheerfulness in her voice. While the dark haired girl still smiled good naturedely and sailed towards the front entrance through which he had arrived and began polishing the steel rococo trimmings of the outer door.

"I apologize . . . . I thought . . ." Charlie Roberts stuttered as he walked behind the swiftly moving Petra Gordon up the stairs.

"Don't worry about it . . . she's Lithuanian and speaks only a few words of English!"

"That's not what I meant! . . ."

Mrs Gordon ignored this comment as if it were beneath her contempt. The fact that men of various rank and persuasion would rather address the cleaner on first glance than herself—despite the fortune she spent on her grooming and make-up—was something she largely chose to ignore.

Aware that he might have annoyed her Charlie Roberts wondered how he would ever manage the next hour of torturous supplication for further time to meet his rent demands and stay in business.

*   *   *   *

Richie Southern saw Tess running from a mile off—her weight had increased since christmas and she had gained half a stone at least. He wondered with trepidation if she were perhaps pregnant.

As she came closer he turned away and concentrated on Titch, his peregrine falcon, caressed the bird's head; the thought of this possible new development made him seek distraction in something or someone who did not disappoint him. He pretended not to have noticed her and heard her panting as she lurched to a halt three feet away.

"I've been fired . . . the bastard fired me!" she gasped, and her panting became a prelude to tears.

Richie held his reaction in check and the bird on his wrist. He declined to comment.

"You hear?" said Tess.

"I don't know why you're surprised . . ." He lifted the bird and threw his arm forward, allowing her to make flight, "the amount of liberties you take!"

"That all you can say?"

"What do you want me to say?" The skyline was silver blue darkening to pewter in the far south. "I'm not one for lying Tess . . . you know that!"

"You could be more sympathetic!"

Tess was hot and flustered and her cheeks were tinged with the shade of pink beloved of nineteenth century artists. She had moist sprigs of hair on her forehead, her full mouth opened to reveal perfectly white teeth. She should have been madly desirable to him, but she wasn't.

She watched him with china blue eyes and waited for him to say something ameliorating. He was staring at the sky and the amazing swoops and whirls of his bird as it rose and fell and made patterns his eye delighted in. His eyes expressed that kindling warmth of constrained love, the sort of love a man has for his child perhaps; the kind of look Tess knew he would never have for any child of hers because she just would not have one.

"Fuck you!" she said and turned on her heel and headed slowly back to the caravan.

*　　*　　*　　*

Behind the bar at the Golden Hind Glen pulled a pint of lager for one of the regulars and at the zenith of the pump action craftily looked at his watch. The barmaid was late—again!

". . . . so you reckon it's all tabloid hype then?" enquired the regular, a man named Ross who frequented the Hind more than he frequented his own kitchen.

Glen nodded briefly and cleared his throat. "Maybe . . . I can't see it being the case myself!"

Glen was a young man of few words; he was not the jovial host, but it didn't matter because neither was he the landlord so it was not demanded of him. Expected at times, but not obligatory. Charlie, as landlord, was hardly the jovial host either, so the tone was already set.

Charlie himself was more the efficient proprietor of a modern bar and the regulars accepted that, in the way they accepted that they could no longer sleep it off on the seating after closing time; it was part of the changing modern world.

"It's got to have some basis to it . . . it was in one of those magazines with the inside gossip on the soaps!" persevered Ross.

Glen seemed unbothered by this elaboration and his eyes slid from right to left—but not at the level of Ross's face—as he considered his job here should the rumours be correct. He considered also the fact that the barmaid might not show at all. He was going to have to have words with her, she was proving more of a nuisance when Charlie wasn't around.

"You heard the rumours? . . ." Ross was saying to another regular.

"What are those then?"

The other regular was pleased to find there was something to talk about that was all inclusive and gave an uplifting feel to the 'happy hour' refreshments.

"They say they're writing Heather out of that series . . . . dramatic ending where she dies!"

"Get away!" The newcomer looked to Glen for confirmation. "There's only just been the storyline where she married that Italian!"

"Means nothing . . . . you know how far fetched these soaps are!"

They both looked to Glen for support and were unsurprised to see his expression set as always in neutral.

"Bet that'll be a dip in Charlie's income if it's true!" Ross said.

"You can say that again!" affirmed Glen impassively.

When the side door opened Glen looked up expectantly, it was the entrance Charlie always used, but his vision settled on Tess instead. She seemed to be dressed more for the stables than the bar, though he couldn't be certain because the pub interior was dark against the stark contrast of the daylight.

Tess smelled of horses or dogs, or some other kind of four legged animal. Glen pulled her elbow and guided her to the tiny room where the dartboard and flatscreen television were housed.

"What time do you call this? I should have gone home half an hour ago! . . . and why've you not showered and changed? This is a pub, Tess, not the beer tent at a gymkhana!"

"Sorry! . . . there was a problem with one of the geldings and I had to go down the vets! . . . ."

"There's always a problem!" Glen said. "If it's not the horses it's the boyfriend . . . . I'm reporting it to Charlie this time!"

Tess stuffed her bag beneath the till and straightened her hair, perspiring and flushed from the dash to get here. She smiled weakly at Glen's retreating back. "I'm going at the end of the week anyway!"

The lack of malice in her voice made Glen immediately contrite. There was never any malice to Tess, she was entirely without edge and eternally on the wrong end of things. She was one of those nice people who make others want to help them and end up exasperating with her lack of common sense.

Glen stood with his back to her. Questions formed in his mind about whether any other reason besides her own work failings had been given by Charlie as a reason for her dismissal—like a deficit in his private income, for instance, caused by Heather being axed from the t.v. series.

"What can I get you?" asked Tess pleasantly of a complete stranger at the bar. Things would work out, they usually did. It was just a matter of waiting to see the next big idea life threw at you.

*　　*　　*　　*

The land Richie used as a short-cut to Rookeries belonged to Norrington's Dairy & Poultry Farm, the biggest in the county. Relations were strained between Norrington's and the smaller agricultural farm on which Richie rented the land for his caravan, for no better reason than no-one could recall a time when it hadn't been so in the last two hundred years. It was almost a point of honour that the rivalry felt since some long ago feud be held in perpetual regard. Norrington's Farm had little to gain from this and not much to lose but was ruled by a man who lamented the passing of the Feudal system without actually knowing it.

Rookeries was situated on a stretch of land owned by the smaller farm, for whom Richie also worked part time. Rookeries was a falconry and bird of prey sanctuary, open to the public. Founded twenty odd years before by Scott Brangle, a New Zealander who found himself getting married in the middle of a hiking tour of Britain and settling in the country of his in-laws.

Rookeries struggled financially at first, their income augmented by Scott's knowledge of forestry and the casual employment offered to him by neighbouring landowners and farmers. Then suddenly a massive resurge of interest happened in the countryside and nature issues generally and the business had taken a new direction.

Rookeries had expanded, renting from Chester's a further swathe of woodland, the rights to which were somewhat disputed by Norrington's as being actually theirs by historical covenant and never properly transferred to Chester's at all.

This contention met with little success and was enjoyed more as a hobby horse by Ged Norrington than any serious lawsuit at which money should be thrown.

Larger-than-life Ged Norrington was as usual at this time of day out with his German Shepherds and overjoyed to see Richie in the distance with Titch on his arm, skirting the acreage where Norrington cattle grazed.

He watched them cover an eighth of a mile, now and then raising his binoculars and zooming in as if he would learn something new. It felt like a satisfying itch he couldn't scratch, a wholesome reaction to some familiar irritation; letting him know who he was and what was dear to him. He couldn't at times like these fathom his own reactions and he seldom tried. His wife did that for him, though not very successfully.

Suddenly he ran, with surprising agility for someone of his size and bulk, and covered half the distance between the younger man and himself in less than three minutes.

"Oi . . ."

Richie stood stock still, Titch squawking at the intrusion into the otherwise silent landscape.

"Get off my land with that bird!"

Richie felt no inclination to react.

"You hear me? . . ." Ged roared.

"I'm taking the short-cut." Richie did not move, his eyes fixed on the farmer's face. "Not harming you is it?"

"Get that bird off my land now . . . it's already had two of my nieces' rabbits!"

"I doubt it . . ." Richie felt the impulse to move, turning in readiness but not taking his eyes off the older man. "She's either with me or she's tethered!"

"A bird was seen near the garden . . . one of your birds . . ."

Richie walked on and Titch squawked, upset by the tension in the air.

Ged Norrington moved closer. "Don't bring that fucking thing over here again . . . you got no right of way, no more than anyone has!"

Richie walked on, ignoring the comment, refusing to rise.

"If any more rabbits go there'll be war!"

"Won't be none of our doing if it's the case!" Richie called. "Anyway, you personally shoot enough of them on your travels . . . ."

"Them's not the rare expensive variety and well you know it!"

"Animals are animals to me . . . I don't put price tags on 'em!"

Richie increased his stride. Titch screamed loud enough to deafen him.

Norrington turned and retraced his steps. He hated Rookeries and its henchmen and its nature-struck admirers. Scott Brangle and Richie Southern he hated particularly; not only were they full of their own importance, they were that detestable breed—Animal Rights advocates. Up to all sorts, especially the younger one passing currently.

Ged Norrington spat at the tangled and sodden brambles of the hedgerow and pushed his decrepit trilby hat to one side. He whistled his dogs and waited for them before carrying on his way.

From the distance, to any stranger, he looked like a shambolic sort of vagrant or an eccentric rambler, wearing the same clothes outdoors he'd worn for ten years or so. In reality he was wealthy enough to renew his wardrobe monthly and employ a valet to keep it in trim of he felt like it. But his background and heritage rejected most kinds of vanity, not necessarily because of the expense but because it was a feminine habit. In his view men who were real men spent their money on other things and looked in the mirror only when shaving.

Once Richie had gone a further thirty yards in a steady tread he darted to the west and nipped through a hedge and entered the field inclining upward and left, to the Rookeries.

As he skirted the outer perimeter the smell hit him like a smog.

It was from the large corrugated iron structure on the mound of the westerly point. It was the shed in which Norrington kept his turkeys, enclosed now until the killing season near Christmas.

Richie felt that numbing mix of physical reaction—partly nausea and partly emotion.

Norrington's farms had been investigated by the correct authorities, at the behest of several complaints from people compassionate to livestock well being. They claimed they held no more than the required amount of birds in the enclosure. Perhaps they did—when the inspector called—or perhaps the inspector left with a heavier wallet than when he entered.

Richie picked up speed and the falcon complained loudly at the jerky movements. So he slowed for a second and pitched his arm forward and let her fly off.

She soared swiftly and with ease.

Richie did not want Titch to sense the turkeys and their misery. He felt it was like allowing children to see other children less fortunate than themselves trapped in some obscene death-camp. Some people might think him weak and sentimental, and maybe he was. He did not talk of his feelings on the matter to anyone except Scott, and then in a small and unemotional way, and Scott concurred.

Their mutual dislike of all things 'Norrington' was a silent and comfortable tenet in their working bond. A man's feelings were his own and there was no changing them.

*   *   *   *

Charlie was trying to reach Heather as he drove through the usual snarl-up in the centre of the town where the ancient roads and thoroughfares to and from the high street were clogged with traffic following some minor incident.

He wanted to give her the bad news so that she could be digesting it before they talked about it face to face. She was constantly engaged and she had switched her answering service off. Heather's phone was always engaged. Her ongoing dialogue with the public relations people about social engagements and off-screen appearances filled much of her phone time when she wasn't rehearsing or shooting. Then there were her charity bookings. And when those were out of the way there were her mother and sisters.

Charlie dreaded telling her the news, because if rumours were true that her part in the soap was coming to a close they could no longer rely on her salary.

In her Merc convertible and stuck in traffic at the other end of the city, Heather was on speakerphone with the assistant producer, a young man who was also now her part-time lover.

"Dean, why can't you give me any updates? . . . it's not like I'm going to broadcast it! You know me better than that."

"When there's any news H I'll tell you!" said Dean in patronising dictatorial tone.

"Like hell you will . . . I'll be the last to know . . . and don't call me H!" said Heather, disconnecting the call.

Dean was younger than her by some twenty years. He would not have looked at her if she had not had that allure of being in front of the camera and lauded as a household face, an attractive one for somebody over forty.

Heather played a woman five years older than the age she pretended to be. And in reality she was ten years older than her on screen character. Dean did not know this, but suspected she had knocked a few off, as they all did.

The feeling in her bones told Heather that it was bad news; she had that slightly breathless feeling she always got when things were going to become tricky in areas beyond her control. It was a feeling of being out of sync, of being a little bit dizzy and not quite in touch with life.

She drove too quickly and was snapped by a speed camera on the road close to the pub. That was now nine points on her licence in total. She slowed down considerably because if she was stopped and done for being also over the limit she would definitely lose her licence.

She noticed that Charlie was trying to reach her on the mobile and she flicked it off. That was another offence these days, using one's phone while driving! One couldn't breathe lately in this damned country without infringing some petty law.

It was insufferable, more and more like a Stalinist state.

Her mind returned to the soap. It was over for her soon, she could feel it. The problem that would cause now in their lifestyle was considerable. She was not one for saving and neither was Charlie. The pub was losing money, like so many of them, and she had foolishly agreed to subsidise it instead of talking him into letting it go.

She pulled the car to the side of the road and lit a cigarette. Her nerves were causing her to lose her centre, as Gita would say. The chattering voices in the head that diverted one's attention and made one do the most foolish things.

If she were honest—she realized on her fourth deep drag—she did not want to lose the pub any more than Charlie did. Heather wasn't a Prima Donna—neither was she an egotist. She was a realist and a people-person and treated everyone the same. She just enjoyed being recognized for something good, and her on-screen character was fundamentally very good: Wendy Tridmore, a hapless divorcee and trained nurse who worked sometimes in the doctors surgery and sometimes on the district, two teenage children from an early marriage, having romantic entanglements all the time and then getting fed up with them or falling foul of their cheating philandering ways and starting the search all over again. Wendy had some debts from her days as a compulsive online gambler, but really at heart she was a good person, and the viewing public could relate to her. She inspired ordinary people who were suffering or lonely. Heather knew as much because the emails and letters the viewers sent told her so. How could they axe such a beloved icon as Wendy Tridmore? They probably couldn't! That was the answer.

Heather stubbed out the cigarette and started the car.

She had been driving for perhaps a further two minutes when a stray horse galloped into the road.

Having just the time to see it she pulled up sharply with a skidding motion and an awful grinding of brakes on the damp road surface and she screamed in horror as the horse seemed to rear and freeze in mid air.

The car stalled as she lost control and as a reflex reaction she closed her eyes and put the gear into neutral and applied the hand-break.

A vision of this grey stallion or whatever it was—she was not herself a horsey person—blurred behind her eyelids. She had the notion for about ten seconds that she had hit it; she remembered a reverberating motion as the car had stopped.

The newspapers would have a field day.

'Well Known Soap Star Kills Horse & is Axed from Series!'

The vodka cranberries she had consumed at lunch with her agent had taken the edge off her clarity and made her reactions slow. The police would arrive for certain and she would be breathallzed.

Momentarily she dallied with the idea of reversing and driving in the opposite direction and going through the nearby avenues of a small select estate of seven or eight properties. Saw herself doing it, passing the house with the covered swimming pool and the Feng Shui styled garden, and the one that had not yet removed its Christmas lights from the eves. Then she realized she would be seen. Her t.v. personna was too well known, and some people might be out on their front lawns tending their roses or washing cars or whatever, on this now fine summer evening.

Nothing for it but to face the music.

She expected to see the horse on opening her eyes, maybe slightly grazed, or lying there on the road injured and writhing.

There was no horse.

She leapt out of the vehicle and scanned the fields and the road to the front and to the rear. No horse, not one single sign of one.

She was perhaps having the kind of hallucinations people have when they drink too much over a long period of time and begin to imagine things. She did not really think so, but it was the only possible answer. That or the horse had galloped very quickly and escaped. Perhaps it was an expensive race horse with a legendary reputation. Perhaps it was simply hiding behind the higher hedges further along the lanes.

She got back into the vehicle, lit another cigarette and cleaned her sunglasses while she thought.

Should she report it? But to whom? If she did not report it maybe it would cause more accidents! but was that her business? She had enough to worry about without running around tracing the correct authorities dealing with stray animals.

She alighted next on the idea of asking Tess, who would undoubtedly know. It could even be a horse she was in charge of grooming or riding or something. Tess being the horsiest female Heather had ever met. Living for them, thinking of them constantly and sacrificing most of her life for them, including her extremely fit boyfriend who was always put on hold while Tess went out to see to some sick horse or take somebody else's to the vet.

Heather was about to drive off again in calmer mood when her phone rang. This time it was the director's P.A.

"Word from Head of Scripting . . ." said the girl without preamble and a questioning lift in her voice. "Dean says you want an update as quickly as possible because you're worried sick . . ."

"I wouldn't exactly say I was worried sick . . ." Heather interjected, but wasn't listened to.

". . . . they've handed in a storyline which Roy is approving . . . it's rather interesting and it would see you go in October!"

"What? . . ." Heather was caught between two shocking and bemusing life events and she struggled to get her senses back into the moment.

". . . It involves you going out in a boat on the river and losing track of time and getting lost at sea . . ."

"What? lost at sea from a boat on the river! . . ."

"That's a detail," said the p.a. hurriedly, "leave that to the writers . . . it's most probably a river leading into an estuary!"

"But why would I do that?"

"To be alone to think . . . having discovered that Enrico is already married back in Tuscany!"

Heather was unable to get a hold of the moment and the horse was now visible again some fifteen yards away, grazing and snuffing at the road surface, a leading rein hanging loose.

"What about that episode last year when I refused to go with Enrico on a cruise because I hate water!"

"Well . . . that's just . . . just . . ." the p.a. searched for the right description to enhance the dramatic licence.

"Ridiculous!!" supplied Heather. "Is that the word you're looking for?"

"Possibly!" concurred the p.a. blithely. "But it's been tabled and Roy's buying it!"

"Fuck Roy!" Heather experienced one of those debilitating moments when it's almost impossible to keep one's eyelids open let alone talk with clarity. "He must be more stupid than the writers to even buy it!"

"I was only obliging Dean by letting you know . . . ." the girl's voice hit a void as Heather disconnected.

She drew on the last of her cigarette, threw it onto the road and gave in to the need to close her eyes. The horse still engraved behind her eyelids and contentedly grazing.

Perhaps only half a minute passed; she thought of telling Charlie the news. It was excruciating to even mentally go there.

When she opened her eyes again the horse had disappeared.

Stress! Delusional states caused by stress! That was the problem, unmitigated and unending stress from life worries! Mostly of her own creation.

*   *   *   *

At the Golden Hind Charlie was in the kitchen fielding a row between the evening chef and the kitchen assistant. Charlie was the kind of person who didn't like rows of any kind, especially other people's; preferring wherever possible to have a stand-off or a growing indifference. He felt now that any moment there could be a walk-out by one of them. Based on this premise he took the side of his chef.

"You're both wankers!" The assistant chef, Lisa, swung round on Charlie. "You don't even know the facts of what we're rowing about . . ."

"I do . . ." lied Charlie glibly. "I followed the argument from the bar . . . . it was loud enough to hear from the car park!"

"No it wasn't!" Lisa was pulling the sort of face that turned his stomach, he knew it so well from his female staff over the years and what it portended. "You're a head-worker Charlie, you know that!"

Charlie blinked dismissively. "Talking of work, can we get back to that please? Customers are waiting for their meals!"

Lisa flung down the cloth she'd moments before conducted the row with.

"Okay but I'm not working Friday night . . . I've told him and now I'm telling you!"

Charlie smirked and partially turned—some of his best lines were delivered whilst in the act of turning. "You may not be working at all soon!"

Lisa called after him. "What? . . . what did you just say?" and then to the chef. "Did you hear that? I think he just threatened me!"

"I think he just warned you!" said Barney.

Through the opened side doors of the public bar Charlie saw Heather walking over the car park. Her head was down and her dejection was evident. A bad day on the set! A bad news day! He braced himself and began sorting the mixers under the bar unnecessarily.

"Can we talk upstairs?" she said, falsely bright, smiling at certain people round about.

"Sure . . . I just have a couple of things to do!" He always needed time to prepare for these kinds of show downs. "You go up and I'll follow in a minute!"

Heather made her way to the private quarters and then stopped on seeing Tess. "I need to ask you something in a while . . . about a horse!"

Tess managed a weak grin; she was not sure how involved Heather was in her employment termination. Probably not at all since Heather didn't concern herself much in the running of the business.

"I hope you're not thinking of buying one . . ." Charlie's voice came from beneath the bar, "that's all we need!"

"Charles don't be ridiculous!" Heather said, and then disappeared through the private doorway like a magician's assistant into a cabinet.

Heather and Charlie lived in a bungalow some fifty yards away, and used the upstairs flat at the pub as their domain.

"I need to talk to you too . . ." Charlie was entering the room in which Heather now sat.

She lit a cigarette and jumped in. "No let me talk first please! . . . I always take longer than you!"

"Yes but I've got really bad news!"

"Then get to the back of the queue!"

They fell silent and stared at each other. They had been together for ten years and everyone was amazed they had stayed. Charlie, the taciturn and sometimes less than hospitable publican, and Heather the local celebrity actress. They went back a long way, to when they were kids, and it was sort of inevitable when they met up after years that they would try the romance thing, having tried everyone else and encountered many other types of people.

In a strange and wonderful way their relationship worked, it made them reasonably happy. Charlie believed that it was unreasonable to expect more than 'reasonable' happiness. In this he showed an uncharacteristic modesty, not quite obvious to him, and not in evidence in the rest of his make-up. Charlie was more astute than people gave him credit for.

"It's the programme is it?"

"The director's p.a. rang while I was driving home . . ." Heather said tentatively.

Charlie was dismissive. "Couldn't it wait until you were back in the studio?"

"He thought I was very worried!" She avoided using Dean's name. "It followed a previous conversation with the assistant producer!"

"Naturally you're worried . . ."

"Well anyway . . . it looks like I'm out in October!"

"October!" Charlie sat down before his legs gave way. The shock was uncompromising. "I thought it was early next year!"

"So did we all but they now want me to go out in some rowing-boat accident, lost at sea, or something! . . ."

Charlie screwed up his face and raised his brows, a pantomime demonstration of someone moving through horror to incredulity while conserving their vocal chords.

"I know . . . it's utterly ludicrous!" Heather stubbed out the cigarette, grinding it intensely into the ashtray.

His eyes closed, Charlie spoke with considered slowness, as if to an invisible audience of dim-wits. "But Wendy was heard and seen only last year refusing to go into the local swimming baths to tend an injured lifeguard on account of her phobia of water! *Now she's out at sea in a boat!!*"

"The river apparently . . ." offered Heather. "A river leading into an estuary . . . which then leads to a . . ."

"I know all that!" said Charlie impatiently. "God, you're beginning to sound like it's real!"

"Of course I do . . . it is real. It's part of my life and I'm an actress!"

"Yeah . . . too good for that load of shite!"

"That load of shite keep us afloat!" Heather compressed her lips and looked at him with a lightning splutter of amusement. "That was an unconscious pun!"

He gave a sour laugh, as brief as hers, and put his feet up on the old sofa. "So . . . that's it . . . we're finished then! . . ."

Heather looked up and her face darkened. "Are we?"

"Yes . . ." He nodded in resignation to the facts with a dignified acceptance, his tone one of dignified weariness "The brewery will fold on us. They won't wait much longer for the arrears!"

After a brief pause she said: "Of course, it's only a shift in lifestyle . . . It's only the end of this particular phase . . . the pub and the series and so on!"

Charlie looked at her pityingly. It was impossible—even for someone of his candour—to retort in the negative to someone of her optimism.

"I mean it's a financial blow . . . it may even be a major set back but it's not the end . . . we'll do other things, we'll start again and make good!"

Charlie wondered whether to tell her the extent of the problems, or whether it wasn't worth the risk it posed.

"Anyway it's not happened yet . . . maybe Roy will have a change of heart and dismiss that storyline . . . maybe they'll think of one which strengthens Wendy's part instead of axing it . . ." she said.

Charlie stood and stretched. He worked long days and often longer nights. "Maybe he will, but the brewery won't have a change of heart!"

"But I thought you said the debts or arrears or whatever would be met by the end of the year!"

Charlie sighed extravagantly. "It's a bit complicated . . ."

Heather's mind had switched off, a reflex reaction in tune with her character and nothing to do with her tolerance of her partner. "I nearly ran over a horse on the way home . . . and then it just disappeared!"

Charlie feigned massive interest; as a change of subject it was rich in potential. "You did what? How did that happen? . . . ."

TWO

Some hour and a half later Heather re-emerged into the bar area, having consumed a mushroom omelette with a salad followed by a summer pudding and ice cream, all prepared for her by Barney.

Lisa took the tray from her and smiled in her cold pinched way, so that it was hardly a smile at all. Heather arched her brows by way of response. "Where's Tess?"

"On her break!" replied Lisa. "Most likely in the garden smoking!"

"I'll go and find her . . ."

Barney appeared and grinned at Heather. "Omelette alright for you Mrs T?"

"Wonderful Barney . . . thanks!"

"Who's this Mrs T you're always on about anyway?" queried Lisa after Heather had departed.

Barney looked at Lisa pityingly before replying. "Her character on the telly is Wendy Tridmore."

Lisa gazed for a second even more pityingly at Barney.

A small cluster of people were approaching the bar wearing the sheepish and intimidating gape of the collective fan base intent on reverse recognition. Charlie saw it covertly but said nothing. It took Heather by surprise.

"You're Wendy Tridmore aren't you?"

Sometimes Heather was witty in retort, and effusive, sometimes she was shy and reluctant. Tonight she said nothing.

Charlie stepped in. "No she's actually Heather Gilbert . . . Wendy Tridmore is a nurse!"

Obliging laughter was heard followed by some harmless and totally inane comments and Heather was gracious in the midst of them until finding the opportunity to slide back behind the bar.

She waved and went through a door that actually led to the cellar, behind which she could lurk on an upper step some three square feet in measurement, dank and chilly, pretending it led somewhere sensible, until they had all dispersed.

When she emerged Tess was back on duty.

"I need to talk to you . . . professionally!" Heather said to her.

"Professionally? . . ." Tess was immediately hopeful; maybe Heather was going to offer her another job or point her in the right direction.

"About horses!" elaborated Heather.

"Horses!"

Tess felt she was being *sweetened up* by the phrase 'professionally' and was clearly deflated. She followed Heather to a small cubicle seating area where usually the lovers and the courting couples sat.

"I saw one today when I was driving . . . it reared up in front of me and I almost had a heart attack!"

Tess seemed to find this incomprehensible, as if she couldn't imagine the animal doing such a thing.

"You know . . . like they do . . ." continued Heather encouragingly. "They kind of stand on their back legs and whinny . . . or whatever that noise is!"

Tess managed to get a grip on the disappointment regarding no new job and turned her attention to horses. "Where was this?"

"About three miles down the back road . . . . close to the railway bridge!"

"Where did it come from? . . . which direction?"

"I don't know! . . . that's the thing! I didn't see it coming . . . but worse than that is that it just disappeared!"

Tess took an age to digest this information and then looked Heather in the eye: Heather was known to take a drink and then drive, it was what famous people did, they believed themselves untouchable.

"What size was it? . . . how many hands?"

"Hands?" Heather blinked hazily, sensing Tess's suspicions in some foggy area of her mind. "Oh those kind of hands! . . . I don't know . . . medium size I suppose!"

Tess tried not to sigh or roll her eyes. "Colour then?"

"Sort of grey . . . . blotchy . . ."

"You mean dappled?"

"Yes that's it, dappled!"

"Which way did it go when it went?"

Heather sighed. "Tess, I just told you . . . it disappeared!"

"It can't have done! horses are big animals Heather!"

"Well it did!"

Mentally Tess ran through the list of likely suspects; the horse owners and riders she knew of. The likely places it might have escaped from. There were a number of stables and riding schools in the area. "Was it a gelding, a stallion or a mare?"

"I don't know! It was a horse! I'm no expert . . . anyway I just thought someone should be aware that's all . . . you know all the people with horses . . ."

"The police should be informed!" Tess said.

"God no!" Heather's shriek caused several customers and Charlie to turn and look at her. "Not the police . . . not until tomorrow anyway!"

Tess smiled and nodded—definitely the drink. But then it didn't mean there wasn't a horse.

"I'll talk to people and see if there's one missing . . . it might take a few days so I'll ring you or text you if there's any discovery!"

"No need . . . I'll be in here most evening over the next week!"

"I won't!" said Tess. "Charlie sacked me . . . I'm gone Saturday!"

"What? . . . why on earth did he do that?"

Heather's voice had again risen. People stared. She took the pitch down to almost a whisper. "What on earth did you do?"

"Nothing . . . I was just late a couple of times!"

"Well I'll . . . I'll . . ." Heather trailed off—in light of the brewery dilemma there was not much point in promising too much. ". . . see what I can do!"

*   *   *   *

Richie looked around the interior of Scott's converted barn and admired his minimalistic decor as he swallowed lager. He could tell that Scott thought him drunk.

"Not a good idea Rich . . ." Scott concluded. "Think on it again tomorrow mate . . . when you're sober . . ."

Richie was disappointed with Scott, he had grown middle aged and lost the passion of ten years ago, when Richie first met him and haled him as a paragon of all things good in the natural world of conservationist pursuits. Scott had gone soft and was walking—yawning even—into middle age. He *was* middle aged in fact, but it was still no excuse.

At forty three Scott looked younger than his years. He had the sort of hair which retained a nondescript sort of hue redolent of any age of man. A lean angular body, shorter than Richie but possessed of a sort of vitality which gave an appearance of strength and endurance. Over the past four years he had grown a slight paunch and seemed unbothered by it.

Richie regarded Scott with a hurt look.

"Listen . . ." Scott put his injured leg onto the polished flag floor of the large living room. "Talk with Andy . . . he'll set you straight about regulations!"

Richie didn't want to talk with Andy . . . jaw, jaw jaw, and no action to help the actual birds.

The large room was adjacent to a smaller living room where Scott's wife was undisturbed while he watched television and spoke to his family back home in Auckland on endless calls about their offspring and the state of their crops.

Richie drew breath, he hated being patronised. "You think Norrington gives a shit about regulations! . . ." He stopped, sensed the impasse and changed tack. "His nieces' rabbits have gone . . . he's accusing us!"

Scott's attempts to get his gammy leg working were futile presently, he gave up and stared at Richie. "Did he actually say that?"

"He said it today!"

"Could it be right?" Scott averted his eyes to allow a truthful reply.

"Well as a matter of fact . . . . the work experience lad left Eddie's pen open Wednesday night . . . ."

Scott was sighing and scratching his scalp.

"He was back in next day though . . . ." Richie added.

"Who? Eddy or the work experience lad?"

"Eddy!"

"Doesn't mean he wasn't awol in the early hours!"

"So!" Richie was defiant. "They should have secured the rabbits!"

"He should have secured Eddy as well!" said Scott in finality.

Richie stood up too abruptly and the room spun. He was wasting his time if Scott was going to side with those scum.

"Who's checking that lad?" Scott rose painfully and limped across the floor, delved in his jacket pockets.

"All of us!" said Richie. "Accidents happen . . . . they're birds Scott, they don't actually speak English!"

"Does Norrington know about Eddy being unsecured?"

"What do you take me for?" retorted Richie sourly.

Scott hobbled out to the kitchen and grabbed his boots.

"Where you going?"

"To check on the pens!" said Scott. "I can't rest now . . . not after that . . . if Norrington gets wind he'll have us by the short and curlies!"

"He won't get wind . . . who's going to tell him?"

Scott was impervious. "Eddy would have had that rabbit you know! He could've clawed and ripped his way through the wire!"

"Get out of it . . ." Richie lurched slightly to the door. "I know he's bright but he ain't that good!"

"Isn't he! . . . he had the latch up last month between him and the buzzards like he was Houdini! . . . Going out hon!" called Scott in a louder voice.

His wife's head appeared around the partition door. "What? . . . on that leg? Where to?"

"To see the Empire's in tact!" joked Scott.

Julie gave Richie a withering look.

"Nothing to do with me Jules!" Richie caught the large bunch of keys Scott threw to him. "I'm just the messenger! what can I do?"

"Stay sober . . . go to bed . . . or watch the t.v . . . . like other people this time of night!" she said and the door closed on possible retorts.

"I'll drive!" Scott was irascible.

"What about your knee?" Richie wasn't hopeful.

"What about your alcohol levels?"

Scott was already limping at a high speed out to where the Land Rover was parked.

*   *   *   *

Heather entered the bedroom and peered to see if Charlie was asleep or just pretending. Then his eyelids fluttered and she knew he was awake.

"Why did you fire Tess?"

Charlie remained mute.

"Charlie why did you fire her?

"She's always late!"

"There are worse sins . . . she's a really good girl!"

"She lives in cloud cuckoo land!"

"She's a natural behind the bar! . . . being late isn't a hanging offence!"

Charlie considered for a moment this idea women had about timekeeping—that it was somehow elastic to individual whims. He had met very few who didn't subscribe to the theory. But some were just worse than others.

"When people are waiting to go off shift and give me ear ache! . . ." he paused before complaining further, but then reconsidered. "Glen for example!"

"Oh he's a complete . . ." Heather couldn't find the word.

Charlie opened an eye and raised his head. "Complete what?"

"Moaning Minnie!"

Awake with no choice in the matter Charlie began to laugh. "Have you been reading the Girls Own Annual again? . . . who these days says Moaning Minnie?"

"Glen takes chicken legs and salmon steaks from the kitchen and puts them in his pockets!" said Heather without emotion . . . "Did you know that? . . . and all he ever talks about is skiing and how to become a professional instructor . . . he's a boring, miserable son of bitch!"

"He's a tosser by anyone's standards . . . I know! . . . personally I can't stand him! . . ." Charlie raised himself on one elbow. "But at least he can change a barrel and deal with trouble late at night. He's the only other male here besides me!"

"At present!" persisted Heather, removing her eye make-up with cotton wool.

"At present? how long do you think we've got? . . . didn't you listen to what I told you earlier?"

She blinked rapidly and refused to look at him. "I want Tess kept on . . . and I do have some say here!"

Falling back onto the pillows he closed his eyes again. "Is it about this horse business?"

"I need to get a handle on it and Tess will have the inside info! Animals do not just appear and disappear at random! I may be having hallucinations!"

He was cautious. Cunning by nature, Charlie saw a dilemma: Tess or Heather's amenability.

"Sweetheart, four or five vodka cranberries might do that to anyone. I wouldn't worry about it!"

Heather flung a packet of cleansing wipes at the bed. "Stop exaggerating! . . . I want Tess reinstating!"

"I'll think about it!" Charlie said placatingly.

Heather slid into bed, putting her hands on his buttocks and cuddling close to him, smelling of the enticing essences redolent of this time of night.

*　　*　　*　　*

When Scott and Richie drew up at Rookeries the night was ultra silent. There was some keening from the hawks and the owls were giving vent, but that was usual at this time. Scott climbed cautiously out of the driving seat and tested his bad leg, refusing the arm Richie offered.

"Get off me!" he said testily "I'm not an old fart yet!"

"No, you're a middle-aged fart!"

Riche watched Scott's progress and walked a bit behind, training the flashlight beam against the rough path ahead of them.

It was not until they reached the wrought iron gates, padlocked and chained, that it became obvious something was tied to the fretwork of the left hand gate.

It was a dead foul of some sort. Probably a pheasant. Scott looked away and shook his head to clear his vision as though he'd imagined it.

"Jesus Wept!" said Richie. "Look at that . . . . Norrington as I live and breath!"

"Let's get in and see if there's anything else gone on!" growled Scott.

As they entered the grounds several birds began to rustle and make noises of unrest. Birds of prey were notoriously good security creatures; they were alert at all times and slept almost with their eyes open.

The compound held several arc lights which triggered automatically as they stepped near to them. It was an enclosure the size of a small urban park and it housed over eighty birds of various species.

They were accustomed to the strange intermittent bursts of noise—the squawks, the inhuman sounds of life—but Richie was thrown off balance by the presence of the dead foul. He was certain where the blame lay.

"It's a declaration of war!" he told Scott as they prowled, shining the flashlight round about, scarcely breathing because they were listening so hard.

"You can't be sure it's him!"

In the pitch blackness behind the torch Richie rolled his eyes up toward a colourless charcoal sky relieved a little by the half moon appearing occasionally from behind darker cloud formation.

"Well put it this way Scottie, the fat bastard might not have been down here himself but one of his henchmen certainly has . . . ."

"If you say so!" Scott struggled not to show pain as the recently torn leg ligaments screamed with the agony of too much movement.

They were near Eddy's enclosure. Eddy was one of their star attractions. A Tawny Eagle some twelve years old weighing around four pounds with a wing span of roughly five feet; a seasoned veteran, entertaining the crowds in displays and personal encounters Eddy was a law until himself, a king among his cronies, and was not averse to escaping for several hours to prove a point.

He always came back.

He was here now, in tact, in his enclosure, impervious to their voices but somewhat disconcerted by the zig-zagging flashlight. He watched them with a jaundiced stare from one eye.

"He's here!" declared Scott proudly, like a parent discovering an errant toddler.

"Of course he's bloody well here!" Richie was becoming more and more enraged by events. "I told you it was just a fluke . . . the lad just got careless . . . he isn't one of the regular team and I suppose he deserves some slack cutting"

"We can't afford that kind of slack . . . we'll lose our licence if he goes off during the night and savages neighbouring mammals . . . beloved pets of little girls and the like!"

Richie groaned and lent against the enclosure wire. "Will you listen to yourself! There's no evidence to say Eddy even went that night . . . he was in his enclosure when we opened the next morning! He doesn't scavenge much these days, he's too well fed here! . . . and there's nothing to say Norrington's telling the truth about the rabbits anyway!"

"That's not my point!" Scott was bent double over his injured leg.

"Look . . ." Richie grabbed Scott's arm to support him, "let's get back . . . Jules'll blame me if you do further damage to that leg!"

"Since when did you worry about what she says? . . . . and get the fuck off me . . . I'm not an invalid!"

Even so Scott allowed himself to be heavily supported as they went back towards the gates.

The entrance lay to the east side of the acreage and led out onto a path bordering meadowland used for grazing and growing. Richie's flashlight swooped up and down the acreage as his gaze kept track with it. But suddenly Scott stopped and pulled Richie to a halt. "Am I seeing things or is that a horse over there?"

"Where?" Richie trained the light in a new direction and noticed some distance away a shape which might have been a horse but was certainly a large animal.

"Might be . . . . can't see . . . could be a bull!"

Scott let out a burst of laughter mingled with his subdued agony. "You need an optician if you think that's a bull . . . . look at it's head movements!"

"Well whatever! . . . We can't get caught up in that now . . . let's just get back!" Richie, Scott noted, was sobering rapidly.

Scott limped forward, shaking Richie's arm away, keeping his eyes on the far field. "What's a lone horse doing out here at this time!"

"Who knows! . . . but it's a horse and it's in meadowland . . . so it's happier than we are at present!" Richie shoved Scott upwards into the passenger seat, climbed in the other side, took a large swig from a water bottle on the floor and then switched on the engine.

"You sober now?" enquired Scott.

"I should think so . . . 'sides who's going to nick me out here?"

"You never know!"

"Take the chance won't we man! . . . can't sit out all night!"

Scott looked back over his shoulder and squinted. The horse wasn't there, it had probably wandered off to the back of farther than yonder. He let the problem go, the better to concentrate on Richie's driving in what was still a semi alcoholic state, although it was a mere four minute drive from the house to Rookeries.

"Should we report this to the police?" Richie asked as they drew up outside the garage.

"What, the stray horse?"

"No, the dead pheasant!"

Scott stared at him in silence. "And say what exactly? A dead pheasant has appeared on our gates?"

"There's laws against shooting wild birds . . . and certainly against nailing dead ones to other folks property!"

"Reckon they've got better things to think about, the police!" Scott moved his body slowly and painfully, his back was taking the toll for his injured leg.

"We could direct them straight to Norrington!"

"Oh yes! . . . . and there were how many witnesses?"

Richie was out of the Land Rover and opening the passenger door to assist Scott down. "We can't just ignore it!"

"What else do you suggest? Anyway, could have been someone who doesn't like us!"

"Ain't no-one doesn't like us besides Norrington and his crew!" Richie put Scott's arm around his shoulder and began to half carry him as Scott limped, dragging his leg.

"Well . . . I dunno . . ."

"No, because we don't harm no-one is why! . . . folks mostly like what we're doing!"

"So it has to be Norrington does it?" said Scott.

"Sure as daybreak comes tomorrow!"

"Cops isn't the answer!" said Scott in finality.

"No you're right . . ." Richie saw the door fly open and Julie standing in the threshold, the inner lights bright behind her. "There's other ways . . ."

"Now look at the state he's in!" she called. "Just look at him!"

Richie helped Scott into the house and smiled a pathetic winning sort of appeal to Julie. "Sorry Jules . . . but he would go!"

"Of course he would!" agreed Julie in perfect sarcasm. "If his life depended on it he wouldn't be able to resist!"

She shouldered the burden of her husband with Richie and they lowered him to the sofa. "No work for you tomorrow then!" she announced triumphantly.

"Whatever you say dear!" said Scott in similar bleak tones, and grinned with the relief of the sofa—the mixture of pain and pleasure in extreme measures.

"Yeah . . . we'll leave the police out of it! . . ." said Richie decisively and almost to himself, righting his jacket and tying his shoe on the arm of the white leather armchair. "There's other ways!"

Julie knocked his foot off in passing. "It's like living with barbarians . . ."

Scott was resting his head against the back of the sofa and opened his eyes wide. "That's twice you said that Richie! . . . just go easy . . . whatever you're thinking of doing . . . it's like I said earlier . . . think before you act!"

Richie moved to the front door, saying absolutely nothing.

"Richie . . ." Scott yelled in aggravation. "Julie tell him to come back . . . I've not finished discussing matters . . ."

"Tell him yourself! . . . phone him on his mobile!" called Julie. "I'm going to bed."

*   *   *   *

Tess was not asleep when Richie returned to the caravan. She lay in their bed—and because it was a chilly night for late August—looked less than alluring in an old woolly cardigan much faded by washing, staring at the tiny portable t.v. up in one corner of the sleeping area which was almost invisible to her from the angle at which she was lying.

"Where you been?" she asked him, as if it were still something concerning her that she had a right to know.

"Had to check the enclosure !" said Richie, too tired to enter any arguments. Some instinct warned him to keep the information regarding the dead pheasant and Norrington to himself. Tess served Norrington in the pub and there was no telling what she might say to him now she was leaving.

"You reek of lager!" She sat partially upright in the bed and shrugged off the cardigan and then pulled the sheet up around her neck, modestly. "You been with someone else?"

"No!"

"You're very late!"

"There's a horse roaming in the field next to us, we got delayed by it!" Richie said cagily, and the excuse felt false.

Tess let the sheet fall and sat bolt upright. "What horse? What did it look like?"

"It was dark . . . how do I know? . . . birds are my expertise not horses . . ."

"Heather spotted a lone horse earlier . . . she almost crashed the car because of it!"

"Oh?" Richie was yawning, dead on his feet.

"I better go and have a look!"

"It's one thirty five in the morning girl! . . . you better get some sense!"

Tess was pulling on her discarded jeans as quickly as he had taken his off. After a minute or so she closed the caravan door behind her and Richie fell immediately into near oblivion on his side of their inadequate bed.

*   *   *   *

Once at Rookeries Tess came to a halt, panting with the exertion of her quick jog. She was sweating and her ankles had swollen from a long day's work, but she stood to the front of the enclosure and used a similar flashlight to the one Scott kept in the Land Rover.

She scanned the darkness, unafraid of it; she knew darkness to be a friend not a foe. Only townies feared the dark, and those with a bad conscience.

A country girl at heart, Tess knew her own mind and her own morals. She loved horses with a passion, the sort of passion that only enthusiasts of one kind another could appreciate.

She took a step or two closer to the boundary fence, beyond which lay the meadow where Richie said he saw the horse. She clambered over and negotiated the thorny scrub on the other side, freed her feet to stride onto the softer lush grass. Everywhere was a noisy silence, the sort of silence only known in the country.

There was a brighter half moon now and clearer skies coming in from the east. It threatened to be a sunny day later, the sort of day which would begin hazy and then brighten to a sultry hot heat. She strolled the field, not at all bothered by either the solitude or the time.

Suddenly out of the tress to the right, on the slight incline leading to the back end of Rookeries, a man appeared.

Tess stopped.

The man seemed to falter, as if he had seen her, but he showed no sign of concern. She pondered on whether to run towards him and enquire about the horse, then saw that it would seem illogical and eccentric at this hour of night.

It occurred to her also that he might actually pose some danger, that he might be deranged or up to no good. She turned and went back towards the fence.

A few moments passed and she heard him coming after her. She gripped the flashlight at the hilt and swung it by her side to test things—if necessary she could heft it and hit him with it. Or at least she could try; it would serve to warn him off, or catch him off guard. It went through her mind that Richie would say this served her right. That she shouldn't be wandering in the open on her own in the dead of night. He would have no sympathy, he may not even bother to voice his discontent, he would shrug in that '*what do you expect*' manner and turn away, the way he turned away from her in bed, because he had ceased to care for her.

These thoughts made her want to cry and she felt some initial wetness on her cheeks as she picked up speed. She tried not to run, tried not to become a victim and turn the stranger into a predator.

Suddenly she tripped, or stumbled, she did not know which. She was tired to the point of exhaustion and her limbs were becoming numb and refusing to obey her brain. She felt the damp grass beneath her and the turn of her ankle gave off a sharp stab of pain. She lay flat on her stomach and filled her mouth with the soft bitterness of the grass, clamped her teeth around a clump of it to stop herself screaming. She was stupid and things were out of control, she was in a nightmare of her own making.

She deserved no sympathy, not her own, not Richie's, not anyone's.

She closed her eyes and wondered who she might pray to. She was not religious and not in the habit of praying but circumstances were at a crucial point: loss of job, loss of boyfriend, loss of direction. It was too much and in the growing state of despair experienced at times of accident she could not stop herself from believing she had to deal with all these points at once.

The roiling waters of some kind of emotional hell were closing in on her.

And then the man was next to her. He was crouching over her, lifting her left shoulder so that she could look up at him. Then straddling her he managed to pull her to a standing position. She was no lightweight these days and she knew it. She heard him rasping for breath as he heaved.

She felt herself sag against him. "I'm sorry!" she said in a fretful whispering voice. "I'm terribly sorry . . . I fell!"

He mumbled something in a strange tongue and she realized it was a language she did not understand. He was a tall and slender person, not thin, but with that angular tautness giving the impression of slim.

"I can go now . . . I can walk . . . don't worry about me . . ." She pulled away, tugged her arm from his hold. She was terrified and her natural instincts regarding fear and danger had kicked in.

"I help . . ." He held onto her arm as they walked to the fence.

"There was a horse! . . ." Tess began, after an age of their slow silent uneven ambling. "Two people saw it earlier today . . . I am involved with horses . . . I work with them . . . so I have to see what they are talking about! . . ."

She felt she was rambling and stupid and must sound ridiculous.

The man seemed to not care. It was moments before she remembered he could probably not understand her.

And then as they came out from the field by the correct entrance, the official gate used for Chester's Farm, she saw the horse . . . a beautiful pale dapple grey, an adult gelding, wearing just a leading rein. Illuminated by the brightness of the moon.

She was arrested by the sight and for a moment forgot about the man.

He made a sound she was familiar with, directed at the horse. The horse came trotting in their direction.

"It's your horse then?" enquired Tess.

He guided her to the pathway, pushed her through, closed the gate, and the horse roamed further towards them and put its head over and allowed the man to fondle him.

"Your horse?" asked Tess again.

"No!" he said at last.

"Then whose horse is it?"

They were in front of Rookeries and two cars passed in quick succession on the main road yards away from them. It was apparent to Tess that he once again could not understand what she said. She pointed to the horse and he smiled. He had a nice smile. She estimated him to be in his forties, perhaps European.

"I'll go now!"

She was half fearful he would not let her free. But he vaulted back over the fence and took the horse's rein and began leading it back over the meadow.

After several yards he turned. "Be careful!" he told her. "Be careful out at night!"

His English seemed fine, accented but fine. She was no longer sure of what he understood and what he did not.

"Who are you?" she called.

He ignored the question, waved, turned away and began leading the horse again.

Tess walked on, dejected, back to the caravan and thought about where he could be heading; other than Rookeries there was no civilisation for several miles. She could not recall a convenient right of passage to anywhere sensible. The puzzle that this presented was dimmed by an overriding realization that someone had been kind to her. In the midst of an oceanic time of bleak emotional despair someone had cared about her.

She reached home and fell into bed beside Richie who snored and moaned and moved about fretfully without waking. Despite a revolutionary happening in the territory that she knew like the back of her hand, there was nothing new in these four walls.

THREE

Heather sat and stared back at the producer in near incomprehension. "So it's changed again then!" she said blankly. "It's gone from being a boating accident to a disaster in a mineshaft!"

"No, no . . . not exactly . . . Heather, don't label things so literally! We have not settled on anything definitely yet . . . . and it wasn't a boating accident that they proposed . . . it's an open incident . . . a *missing-but-not-pronounced-dead* scenario!"

Looking at him with the same blankness Heather wondered whether she dared smoke, but decided against it.

"Equally stupid! . . . why can I not just go abroad for several months and then come back . . . or decide to stay there when it's convenient to your writers, or whatever?"

"Because there isn't any dramatic impact in that . . . you and the Tridmore family are outlined for key pivotal emphasis at that time in the schedule . . . . what you suggest would be incidental background stuff only!"

"Better still why can I not just stay? . . . I don't see what I've done wrong . . ." said Heather as if he'd not spoken.

"You've done nothing wrong! . . . stop taking all this so personally!"

"Well Wendy then! . . . . I can't see what Wendy did wrong!"

"Nothing! she does everything right . . . that's the point! It's time she did something a little daring . . ."

"What like going out in a boat and getting lost!"

"You're doing it again Heather . . . no-one goes out in a boat and gets lost . . . they forget to navigate or get blown off course!"

She looked at Roy Preston and wondered which one of them was mad. If he couldn't understand what she was getting at he should go and take a sabbatical from his role as producer and live more in the real world for a while.

"Well . . . I need to know . . ." Heather removed her cigarette pack and Roy Preston lifted a warning finger. "Not in here please? I already got my arse kicked for it when Dudley lit up last week! It's a health and safety no-no . . . and against the law!"

"Screw the law!" said Heather peevishly, but she put the cigs back in her bag. "I need to know which way I am going out . . . . in a boat or down a mineshaft!"

"It depends . . . ." Preston slit open a piece of gum and dropped the paper to the floor, like a lager lout in the pub, thought Heather. "What difference does it make! You're an actress . . . a good one . . ."

"Don't patronise me!" she said before she could stop herself.

Preston raised his brows and looked at her quickly.

"It matters to me . . . Wendy is my alter ego. I've been playing her for eight years and I need to know which way she is going to die!"

"She may not die of course!"

"She will if I refuse to go along with this!"

"Heather listen . . ." Preston leaned forward and assumed a weary and avuncular tone. "Don't do anything hasty . . . and don't make any announcements to the press or anyone . . . just leave it with us!"

"No!" said Heather, defiance coming from where she knew not, but deep within her.

"I want to know in the next three days . . . how she is going out!"

Roy Preston sat back in his chair and watched her. He liked Heather Gilbert, she was one of Britain's finest. She could have gone on to great heights. Possibly still could, but he personally guessed her age to be in excess of fifty five.

She'd been a theatre actress of the best calibre. One who could turn her talents to television. Why she had sold out on greater things he did not know. Only that she had been invited to do a cameo spot for a few episodes nine years ago and then been written in permanently after agreeing to stay. No-one knew why. No-one knew the full story.

She was a little past her prime now, but then so were many of the greatest actresses. Make-up was a wonderful thing. Better than that was good script writing.

"Leave it with me . . . I'll get on to scripting this afternoon and call a meeting with everyone and we'll make a decision!"

Heather stood, collected her bag, stared from the window at the car park way down below. "A mineshaft seems even more improbable than a river!" she said vaguely, more for her own benefit.

The producer cleared his throat, hesitated and weighed his words. "Well . . . by the time they've finished with the storyline it will seem normal and routine . . . it always does . . . that's what they do!"

"Routine?" Heather swung round to look at him. "How can falling down a mineshaft be routine!"

"Oh . . . I give up!" said Preston. This overly literal woman before him who was at the same time talented and adept. "Not the death itself! the circumstances leading up to why it happens . . . that's the routine part!"

Hoisting her bag, Heather left the room, saying nothing else whatever and staring at him as if more words might be wasted.

Just outside the door she collided with Dean. He steadied her slightly, his hand lingering on her hip. "You finished in there?"

"Yes!" She looked past him and along the corridor, she was weary.

"Fancy a drink?"

"'Not really . . . I think I need to go and digest the latest info!"

Dean put his head near hers, as if he was saying something confidential that anyone passing should not hear. He touched her nose with the tip of his own, then sighed audibly. "Soon then!"

Heather stood very still and did not react. The faintest of smiles lingered about her features and he took it as a good sign. He pulled back from her and reached for the handle of the producer's door. "I'll call you!"

Heather widened the smile to a more warming facial angle, convincingly but nonetheless false, and then moved to the lift.

*   *   *   *

In the Golden Hind Charlie watched as Richie conversed in a low voice with a character whose name Charlie couldn't remember. The character was somewhere in his late thirties or early forties and wore his hair in a long plait, oiled and slicked and appearing jet black. He had sideburns turning very slightly grey and a highish forehead which suited him. He wore a long leather coat and at other times a suede jacket in an indistinguishable colour with gnarled fringing. It occurred to Charlie to wonder how an Animal Rights devotee could wear a leather jacket, but maybe it was faux. He was clean shaven but now and then wore a small neat goatee beard. His hair tonight seemed different although Charlie couldn't have said how; maybe the plait was shorter or something. He had an earring in one ear, a small solid gold loop with a silver ank dangling from it. It was a trademark kind of piece and he was seldom without it.

For all his meticulous wildness there was a respectability about him, a sedate and tranquil air, as if he knew how to conduct himself and how to preserve his own standards. He could have been anything . . . a poet, a musician, a modern philosophy professor . . . or just a gypsy. Charlie knew only one thing for sure, he was Animal Rights in a big way. Apparently he had done time for some of his activities. How he knew this Charlie had forgotten; it was not Richie had told him. Perhaps it was Tess. She was very free with information when she wished to be.

Charlie didn't have an opinion on animal rights much himself. He lived in the country where there was strong opinion against it rather than for it. But he personally could see where these people were coming from.

Charlie was circumspect. He never said anything to anyone else of what he learned about his clientele. He was not a gossip, not one of those gabby landlords who forms a clique from which some are excluded unless saying the right things or holding the right opinions. He could not stand set-ups like that.

He was a private man And as he looked at this character he saw a kindred spirit in that way: another private human being with a mind used to form his own opinions.

At present the customer in question was listening carefully to whatever Richie was saying, and Richie was saying it very vehemently and with a look of venom on his handsome young man-of-the-rugged-outdoors face.

Charlie moved closer to the pair in the pretence of reaching for wine glasses on the shelf above the bar adjacent to where they stood on the opposite side. Charlie's face remained not just impassive but with a look of remote absorption to his own thoughts. No-one would ever imagine he could be eavesdropping, or even be interested in anyone other than himself. The makings of a good spy, or an investigator, Charlie could have been either but he preferred a more predictable and an easier life.

". . . . I could tell from the fucking smell! . . ." Richie was saying. "It was the same last year . . . . he's got twice at least the permitted amount of birds housed in that shed!"

Charlie realized they were talking of Ged Norrington, whom Charlie did not like very much. Norrington was loud, opinionated and thought he owned the county just because his ancestors had lived there since the sixteen hundreds.

Who gave a shit!

Norrington felt he had a duty to the unchanging face of rural England to speak out, meddle, or generally bully people with less money than himself into having things his own way.

Charlie was now very interested in why Richie was suddenly telling this character all of this stuff and he moved with rapidity to fetch a carton of crisps from the top of the cellar steps and then deposited it below the bar and dropped to his knees so that he would be forgotten about as he listened in.

". . . he was there with his dogs when I was taking the short cut across his land . . . and he accused me right out of letting Titch free to kill his relative's rabbits . . ."

Richie paused and Charlie waited.

Pigtail had not uttered yet, had left the pauses unfilled so that Richie would be encouraged to continue at his own pace.

". . . it ain't true . . . Titch is locked in . . . . and it probably weren't Eddy . . . even though he had the chance a few nights since, owing to a balls up by the young lad on work experience . . ."

There was an interruption as Glen came up and towered over Charlie and asked if he could take fifteen minutes off now rather than later to go ring some girl he had fallen out with and now wanted to make up to.

Charlie waved him away and said briskly: "In ten . . . I'm due a pee myself!"

"Too much information!" said Glen hilariously.

Charlie made a face at the crisp carton, denoting his opinion of Glen's idea of humour. All sociability was wasted on Charlie, even from people he did not dislike, though he made some attempt to hide the fact. He watched Glen move back to the other end of the bar as he closed the crisp carton.

". . . . Scott wasn't fit to be walking on the leg . . . torn tendons . . . fucking agony . . . and then the appearance of that on the railing . . . . it was almost too much for him! He loves birds like I do, probably more so. He was nearly throwing up! . . ."

Now Charlie had missed a vital piece of the puzzle because of Glen's interruption. Missed what it was on the railings they had found last night.

At last, after a lapse during which there was only throat clearing and the sound of glasses being put down on the bar, the pigtail character spoke.

"Can you show me the location? . . ."

His voice was deep, educated and rich, an orator's voice. It wasn't the sort of voice Charlie had expected to hear from the man.

This pleased Charlie; he liked the world to surprise him as it came through his doors with its out-of-the-ordinariness and presentation of opposites from what you would expect.

"We'll have to think about it . . ." said Pigtail. "Don't worry yourself anymore Richard!" This was said in a light familiar tone. "These things get sorted in the fullness of time, as you know!"

Richie laughed, and the sound of his hand slapping the guy's leather clad shoulder was audible as Charlie stood up, stiff from all the bending and crouching.

"Good man!" said Richie and was alarmed for a second as Charlie's head appeared before them, rising up like some pale faced spectre from below the bar.

Guilt was all over Richie's face at what Charlie might have been party to.

Charlie feigned ignorance and almost smiled. "Anything else lads?"

"Another pint of the excellent Guinness Landlord . . . if you please!" said Pigtail in the same light and jocular tone as before.

Some minutes later Tess appeared, late as always.

"Charlie I'm sorry . . . ." She opened her mouth to reveal her pearly white teeth, shining invitingly between her naturally pink and healthy lips. "I tried to be on time but this woman stopped me . . ."

Tess's voice was quite pleasant with it's west country drawl that she did nothing to disguise or alter. Charlie thought it was like going back in time and listening to 'The Archers' on the radio with his gran when he was a kid. It pleased him somewhat. But nonetheless he put up his hand to silence her.

"Save it Tess . . . please! I don't need to hear it"

"Anyway it don't matter now really . . ." Tess looked apologetic. "I mean, I'm going tomorrow so . . ."

"You've had a reprieve!" he said briefly and then he turned and walked into the back area before she could pursue the topic. "Heather will explain . . . " he called over his shoulder.

For a minute Tess wondered if she had misheard and she stood perplexed, staring at the photo of the darts team on a weekend in Prague nailed to the beam over the bar.

She started for the door to the kitchen area, stopped, turned, considered going to the Ladies, changed her mind and turned again.

Lisa rushed past her, carrying dishes to the kitchen because the waitress hadn't turned in to do the service. "Richie's over there somewhere . . ." she announced and Tess felt even more confused. He had told her he was doing an owl watch, out of Rookeries and in the nearby woodland.

He was lying to her obviously. She had thought it suspicious at the time; why he would want to watch owls in the countryside at large when they had them of their own in the enclosures, presumably more exotic ones! He must think her stupid.

She stared around the crowded pub and looked in and between and around the clusters of people for signs of her boyfriend but could not see him.

*   *   *   *

Richie was using the pay phone next to the toilets, situated round a corner passage, invisible from the main room. His mobile would not get a reception here, not many could; it was necessary to go up the hill and stand on the low wall next to the Chester Farm tea rooms to get any sort of signal.

Tess gave up looking for him and headed for the bar.

Charlie rushed past her with two plates of lasagne steaming hot and burning his hands.

"Tell Glen to get his arse in here! Hurry up while there'a a lull . . . he's out in the smoking area phoning some woman . . . tell him we're too busy for his love life!"

Tess went quickly. She still could not believe her luck and the reprieve.

Glen was walking about, as phone users do, nodding to himself and making animated facial expressions as if being secretly filmed. He stared at Tess and held the phone away from his ear.

"Get your arse in here! . . ." Tess called. "Charlie's words not mine . . . it's getting busy!"

She was about to go back in when she saw Heather, captured by a group of customers giving their opinion of the soap and what should happen next. When she caught sight of Tess she made excuses and came across the tiny lawned area bordering the smokers from the rest of society.

"I have to go and serve . . . but Charlie said something about keeping me on after all!"

"Yes . . ." Heather grinned. "You're hired again Tess . . ." They went back into the pub. "Did you enquire about the horse?"

"Better than that Heather, I saw it!"

"What? . . . Where?"

"I'll have to go behind the bar . . . if you come with me I can tell you!"

Heather hesitated and made a face. "I don't feel like being gawped at any more tonight . . . I'll catch you later!"

Richie had still not left. He was oblivious to Tess, having forgotten his lie about the owls, and had stopped to play the fruit machine, a ritual he always indulged before he went home.

He watched the rotating colourful emblems in the machine in a glazed kind of way, his thoughts whirling. He held the almost empty beer glass aloft to his right while he operated the machine with his left hand, and he suddenly became aware of a girl standing near him, watching him.

Attractive and young, short dark hair, gamin features, large dark eyes. She was smiling at him in the way that told him she had him in her sites.

At twenty nine Richie knew there were females who thought nothing of selecting a man at random and making all the moves. He muttered something incoherent in her direction, terse acknowledgement without invitation—or so he thought—and she stepped nearer.

"You're from Rookeries aren't you?"

He continued to gaze at the screen of the fruit machine. He didn't much like being lured by females of any age. He liked his women more demure, although preferably a little more self aware and sophisticated than Tess had proved to be. It baffled him completely now as to what he'd ever seen in her beyond her generous bosom and inviting mouth, her countryside wholesomeness

"You are aren't you? . . ." the girl was saying. "From that bird place!"

Richie glanced, took in her immediate appeal a second time. "Yeah but I ain't one of the inhabitants!"

She stood very still and frowned at him. "What?"

He glanced again, she was genuinely mystified; not very quick on the uptake or not used to sarcasm?

He grinned slowly. "I mean I don't like being stared at!"

She lowered her eyelids and looked, for a second, crushed—the truth behind the veneer maybe.

He felt himself coming round to something unknown, seduced by his conscience more than by his desire. "You been over our place then?"

"No . . . I've watched you walking your hawk!"

"She's a peregrine falcon not a hawk!" He allowed himself another feint smile of fondness, the fruit machine still his object of attention.

"Whatever! . . . I don't like birds very much personally, specially not those big ones you keep . . . ugly squawking scary things if you ask me!"

"I didn't actually!"

She was lost for words it seemed, but still intent on knowing him. He was growing embarrassed and uneasy. "So you been stalking me through the woods or what?"

"Get over yourself! . . . I see you from our land, that's all!"

"Our land? . . ." He turned his gaze on her then and she had to stop herself from blushing. "What land's that then?"

"Norrington's Farms . . . my mother owns the paddock and grazing land out to the motorway intersection! . . . she's Ged Norrington's younger sister!"

Richie froze a little. He looked at the girl, a long cool appraisal. She was beautiful, without a doubt. But she was young and she was a Norrington.

"I'm Francine . . ." she said hopefully—the kind of guileless entreaty better men than him had been unable to refuse—and then she held out her hand.

He looked for a few seconds at her hand, dark green nails embossed with tiny white stars—how the hell was that done! Rings that were inexpensive and fashionable, but a watch that was probably worth the value of his entire caravan.

"Who are you then? . . ." she said next.

He didn't speak. He was weighing up the odds, ignoring her outstretched hand.

"I mean what's your name? . . ."

"Not one you need remember!"

He turned away from her and pushed more silver into the machine. He hadn't meant to spend this much, didn't have it to spare, but he was embarrassed and alarmed and if he left she may follow. Something was occurring here, something coincidental or contrived. He couldn't clutch at his instinct, couldn't read any of the signs. He wasn't a believer in coincidence. He had read a book once about synchronicity and the Law of Attraction, and some of it had gone over his head but some of it rang infallibly correct. Not to be denied.

"Why are you so rude? . . . I was just making conversation!"

She stepped nearer to him and he had the urge to yell at her, to trample through her confident innocence. He saw himself reflected in her navy blue eyes, and for a nano second he disliked himself.

However, it was no reason to court disaster. "Did he send you to spy on me?"

"Did *who* send me to *do what*?"

"Your uncle! . . . Norrington-in-chief!"

"No . . . why would you say that?"

She had taken her small delicate hand away, snubbed, and trying not to feel bad or let it effect her.

"Why would he do such a thing?"

"He hates us!" Richie spluttered a laugh through the last slurp of his beer. "Hates what we stand for!"

"He may do, but I don't!" Francine said. "I actually agree with Animal Rights!"

"How do you know I'm Animal Rights?"

"He told me!" She turned half a circle, felt she had had the final word. "But I can think for myself . . . to tell you the truth, I don't even like him!"

So saying, Francine walked to the door, two or three longish loping strides in a dainty female. It was irresistible. "You need to get over yourself . . . Mr whatever you're called!"

Richie moved quickly. "Francine . . . sorry . . . I didn't mean to offend you . . ."

He held out his hand and she hesitated fractionally and then took it before he could change his mind.

"Fancy a drink? You can buy me one if you want!" she was verbally clumsy now.

Richie hesitated, he had seen Tess pass across the main room several yards behind them.

"Or I'll buy you one then!" said the irrepressible Francine.

"No you won't!" He pushed a last button and the machine made it's game-over noise.

"If anyone's buying it's me . . . I'm very old fashioned like that!"

Francine smiled. "I'll go and find a table!"

"Not here . . . put your number on a piece of paper and I'll call you tomorrow! I got to be up at the crack of dawn!"

She lowered her lids over her dark eyes and she seemed now to be years older. "Early risers these birds aren't they?"

"Somewhat! . . . but I do a shift at Chester's tomorrow . . . that's the pressure!" He smiled and watched as she tore off the back of a stray menu and wrote down her number.

From the middle of a crowd in the main room Tess was now watching them. People were pushing past her this way and that as she stood stock still.

"Tess, get your backside out of the frigging way!" Lisa pushed her with a hip, loaded down with used plates and crockery. Tess lost her balance a little and zig-zagged sidewards into a group of men. One of them steadied her and she pulled back quickly from social exchange with them, fearing she would burst into tears.

Francine zipped her bag and looked at Richie with a newfound shyness. "You still didn't say your name!"

"Richard . . . Richie to my friends!"

"I prefer Richard." She ran through the doors, overwhelmed by her own temerity in the face of some previously untried emotion.

Tess waited until the girl and Richie had both left and then made her way back towards the the bar. She was in a daze, moving on auto pilot, numbed for the moment against the pain she knew would arrive.

It wasn't long before the man Charlie thought of as 'Pigtail' arrived on the scene.

"You look like a lady in need of cheering up!" he said to her.

Misunderstanding his motive Tess gave a weak smile and let her hair fall into her face as she pulled the pint. "Actually that's the last thing I need!" she told him ungraciously.

"We have been formally introduced . . . but you were slightly the worse for wear and may not remember!"

"You mean I was pissed!"

"If you want to put it that way!" He waited for her to lighten up, in vain. "You were with Richie . . . it's okay, I know you're his girl! I'm just being friendly!"

"You're wrong . . ." She placed the pint of Guinness before him on the bar top and he made a familiar hand movement towards the glass.

She placed it back under the pump and topped it up.

"You were with him that night . . . back before Christmas!"

"Yes? Well I ain't with him now!" She smiled again to soften her abrupt tone and moved along the bar to serve somebody else.

*   *   *   *

Tess thought about her failed relationship with Richie for the next two days. Although their paths did not cross above once, when he was at the caravan using the tiny shower cubicle. He had been sleeping in the back office at Rookeries—she thought so because his sleeping bag was gone.

Two days later she was doing a shift in the pub when he came in and ordered his usual pint between working the farm and Rookeries.

"You want some steak and ale pie?" she asked in a friendly manner, but avoiding his eye. "You can have my portion put by for later . . . I'm dieting!"

"Why'd you have it put by if you're dieting?" Richie enquired blankly.

He had thrown her gesture back at her. She felt stupid, flushed a deep pink and looked at him directly. "Lisa put it away without asking me . . . I always have it . . . usually!"

"Why are you suddenly dieting?"

"Because I need to lose weight!"

He swigged hard from the lager and stared dispassionately in the other direction.

"You want it or not?" she said ominously.

Her voice was cooling. She was not about to turn the steak and ale pie into the 'humble' version.

"No thanks . . . I ate the sandwiches Shirley made!"

"Please yourself!"

Shirley was the Chester's Farm cook and Tess was not bothered by her sandwich making. She could cook him full scale banquets if she liked. Shirley wasn't nineteen and elfin featured with a lush body and covetous of liaisons with other women's men.

"Why'd you tell Curt we're not together now?" Richie asked after a length of time in silence while Tess took glasses from the rack and he took careless slurps of the lager.

"What?"

"You told Curt the other night that you were not with me anymore . . . using the past tense!"

"Who's Curt?" Tess said.

"Curt Chambers . . . long plaited hair, earring . . . my colleague . . . you know bloody well who he is!"

Tess heaved a large sigh, her generous breasts stretching the fabric of her tee shirt—pristine white for a change and spotless over her best jeans.

"Because I got my pride . . ."

"What's that supposed to mean? . . ." said Richie.

"It means I know the signs . . . and I'm not going to be lied to . . . you've gone off me!"

She looked around the pub diffidently and then met his eyes, sure that no-one was near enough to hear them. "Deny it then!"

Richie stared at her for an age before swinging his attention to the opposite side of the room where Charlie was talking in a low voice to one of the draymen and checking the delivery sheet.

"See!" said Tess. "You can't! That's why you were cosying up to whatshername from the Norrington clan the other night!"

"I wasn't cosying up to nobody . . . and it would have been nice to have been consulted!"

"About what exactly Richie? . . ." She threw down the tea towel and prepared to move off. "About the method you'll use when you leave me?"

"You're making it too easy for me!"

Richie muttered the remark softly but it still sounded like a veiled threat.

"I've got my self respect! . . . . if I'm making it easy you should be thanking me!"

Moving away, Tess wondered about Curt Chambers. He must have told Richie all that on purpose. She thought only her own sex did that sort of thing and she smiled a wan and painful smile for her own benefit.

Richie finished the last of the lager and watched her serve two strangers at the other end of the bar. Then he left the pub and cut across the field to the bridle path to Rookeries.

Francine was in the paddock land with her mother and saw him from the distance as he sprinted. She gave a loud whistle which she knew wouldn't reach him.

She wouldn't push it with him. He was not that sort of man. But it felt good to be able to make some sound that he might hear, and if he did it would be okay. Then she could just wave, or deny she'd whistled at all. It was a good feeling, to be freer around this man she'd watched for weeks before plucking up the courage to make an approach. She was experiencing her first real taste of serious intent on closeness with a stranger. *Real closeness, real intent.* It felt heady and unnerving and more than a bit daunting: the wondrous suspicion of being the first person ever needing to go down that route.

Richie rambled on, oblivious of her surveillance, his mind full of Tess and not looking for or sensing her. The girl was an obvious move, but Tess was his past and the reality that had made up his life for three years. It was always that kind of familiarity which claimed attention.

To the right and beyond the tree line on the old stone bridge joining the two halves of the narrow road over the old canal Heather was parked in her car on the verge close in to the wall. She saw the figure emerge from the scrub and into open grassland and she vaguely recognized Richie.

She ducked down into the well of the car.

"What are you doing?" Dean demanded from the seat next to her.

"There's Tess's boyfriend!" Heather said in a whisper, as if Richie might hear her across the expanse of land.

"So!"

"So I don't want him to see us . . . me! I don't want him to see me! . . . in fact lean forward so he won't see you either!"

"He doesn't even know me!" complained Dean, but did as he was asked, cramping his back as he bent, his voice croaking with the effort.

"Who the hell's Tess anyway?"

"She works at the pub . . . Richie may recognize my car!"

"So?" Dean was put out; anyone would think she was ashamed of knowing him. "We're only sitting here talking!"

Richie walked on without looking from either right to left and Dean straightened his posture in the seat and informed Heather of the man's disappearance from the landscape. Dean's own car was parked some few minutes walk along a lay-by in a field.

Heather was still wrestling with the understanding of what Dean had just told her about Roy Preston and the programme. "I have a medical appointment so let's get back to the subject in hand . . ."

She twiddled with her various rings and resisted yet another cigarette; too many played havoc with the larynx and aged the voice, it didn't bode well for any reputable actress.

"I am not going to be written out like that!" she declared for the sixth time in half an hour.

Dean took on a helpless and beseeching expression and could think of nothing to add or to offer. "But if you don't want a boating accident and you won't consider the mineshaft and you have left things absolutely up in the air with Preston, you've given them little choice . . . ."

"I expect to be consulted!"

Dean lit a cigarette of his own and opened the car window wider. "You were consulted on Monday! . . . ultimately we don't have to consult you at all!"

"Oh . . . it's *we* now is it!" Heather grabbed the cigarette packet from his hand and took one. "I can see which side you're on!"

"Well of course its *we*! I work for them . . . I'm assistant producer! What do you expect from me?" Dean's tone had become bleak and unsympathetic.

Heather looked away and over the fields—Richie's silhouette was a tiny figure nearing the far side of the expanse of land inclining upwards to the forested area.

She was upset and growing embarrassed, becoming more and more unsure and vulnerable.

Dean shucked around to face her as best he could in her small car. "Look H . . . Roy's afraid you'll break contract and the storyline will suffer . . ."

"Which storyline? . . . the one on a boat or the one in the mineshaft?"

"Any storyline! He's afraid you'll just walk out . . . many actors before you have done it! . . ."

Heather considered matters. She couldn't believe what she had just heard: they apparently were considering now writing her out next month—just two weeks away—on an arc of fast escalating events that saw her long lost elder brother arrive and whisk her off to the United States to take up a position in an exclusive clinic he was a director of where she would be fabulously paid to leave everything in the U.K. behind her, including her teenage children, at a moments notice, never to return.

It was beyond stupid.

She had made a decision in the last two minutes. She did not know whether to tell Dean of it. He might blow the whistle on her. But to be fair, Dean had risked a lot to come to her with the information today.

"I'm not going back!" she said. "I'm not putting in any appearances next week!"

"What? . . . you'll break contract! I thought you and Charlie were hard up!"

"From what you say they won't be able to run that script without me . . . not if whatshisname is agreeing to play the brother!"

The actor who was to play her brother was a well known film and t.v. star of many years. He had long since wanted a cameo role in the programme and he was eager to sign the papers. The script was already written it seemed, and Preston had agreed it. They were to start shooting on Tuesday when she was next due in. One rehearsal, a quarter hour of dialogue through three episodes and the thing was in the bag.

Heather thought about it. If she just didn't show they would have to delay it or shelve it. They could not let the Big Name actor hang about or be made a fool of. He would sue.

This time, thanks to Dean, she was one step ahead. Without Punch there was no show.

She grinned to herself and folded her arms tightly around her middle. It was one of those times when the practical common sense of the larger situation had given way to a more personal and illogical set of rules which brought their own guidance and reward.

"What are you thinking?" Dean asked warily.

"You're better off not knowing!"

He made to open the car door then realized he was jammed against the wall of the bridge. He made a sweeping movement with his hand to indicate taking the car forward. "Listen Heather, don't do anything silly, anything that's going to mean financial suicide . . . you could come out of this winning if you keep your cool!"

"I don't care about that . . . I care about Wendy!" said Heather suddenly. "Wendy is a part of my life now . . . she deserves integrity! She is like my spiritual sister and I have to protect her! . . . people love her the world over!"

Somewhat horrified at what he was hearing, Dean attempted to play down his mortification. Actors of course were often temperamental and odd in their views, but this sounded like a dangerous edge to have reached for a woman of Heather's age.

"Well . . . maybe not the world over . . ." he retorted, hair-splitting and out of his depth. "Let's not get sentimentally carried away! It's not real life H. Wendy's not real you know . . . and you are . . ."

"Too late for that! . . ." Heather started the engine and moved the car forward. "And I'm sick of telling you not to keep calling me H!"

Dean alighted and leaned back into the window aperture. "Do you want to to come over to mine tomorrow evening?"

Heather looked up at him as he lingered. "We'll see . . ."

Without a backward glance she accelerated past him and drove at high speed towards the village.

He wondered as he unlocked his own vehicle whether he had not gone too far out on a limb for her. Whether she was about to hang him out to dry on her campaign of righteous justice for the fictitious Wendy Tridmore.

*   *   *   *

Richie had about him that cloud of muted misery that Scott found so hard to bear. It was not just Richie—Scott detected it in a lot of Brits, particularly the men. But Richie exuded it on some days like a bad odour.

Scott thought he knew its origins, but he was wrong.

"I just hope you got a good alibi!" Scott said, limping along with arms full of the straw they used in the bird units. He walked past Richie and further into the sanctuary.

"What?"

Getting no reply Richie followed Scott's limping-but-vastly-improved-gait to the pathway between the enclosures. "What alibi?"

"Don't give me that! . . . ." Scott was half laughing but struggled to remain grave . . .

"Man, I don't know what you're on about . . . has something happened?"

Scott opened the enclosure to the hawks and the birds hopped about between their rustic solid perches, the youngest one—resident for only a month—frantic and screaming and shrugging his wings. Scott made soothing noises and then some finger movements and the birds became quieter. He looked at his first in command through the mesh wire of the enclosure door and noted his expression. He decided to give Richie the benefit of the doubt."

"Don't go making a fool of me Richie! . . . that's all I ask . . . Norrington's turkeys have been nicked! . . . nicked or set free . . . amounts to the same thing!"

"The turkeys in the barn up yonder?" Richie was bemused and then amazed and then gleeful. "The turkeys giving off the smell in the field next to Chester's?"

"Well the very same!" said Scott in a loud pantomime sing-song voice. "Would you believe? . . . those very same birds!"

Richie grinned and turned away.

Curt Chambers had acted.

"Just before you crack open the bubbly . . ." Scott continued. "You better think about your stand here . . . Norrington has pointed the finger straight at us!"

"Get out of it! He can't . . . that's slander!"

"Well he has . . . police were on the blower first thing and they want to see you!"

Richie's head was reeling. Tess and now this! He was optimistic for the future but he was weary with too little sleep.

He picked up the last of the straw Scott had left outside the enclosure. "Scottie, I swear to you . . . it wasn't me . . . I don't know anything about it!"

Scott looked at him a long moment, "No but I'm willing to bet you know a man who does!"

*　　*　　*　　*

Heather lay on Gita's couch at the Soul-Light Centre, where Gita, a doctor of Chinese medicine, performed minor miracles and less spectacular feats of healing.

Heather for some reason was crying a lot now. Gita ignored this and worked with her pendulum.

"Your blood pressure is dangerously high Heather . . . it is bad to grow it to this pitch!"

Heather almost laughed at Gita's strange way of phrasing things, Gita was not English.

"I didn't do it on purpose!" Heather said. "But the stress I'm under is awful!"

"Of course!" Gita declared. "Stress always is . . . . but you do well to remember Heather, this is only a t.v. programme . . . it is not real life!"

Heather made a loud and exasperated noise; it was as bad as talking with Dean.

"Easy for you to say Gita, but what if someone had threatened your Centre with closure! How would you feel?"

"Then I would open a new Centre somewhere!" said Gita pragmatically, lifting her brows above her Oriental features and assuming the distant and superior air that she felt was necessary to carry on with her ministrations.

"Well you see, I can't just open a new t.v. series can I?" said Heather bitterly.

"No, but there are other programmes!" replied Gita who scarcely ever switched on a television set.

"Ha!" Heather tossed about on the treatment couch. "Spoken like someone who isn't in show business!"

"Please be still!"

Gita refused to be baited. She had been practising her arts for some thirty years and knew all about people in distress, from one cause or another. She knew enough to ignore what they said and to listen instead to their bodies, and now and then to the wisdom of the ancestors who intervened at moments and helped to expedite healing and the understanding attendant upon that healing.

She continued to do her job whilst Heather ranted about the various plots which she called 'story lines' but sounded to Gita like something from dark fairytales or horror movies . . . .

There was something about going to sea in a boat, and then something else about a disused mine, and falling down into it. Then there was an improbable thing about an elder brother from America and a clinic where the rich went and to where this Wendy (aka Heather) was also to go . . . .

Gita tuned out and thought about her father and mother, long since dead, as she often did. They were Christian missionaries and they had tried to instil such values into their daughter, to no avail. Still Gita often thought of them with love. But not as much love as when she thought of her paternal grandfather in Peking who had taught her the finest of his skills as a doctor.

She was inserting a very painless needle into Heather's elbow when one of the ancestors called her attention.

Gita shushed Heather rather loudly and Heather looked startled and halted in her ramblings of the doings and ideas of these writers and editors and the other silly people with whom she was forced to work.

The ancestor spoke clearly to Gita for some moments then made farewells and left Gita's spiritual presence.

"Begging pardon for that! . . . I did not mean to shush you so rudely . . ." began Gita, "but an ancestor has just spoken!"

"Oh!" said Heather.

She gave little credence to these ancestors that Gita had much respect for, but Heather had so much regard for Gita herself that she was respectful of whatever Gita wished to impart. If someone as intelligent as Dr. Gita needed imaginary friends who was she to argue! After all, she was an actress and imaginary friends were her stock in trade, so to speak.

"What did they say?" Heather inquired lightly.

"They said to tell you that a death in the water and lost at sea is a preferable end!"

"End to what?"

"End to the life of . . ." Gita cast about in her memory for the name—she recalled it from the ancestor better than from Heather to whom she had listened only scantily. "The end of Wendy!" she concluded, sounding proud of her recall.

"But I don't want her life to end!" wailed Heather. "Tell them not to be so heartless!"

"I can tell them no such thing! . . . it isn't a question of that . . . they say what they have to say!" contended Gita. "It is not a programme like your soap opera!"

"Isn't it?" said Heather ambiguously, and then more carefully added, "Gita why are they saying that at all?"

Gita lifted her pendulum and looked heavenward. "I do not know . . . I shall have to get permission to enquire further of whoever that was!"

Only the needles in Heather prevented her springing from the couch. She was still overwrought, but no doubt the treatment Gita had given her would not see an effect for a couple of hours. "I'll be eager to hear whatever they say next!"

"Wait . . ." Gita put up her hand. "There is another of them here . . . very dear uncle to you apparently . . . he has better transmission . . ."

"And?" Heather was beginning to think they might be useful, these people in the nether regions.

"He is calling himself James . . . do you remember him? He gave you your love of theatre!"

"Of course I remember him!" proclaimed Heather, and it was only later she realized that in her eagerness to have information on the programme she had been completely cavalier and unbothered by the fact that her uncle had reappeared from the spirit world at all.

She had almost taken for granted that it was what uncles did.

Much later, in bed with Charlie asleep beside her, she had felt ashamed and less than restful. She had offered up a prayer in the dark and said she would be more humble next time in the face of such evidence.

"Your karma is tied in with Wendy's now . . ." Gita had said. "It could not be otherwise . . . and a death on the sea is better for you personally, you Heather! . . . Better for it to happen to Wendy than to Heather!"

"But it isn't going to happen to Heather is it?" Heather had enquired.

"I do not know . . . I am not an ancestor!" retorted the doctor archly.

"Gita what do you mean? . . ." Heather looked at the little woman as she removed the needles from her flesh.

Gita stared at her. "Do you not understand English? . . . I spoke quite clearly!"

"Yes but . . ." Heather rubbed her arm where one particular needle had left a stinging sensation. "I am not used to this jargon!"

"Jargon!?" repeated Gita imperiously. "What is jargon?"

Heather began to put on her blouse. She realized she had to tread carefully if she wanted more of this information. "Well . . . a way of speaking . . . the language a certain science may use!"

Heather reminded herself of an overly unctuous tele-sales person who had managed to upset someone of a different ethnicity. Or a not very polished speaking version of the Cambridge Dictionary.

"What they mean! . . ." Gita hesitated, "is that the soul of Wendy and the soul of Heather may be entwined now . . . and that the emotional personna of Heather is affected by what Wendy is doing . . ."

Heather tried to follow all this, and then saw a thread similar to her own recent train of thought. "That is perhaps why I am loath to go through with it! . . . why I don't want to die in any way as Wendy!"

"Yes but it may not be as simple as that!" said Gita. "Wendy is part of a collective aura now . . . she has become an archetype in the minds of many!"

Heather put on her shoes, picked up her bag, felt monumental anger towards Gita and glared at her.

"My God, Gita! . . . when I first came in today you were telling me that it was only a t.v. programme . . . and now you are giving me all this metaphysical stuff to think about!"

"The ancestors have spoken . . . it becomes a more intense matter!" said Gita, inclining her head as if still in the presence of the ancestral entourage and Uncle James. "I admit that I do not watch any t.v. . . . it is all very childish and silly to my eyes . . . but the ancestors have opened a wider horizon upon it . . . and I am obliged to listen!"

Heather was ready to leave and she marched to the front doors, impatient to be outside, forcing Gita to hurry after her.

"Will there be more? . . ."

She hesitated at the top of the steps of the converted chapel which was now the Soul Light Centre. "Information I mean! Will they speak again to you, these people? Or will they wait until I am here!"

"We will have to see . . ." said Gita promptly. "Come for your next appointment as planned on Wednesday . . . and we'll see . . . they are not a travelling circus you know, or a cabaret act! We cannot book them in advance through an agency1"

"Yes, yes . . . thanks!" Heather made her way down the steps. ". . . that's enough of the industry metaphors thank you!"

Gita trilled a tinkling kind of laughter, as if the whole thing were humorous, and closed the double doors on the outside world.

FOUR

Ged Norrington stomped around the kitchen of his farmhouse and ranted. His hat was on his head but his shirt and socks were off due to the heat generated by his womenfolk cooking in the kitchen on a warm day. "He'll get away with it! . . . that little shit and his accomplices . . . you mark my words!"

"Who'll get away with what?" asked Ged's aged mother, ninety one and sharp as a tack.

The volume of his voice brought his wife from another room. "Stop yelling Ged . . . for the love of God!"

"I'll yell all I want . . . I've reason to!"

Ged prowled about barefoot and searched for the daily paper amid bills, magazines and assorted pamphlets delivered (despite their remote location) on a frighteningly regular basis by leaflet distributors he could never quite catch in the act.

"I'm not putting up with your bellowing while I've a bad head! . . ." continued his wife of many years.

His wife, unlike many younger farmers wives of affluent heritage, still liked to maintain the old country ways; she baked bread, roasted foul and did all the other things that people thought they should envy.

"Anyroad, which little shit are you talking about now? . . . there's a whole list of them if memory serves me right!"

"The bird fancier over yonder!" said Ged in more moderate tone.

Nancy Norrington produced vegetables in a hot turin and Ged's mood mellowed at the thought of food. "The one who lives with her from the Hind . . . Bess, or whatever she's called . . ."

Nancy put the vegetables in the slow oven and helped her mother-in-law baste three sorts of poultry.

"Not for much longer by all accounts . . . and it's Tess not Bess!"

"She must have given the coppers an alibi for him because they say he was with some girl all the night until leaving for work next day . . ."

Nancy straightened and stared.

Ged watched her.

"What are you looking like that for? . . . spit it out! . . . . what is it Nan, what?"

"Nothing!" said Nancy and ducked down to check things in the oven.

"It can't be nothing!" Ged was again using a rate of decibels which some people might have construed as an abuse but to which Nancy was inured after many years of atunement. "Otherwise you wouldn't be looking like that! . . ."

"According to Mrs York buying eggs this morning Tess has left Richie and they're not a couple no more!"

"And how would Mrs York know?"

"Tess works at their yard . . ." Nancy stopped and thought twice about giving him more information in his present mood.

"What else she say?" He stomped across the tiled floor and towered over Nancy.

Nancy was unworried, she had loved Ged for the last forty years. She gazed up at him merrily. "Thought you was going to kiss me then!"

He brushed her mouth quickly with his own and gave her an even quicker smile and lowered his voice. "You know what this means? . . . It means Tess wasn't the one alibied him! . . . so who the devil was it then?"

"Might have been Tess . . ." Nancy pointed, "but it could have been anyone . . . he's a good looking feller!"

"He let the frigging turkeys out! . . . do you know what that's cost us?" bellowed Ged.

"I'm warning you!" intervened his mother, busying herself with the turnip mash. "I'll not be having that voice in here!"

Ged lowered his voice and inclined his head to his aged relative. "When's she going back to Mavis?"

"Not until Sunday!" said Nancy.

"Jesus Christ!" said Ged more audibly.

"I'll not tell you again!" said his parent in her ferocious croak.

Ged was a double for his father in many ways and his mother ordered Ged around as if she couldn't distinguish one from the other—which many in the family thought completely understandable.

Nancy moved to where the old woman was turning the gas higher than a flame thrower and allowing fat to burn on a separate jet. She was something of a liability now.

"Dora listen . . . you go and sit down . . . Antique's Road Show's on! . . . I'll get you a sherry!"

Mrs Norrington senior shuffled off to the other room, the soles of her slippers squeaking on the floor. "They're all repeats at this time o'day!" she complained.

A pause ensued in the kitchen during which Ged felt comfortable enough to raise his voice again. "It'll be a false alibi . . . ten to one!" he said, subsiding into a chair at the huge round wooden table. "Pity I can't find out who it is!"

"The Police won't say then?"

"Of course they won't say!"

Nancy waxed philosophical. "But if he got an alibi, Ged, then that's it!"

"That isn't it at all Nan!"

"Better for your peace of mind, not to mention your blood pressure, just to let things go! . . . it's done now! I think you should just take it in your stride! . . . you can't win them all . . . no-one can!"

"God give me strength!" Ged levered his cumbersome load out of the seat again. "Call me when dinners on the table . . . I can't sit and listen to this bollocks!"

It was a mark of his rural and rustic ways that Ged still referred to the mid-day meal as *dinner* and not lunch, and that he liked to eat it at around eleven thirty and not later than noon—having been up and about since five thirty, even though he had all the staff he could need.

Often he ate dinner alone; his more modern relations for whom Nancy Norrington liked to cook did not scruple to set their own deadlines and turned up after one in the afternoon on many occasions. He no longer worried about it, they could eat when they liked as long as they didn't expect him to starve himself waiting; it suited him better in many ways when there was no-one to monitor his carbohydrate levels or his fourth and fifth beer.

*   *   *   *

At much the same time as Ged and Nancy discussed recent events, Tess rode a prized horse along the bridle path skirting the forest. The same forest to which visitors came. The forest where mediaeval people had found everything they needed to live off, where naturalists went to study wildlife and where local adults told their children not to roam unaccompanied.

The bridle path was over three miles long and the forest could be accessed at various points along the way where the fencing and other impediments to entry were non-existent.

She had got up to a fair gallop on one of the York Stable mares, riding her hard as she liked to be rode, away from the more popular pathway used by dog walkers and other pedestrians. She rode where the forest and the path threatened to become one and the same but where the ground was even and flat.

Due at the Hind early afternoon she suddenly remembered and slowed and turned the horse to ride back the other way.

The horse's name was Flame, an unoriginal and quixotic choice by one of the York children. Flame was not flummoxed by this sudden change of mind; she was an experienced animal and used to the vagaries of riders.

Suddenly and from nowhere a rider-less horse rode up alongside them, and as Tess pulled the rein to steer Flame to the left she took fright and bucked. Tess struggled to get her under control for several seconds.

The new horse had stopped now some way in front and just as Flame seemed to be growing calmer she reared with ferocity and Tess was thrown from the saddle.

She landed hard on the ground and felt the vital strength going from her body. The strange horse was turning to cantor away as Tess scrambled in her body warmer for the mobile phone. Her vision was blurring rapidly but she recognized the horse as the same one she had encountered several nights ago with the foreign man in the meadow next to Rookeries. Then as the pain in her head became more intense and the nausea suffused her senses she dropped the phone and lost consciousness.

*   *   *   *

"What do you mean when you say you're not going into the studio for a while?"

Charlie turned from pumping out excess beer from one of the pipes and looked at Heather across the room with serious intent upon hearing. It was ominous; usually Charlie heard on an ad hoc basis without any real show of listening.

The pub had not yet opened and Heather was enjoying the vista of the meadowland and hills through the small mullioned window which gave the best view.

"Have they axed Wendy already?"

"No . . . I am refusing to support the storyline or attend the script meetings!"

"But . . . . but that's professional suicide!" Charlie stood transfixed, his hand on the pump. "Have you taken advice on it?"

"No . . . . only my own!"

"Only your own?" He could feel himself becoming very agitated, another unusual state.

"Are you gong to stand there repeating everything I say?" Heather cleared her late morning breakfast dishes and brought them to the bar.

"Heather, you should get some legal advice . . . suppose they sue for breach of contract!"

"They can't!"

"How do you know? Do you know that for certain?"

"Yes!" lied Heather.

Charlie was silent for a full three minutes, during which Barney came in and handed him the menu changes in rough to verify. Charlie looked at it without seeing it and handed it back.

"Well is it okay?" asked Barney.

"Show me later . . . I can't concentrate!"

He watched Heather prepare to leave the pub and pick up her car keys.

"I need to order supplies soon Charlie! Or we won't get any in time for tomorrow!" Barney adopted a wary and warning voice.

"Yes fine! . . . just do it . . . it'll be fine!" Charlie turned back to see Heather going through the main doors.

He ran after her. He couldn't remember when he had last chased after a female like this, probably in his final year at school.

Heather made no attempt to slow down. She was in a hurry to go somewhere, but she had not said where. He felt a chilled and growing desolation amid the flurry of events, as if he were being edged out of things and left out of the equation.

And then the knowledge struck him forcibly, arriving from nowhere: aside from the main event and the overriding worry of the axing of Wendy Tridmore there was something else happening; Heather was having an affair.

He knew it as sure as if someone had told him. Why he had failed to realise it before he did not know. Why it had not occurred to him when it had been apparent in her behaviour—all the signs consistent with infidelity—was a mystery to him.

"Where are you going?" he demanded of her a second time from the top of the steps leading down to the car park.

It was a well laid out plot on which the pub stood. Landscaped around the perimeter of the building. Flowered borders raised in deep low stone walls. Wide access points to admit vehicles. A nicely designed smoking area with metallic tables and chairs on a raised patio separating it from the rest of the land.

"Just out . . ." Heather called eventually, her voice faint as she neared her vehicle at the far end of the car park.

Charlie realized he had two choices; he could stand there and feel foolish—having made the initial attempt to catch up with her—or he could finish what was started and make sure he claimed her attention.

He was panting by the time he got to her car and she had actually put the vehicle into reverse. She jumped when she saw him at the window.

"What for Christ's Sake? you nearly gave me a heart attack!"

"You knew I hadn't finished speaking to you . . ." Charlie felt even more ridiculous now. "Why are you running off so quickly?"

"I'm not running off . . ." and even so she would not look at him. "I just don't want to argue about this script issue. I have made my mind up!"

"Listen Heather, if you do this you might not work again . . . you'll be blacklisted or something!"

"What do you think it is, the McCarthy witch hunts!" Heather angrily re-positioned her mirror as a prelude to driving.

"We have to talk about it!"

"What is there to talk about? . . . I am not going to be written out in a storyline which ends Wendy next week!"

"What? ends Wendy next week! when was this proposed?"

"That is what they now want . . . Wendy going off to America with her long lost brother . . . I want the boating incident instead!"

"It was only last week you said you didn't want a boating incident!" Charlie felt the car begin to move as he leaned against the driver's door and spoke through the lowered window. "I thought you said you hated that!"

Heather did not comment but waved her hand at him impatiently. Suddenly he was not to be included. He was not important enough to warrant an explanation.

"I know you'd earn more money if it went out to October Heather, but don't worry about that so much . . ."

Heather stopped the car's motion. "It's nothing to do with that! . . . it's because I'm scared to tempt fate . . ."

"What?" Charlie stepped back involuntarily. "What do you mean?"

"It is not something you'd understand!"

"What, because I'm not a lovey?" asked Charlie with some hostility.

"No, because you're a pragmatist!" said Heather. "Now Charlie please move . . . I'm late already!'

"For what?"

"An appointment!"

"Where?"

He detested himself; he sounded like a fanatical dependant, or an obsessive who couldn't be left alone without fear of abandonment.

"You're seeing someone else aren't you?" he said next, and for a second he wondered who had uttered the question for him. Directness of this type was not his style.

The car stalled and Heather stared at him, adopting in an instant a false and over stated look of incredulity, the best an actress might produce.

Too late—he had caught the initial look in her eyes before she had wiped it out in one clean sweep like writing from a chalk board. He had seen it and she could not take it back.

"I think you need to rethink what you just said Charlie!"

Standing watching the car pull out onto the road, Charlie registered the fact that she had not made any denial and had not said anything at all pertinent to the sensitivity of the question.

Heather headed for the Soul Light Centre, where she had an appointment with Gita and a colleague of Gita's who was something similar to a medium. They did not like that word, they actually grew uncomfortable when it was used, so Heather was careful not to say it in their presence. She only thought the word when describing to herself what she was going to do. She was getting the best help she could under the circumstances, concerning her inner life and her outer planning. *Medium* was the only term she had reference to in this context.

Hopefully they would shed some light on how her soul-path had become intertwined with Wendy's soul path. Apparently there was a reality somewhere in the wide and diverse universe in which the Tridmores and the rest of the characters of 'Marlborough Place' actually existed. It was in something like a parallel universe, but it was real in that it impinged upon this life and grew more and more influential in reality as it was acted out and witnessed by viewers.

Heather had learned of the aesthetics of all this the day before yesterday by having a long drawn out conversion with an expert on such matters residing at the other end of the country, having been recommended by Gita.

Heather was nothing if not thorough. She had recorded everything the woman had said and Dean had sat in on the conversation; a three-way conference call. Dean using his own bedroom extension whilst Heather used his office phone with the door open so they could see each other and make comments when necessary without interrupting the flow.

The woman in question had degrees in various types of psychologies and one in Quantum Theory and had briefly studied Particle Physics. She was erudite and wide in her approach to the subjects, extremely advanced in what she believed and advocated. The things she said made perfect sense to Heather and Dean, especially after extensive background information and much questioning of the rhetoric.

Heather felt she had travelled over the Atlantic twice without sleep and was jet lagged. She needed to lie down on Dean's bed and felt that her brain was fizzing with surreal data and incredible potential requiring two lifetimes to properly digest.

Two hours later she fell into a deep sleep from which she did not awaken for the next twelve.

Dean left her while he went to the studio, came home again, went for a game of Pool and a meal, returned to the flat, listened to her mobile ringing constantly and then decided to wake her up.

"What time is it?" she had asked, her voice a mere whisper from dehydration and far off activity.

"It's nine o'clock!"

"What, in the morning?"

"No, at night!"

"How long have I been here?" said Heather, her eyes huge on Dean's face.

"Since yesterday afternoon!" he told her.

And then Heather had run from the building, her hair and make-up less than acceptable, and Dean had followed with half her belongings as she got into her car.

"Charlie will be frantic!"

"I expect he will!" said Dean. "But you'll win him round!"

Heather knew she would not be able to relate any of the information she had learned on the phone call; it would be too ponderous and Charlie would stop her and interrupt and she would grow weary and impatient. It was taking her all her time to get her own head around it. She decided to leave a blank where the one and a half day gap in her life had been. He would have to think what he wanted to think.

Predictably, Charlie had not really believed her story of falling asleep drunk with one of the other cast members and losing track of time.

He wanted to, she could see that. And she knew that it was almost as good as him being convinced. Until half an hour ago in the car park of the pub when he had accused her of sleeping with Dean . . .

As she drove up to the Soul-Light Centre and parked in the sleepy little hamlet of Winifred Mead she thought of the last two days as something of a dream state.

She was shocked to discover that there was a little gathering of people present with Gita. They stood by as she lay on the treatment couch and Gita opened proceedings with her pendulum.

"Why are they all here?" Heather enquired with trepidation" I thought there would be just one medium . . . I mean one expert!"

"No, that isn't how we work!" said Gita in her businesslike manner. "We need the combined energy to go deeply into the matter!"

"I see!" Heather felt that her limbs had become weak and had she not been lying down she would have fainted.

Tridib joined them briefly, smiling his omniscient smile but saying nothing—in keeping with his vow of silence.

Some murmuring presently began, lower than the softest of voices, like a chant almost, but more of a keening sound. Heather's eyes flew open and she looked from one to the other. They were oblivious of her, their own eyes closed and their hands joined.

Gita took the floor in front of them all, like a soprano with her chorus line, and she lifted her small hands, palms upper most, towards the ceiling and waited.

Heather watched for a few seconds but whatever it was Gita had done to her with the pendulum made her drowsy.

It was impossible to keep her eyes open, or even to stay awake, she felt herself drifting to the accompaniment of the ululation of the humming, which is what it now sounded like. Presently she dropped into a deep and almost trance like state.

When she came to the gathering had dispersed and were standing randomly around the room, smiling and softly commenting in a foreign language to one another.

Gita noted her conscious state and took her wrist to check her pulse.

"What happened?" Heather asked

"The ancestors spoke!"

"What did they say?"

They all laughed a little in unison, as if this were an amusing joke and not a serious query. "Do not be in such a hurry Heather!" Gita admonished. "All in good time . . . let us first make sure the chakras are balanced . . ."

Gita handed her pendulum to one of the other females attending, of which there were about three, the other four people being male, and then she went from the room while the unknown woman held the pendulum over Heather's body and read whatever it was telling her.

At length Gita returned with a cup of jasmine tea and handed it to Heather.

Heather was by now sitting on the side of the couch and accepted the tea gratefully. Her throat was parched and it was as if she had drank nothing for weeks.

"You experienced on the astral a drowning . . ." Gita said unexpectedly, causing Heather to partially choke on the tea. "What?"

Gita did not repeat herself, knowing that it was a rhetorical question.

"It was so your subconscious can remember the experience for Wendy's behalf . . . ."

"What?" said Heather again, rather stupidly. "I don't understand Gita!"

Gita sighed and waited with a pained expression for the information to make itself understandable to Heather.

"Did you not say that Wendy was to be lost at sea near the end of the year?" Gita enquired.

"Yes . . . but . . . that isn't certain now . . . it might be that she's written out by going to America!"

The group frowned in unison and looked to Gita for explanation. Gita began talking to them in another language, her facial movements denoting her bemusement and lack of patience with the subject.

Eventually she turned to Heather again. "You have decided to accept that story? . . . . the one about America?"

"No . . . I am staying away so they cannot film it . . . but the boating accident might or might not happen . . . that is what I'm saying!"

More exchange of words in rapid unknown language.

"One way or another there will be a drowning!" Gita declared at length.

"You are all sure of that?" queried Heather.

Gita translated for her peers and they began nodding at Heather.

"Yes . . . we are all sure!" said Gita, but her face remained somewhat uncertain.

"So my plan will work then?" Heather leapt from the couch, revived by the tea. "I will get out of the American ending?"

Heather looked at each person present in turn. Their faces remained impassive and they stared at her, as if she were the strangest of creatures and her profession was the oddest pursuit of which they knew little but were mildly fascinated by.

Heather wondered what to make of it, she started several more phrases but stopped after the second word of each had left her lips.

Gita was looking and waiting politely for her to get a single train of thought and stick with it . . . or to leave well alone and call it a day.

"Will there be more news from the ancestors?" asked Heather, replacing her wedged sandals.

"Not in such depth . . ." replied Gita. "I doubt it . . . but if there is we will convene again!"

"I see!" said Heather "Send me a bill Gita and I'll pay it promptly!"

Gita bowed and the entourage bowed also, as if seeing out royalty. Heather knew that in financial terms, and comparative to some of the clients Gia saw, that is exactly what she was in this place.

*　　*　　*　　*

It was gone three a.m. when Heather awoke and remembered Gita's words and saw them in a different way entirely.

"One way or another there will be a drowning . . ."

In the still of the night next to the gently snoring Charlie, the words seemed ominous. They filled her with dread. Was it Wendy's dread or Heather's dread? She scarcely knew which. Of course her common sense told her it had to be Heather's dread.

She rose to make a cup of tea and smoke a cigarette, and opened the patio doors of the bungalow. A nice clear chilly night, a slight wind and a smell of lavender from the house across the road.

She felt peace return.

She felt better, she even felt she could in the fullness of time psyche herself up to letting go of Wendy and to letting her be lost at sea. If that is what it took.

Currently the thought of never being Wendy again filled her with sadness. More than that, it seemed to fill her with trepidation. As if she were losing a sister, or a twin.

Perhaps she needed a psychiatrist rather than a medium.

She returned to bed and saw that Charlie had awoken—she had accidentally left on the light outside the bedroom door and that always woke him.

He looked at her blearily. "What's the matter?"

"Nothing now!" she kissed him lightly and got back into the bed.

"Well I can't get back of!" he said tetchily. "I'll have to go and make some tea!"

In his absence she thought again of the session at Gita's and the strangeness of it all. She tried to recall word for word what had been said and what had transpired, but the trance like state which had fallen over her was too great and so a major part of it was lost to unconscious memory.

Perhaps the group around Gita had seen the future, or perhaps they had seen the future as Heather was going to plan it. Was it the same thing? Possibly! If the future was not fixed, as Gita contended, then they could only be guided by Heather's inclinations herself at the time of them concentrating on her!

But what of the scriptwriters! What of their intentions for Wendy!

Wendy and Heather were separate people, weren't they! No, of course they were not, how could they be!

But Wendy was not a person at all, she was a figment of a writer's imagination and a contrivance of Heather's own further imagination! And then overall Wendy was a part of this imaginary world—which Gita claimed really existed in its own dimension.

But for the purpose of argument per se it did not and would not have an existence without all the actors, writers, producers, crew members etc. It was not a viable option to say that Wendy had inclinations or intentions of her own about her own future. She simply did not have a future! Unless Heather chose to speak for her, she did not exist. Did she?

The very ramifications and the machinations and the various parts of the mind and its take on reality were beginning to tire her and her eyelids drooped.

Then Charlie entered the bedroom and made a clanking sound with the mug of tea against the bedside clock. Heather jumped and came to.

"Sorry . . . sorry . . ." Charlie put the mug in a better position and clambered back into bed.

"No, it's *my* fault for waking *you!*" Heather said politely.

She watched him take tentative greedy slurps from the hot tea and she became fascinated by the ritual.

Silence ensued while Charlie drank and stared into the distance at nothing in particular and Heather followed her own thoughts. Then she knew she needed the loo before sleeping and went into the en suite.

As she climbed back into bed again she winced with some kind of back pain.

"Okay?" enquired Charlie.

"Fine!" she said and straightened out gingerly, releasing tension from her spine.

It was at moments like this when Charlie remembered that Heather was older than most people thought she was. It might be as well that Wendy was soon being axed. What was that saying about people never tiring of the theatre but the theatre tiring of them?

"I hope you can sleep again tonight!" said Heather affectionately and ran her hand up and down his arm in a comforting way.

"So do I . . . I may have to do the whole day tomorrow if Tess doesn't turn in!"

Heather looked at him sharply. "You mean she didn't turn in yesterday after all that trouble last week?"

"Not seen sight nor sound of her since the day before that!"

"And hasn't she phoned?"

"Nope!" Charlie sounded as if this wasn't surprising and had a *what do you expect* sort of tone to his voice.

"But that's odd! She was so glad to keep the job!"

"Yes! . . . but then again you know what they're like . . ."

"No . . . there's something very odd Charlie . . . I can sense it!"

"Oh Good God!" Charlie banged the mug down onto the table. "Not more conspiracy theory! . . . maybe that mystery horse ran away with her!"

Heather tutted and removed her hand swiftly from his arm. He had turned her off again now.

Charlie moved away up the bed and lay with his back to her. He was not yet over the afternoon's painful exchange in the car park and still had no clue where she'd been. Added to which he was more certain than ever that she was having an affair!

FIVE

Richie was enjoying the benefits of an actual building as a residence, a bricks and mortar structure, rather than a caravan.

He looked about him as he smoked his second post coital cigarette . . . the overly fussy curtains which were a definite feminine touch, the tiny central chandelier (mock Georgian but still tasteful) and the picture rail running around the high walls. The flat was converted from an early nineteenth century mansion house and a lot of the period features had been nicely retained.

"Who pays for all this then?"

"I do!" said Francine, wiggling her lithe body closer to him, moulding her contours to his. Her ears were pink in the low warm light of the lamp. She looked almost cherubic. She was drop dead gorgeous, and she knew it.

"What, all by yourself?"

"No . . . I have a flat mate!"

"Even so . . . must be an arm and a leg for the pair of you!"

"Yes . . . but I get an allowance!"

"Course you do!" said Richie and then hoped that his tone was not tinged with any sarcasm. He did not mean it to be; the comment was meant to denote his stupidity in not seeing the probability first off: a rich kid with an allowance and a land owning farming family stretching back generations. Posh daughters and sons, folk educated way beyond their ancestors and predecessors.

"What do you do all day then?"

"Attend college!" she said. "Horticulture and Floristry!"

"You like it?"

"Not that much . . . but I had to choose something . . . one of Ged the Dread's stipulations!"

Richie remained silent; he was unsure how much she knew of the feud with her Uncle or their recent interchange. It was best to say little, blood was blood when all said and done. Even though she'd declared that she didn't like him did not give Richie the right to make derisive remarks.

Francine had skin that was pure and ivory and soft. He was surely very fortunate suddenly; lovely girl in a lovely bedroom in a plush apartment. Did it get any better than this?

No, it probably went downhill quickly!

Richie was not so much a pessimist as a self doubter. Why should this happen to him! Especially when he had treated Tess badly.

He looked down and admired his superlative erection with pride. His penis swollen to enviable proportions and throbbing fit to burst. He could pace himself, he was no longer sixteen, he took as much enjoyment from watching his manhood as he took in executing it.

Besides, Francine was dozing again, her eyes closed and her jaw slack, her body with that dead tired feel against his. It was a tragedy to wake her.

He thought about her generosity in giving him an alibi—she did not have to do it. She could easily have refused, even though he was with her for the greater part of the night she could have told them that he was gone after four thirty a.m.

He had been nowhere near the turkeys at the time they were sprung, but as Scott would say: *'he knew a man who knew someone who was'* . . . .

How perfect was Francine at her tender age! how gentle and soft and girlish in her beauty! Would she improve with age or would she fade? Some women improved with age. He knew it, had experience of some great looking older women.

He had that kind of universal appeal to women in general, and he seldom stopped to question it. He did not always take advantage of it. He liked his other passions as much as he liked women.

Francine stirred and opened her eyes, took his throbbing penis in her delicate hand, the nails of which had changed again: snow white with swirls of red; a raspberry ripple effect. They fascinated him momentarily. Then she ran the tip of one nail lightly, ever so lightly, down the side of his penis and his breath rasped through his teeth with excruciating pleasure. He was holding back from her so he wouldn't begin to climax as he pulled her into place beneath him.

They had just got nicely into rhythm when his phone rang.

Francine swore but tried valiantly to carry on as if the interruption hadn't happened.

He too ignored it, but something was a little lost and they had to retrace the approach to pick up the pleasure pace again. They were just underway with enthusiasm when the phone rang a second time.

"Fuck me!" exclaimed Richie in an unromantic brusque voice.

"I was trying to!!" she purred, her voice a little girly whisper in his ear, her marvellous nails tracing tiny spirals around his scrotum, touching the skin with just the right amount of pressure.

He focused his senses on her totally but the phone all the while was playing its jarring jingle above the strains of 'Whiter Shade of Pale' in the background of the apartment. The phone was muted in the pocket of his jacket but still audible and taking precedence.

"Shit! . . ." he rolled off her. "I can't get it on again after that!"

"Never mind! . . . why don't you answer it? . . . could be important!"

Her tone was still ambient to the intimacy of the moment and it oozed patient understanding, made him feel better.

He scrambled from the bed; pale lemon sheets awry and tawny coloured satin pillows at irregular angles over the bed, expensive silk covered duvet on the floor.

The time was 12.30 in the morning and his voice told the caller of his recent enjoyment, thick with longing and desire for another person.

"Is that Richard?" said the female at the other end.

"Yes, who's this?"

"It's Annabelle York!"

"Who?" He realized he sounded angry. "Who's Annabelle York when she's at home?"

"York Equestrian Centre!"

His brain tumbled pieces into place enough to get the geography and nature of the woman before she continued.

"It's about Theresa . . . ."

"Who?" He was in the dark again, startled and a bit alarmed.

"Theresa Bailey . . . . Tess? . . ."

He had forgotten Tess's full first name some time ago.

"She works for us . . ."

"Look what's this about? It's twelve thirty five a.m.!"

"She's in St. Anthony's! . . . She's unconscious . . ."

Annabelle York had a deeply melancholic tone, slightly embarrassed, as if this were all her fault. "She was riding one of ours when she must have been thrown . . . a hiker found her on the tow path hours later . . . ."

Richie took in the news and said nothing. It was as he had suspected, all downhill from here.

"The hospital gave me Tess's phone so we could tell people but it had been damaged in the accident. My husband had to fiddle with it and recharge it to get it working again, you're first on her list of numbers. I thought you'd like to know. I'm very sorry!"

"Yes, thanks! . . . I'll go over there! Thanks for letting me know!" Richie brought the call to an end in a neutral kind of voice, betraying nothing of his inner feelings.

He went to the bathroom and turned on the shower. He couldn't bring himself to relate any of it to Francine just yet. He needed to come down to earth and to wake up properly.

When he looked in on her she had fallen back to sleep. Two bottles of Chardonnay would do that to a girl.

Hers was the most efficient shower system he had ever known, the water jets comforted his body almost as much as she did. He stayed underneath them for ten minutes and wondered what to write on the note he would leave for her.

*   *   *   *

Much later that morning Dean was looking at Heather closely, she was showing signs of strain without a doubt. She was wearing too much make-up, giving her an older appearance rather than the effect she was trying for.

"They delivered some kind of legal letter this morning . . . but I haven't opened it yet!"

"Who, the studio?"

"Yes, naturally the studio . . . . who do you think I mean?

"Okay, Heather, keep your hair on!" Dean looked about him in the restaurant to make sure no-one of any influence saw them.

They were in the bar area which was obscured from the eating area, but even so one never knew who might pass by. It was a place frequented by the profession and he could not risk being seen to collude with Heather on this ridiculous campaign she had waged.

"Don't you think it would be wiser to open it and find out what's inside?"

"Why? . . . much better to pretend I haven't received it!"

"Heather, you can't avoid the situation forever!"

"I know that, but I can make a stand!"

"You're being ridiculous . . . and unprofessional!" said Dean with some asperity.

Heather made a face so mutinous and enraged he moved back on the seating away from her; she was about to launch her wrath on him, it was evident.

Then his phone rang loudly, he had turned it onto full volume earlier whilst he left it indoors and went out to fix his balcony awning at the flat. Consequently the ringtone was playing a Status Quo rift loud enough to alert the whole restaurant.

They both started as it came to life and Dean grabbed it and jumped to his feet and moved away from the table by a few feet.

It was Roy Preston, and he could not believe the coincidence.

"Listen . . . go and check on Heather will you?" began Roy in a conspiratorial way. "I know you're . . . well I know you two are . . ."

"What?" snapped Dean curiously.

"Let's just say I think you're quite close to Heather! I think you might be the best person to take this forward now, short of a writ and all that . . . which could damage the programme credibility a lot. So can you go round to that pub and see what's happening?"

"What pub?" said Dean, being annoyingly obtuse.

"The pub she owns with her boyfriend . . . . The Golden Fleece! Or something of that kind . . ."

"Golden Hind!" corrected Dean.

"Just call in and try to talk with her . . . she's completely ignoring the letter!"

"Okay Roy . . . got you . . ." Dean tried to ring off quickly.

Heather had moved to the other end of the bench to listen in. She knew of course that it would probably be someone from the studio. Now Preston had launched into a diatribe about the studio's legal policies and his conversations with the Chief Chirpers and so on. Dean was trapped.

"Yes . . . yes . . . yes . . . yes . . . I have to go Roy . . ." he interrupted eventually. "I'm driving!"

At length he was allowed to ring off.

"Was it the studio?" Heather enquired.

"Yes . . . it was Preston!"

"What did he want?"

"Oh, he was just asking me to attend a meeting tomorrow!"

"Took him long enough! I thought he was reading you an entire episode script!" Heather took a cigarette she would not be allowed to smoke out of the packet and tapped it on her lighter in agitation. "It will be about Wendy no doubt!"

"No doubt!" agreed Dean, and sat down again and surveyed the food menu.

He could risk being seen now with Heather; if anyone queried it he could say he had brought her here to talk on Roy Preston's instructions.

Some innate wisdom, however, kept him from telling her that Preston was asking him to act as covert envoy. He felt that would be too difficult a situation to manage for someone of his own overt nature.

*   *   *   *

At St. Anthony's Hospital the ward where Tess lay was one of the quietist. It was an intensive care unit, removed from the main corridor by a longish passage around the corner of another short isolated corridor.

The hum and thrum of machinery and the squeak of trollies and wheeled apparatus and occasional shoes on the polished floor, a distant radio playing in an office belonging to clerical staff.

The sun shone brightly through the extensive windows in this modern part of the building, giving it a deceptively cheery and informal appeal.

For the most part Tess felt she had come to some strange intermediary place where she was still Tess but not any longer of Tess's life. She felt she had been there an age, and although she knew that she was deeply asleep and not connected to anything roundabout she also knew there was a 'roundabout'—just as she knew there was another place where she kept going to, and when she was there the 'roundabout' had gone and nothing from it could penetrate the new place.

Sometimes people from the *roundabout* poked her, or so it seemed, and stuck things into her and lifted and shifted her and came near her face. She felt that any second she might attempt to open her eyes, but then the temptation went again and it seemed absolutely irrelevant to even try.

At certain points a warm scented damp cloth came past her nose and she knew someone was touching her with it, washing her or caressing her with it. It was a very odd sensation, it was happening to her but not to her.

At other points someone took hold of her hand and there was a feeling to her right side of being pulled from the other place, which she fought hard to resist with her mind.

At the other place there was a farm and a group of people whom she knew but didn't quite remember. They were good to her. They talked in an odd way and at first she couldn't remember how to communicate with them. They looked at her strangely as if they thought something had gone wrong but didn't like to question her.

And then suddenly she knew what they were saying. It was a language different to the one she had been used to speaking, although she did not right then have a frame of reference for naming it.

It did not occur to her to reason it against anything other or different. It was just where she was and who she was. It was fine.

She stared at the hills—they were hills she felt she had returned to. But from where? Where had she been?

There was an intrusive knowing that something kept on intervening, pulling her from the constant of this good place. It was an intermission only, like travelling overnight through a tunnel while asleep to a foreign but regular destination.

In the *roundabout* things on wheels (and often shoes) squeaked and she couldn't see anyone and did not know if they could really see her.

Now and then voices spoke to her. They called her name, but it was a different name than the one she knew herself by at the other place. It felt like she was dreaming it all from the the new place, had fallen asleep for a moment or two in the deep rocking chair on the veranda of a house she lived in with others overlooking pleasant mountains.

She no longer bothered, after a while, trying to sort out which was the dream and which was not. Perhaps both states were dream states.

Then a time came in the *roundabout* when they were calling her a name that sounded like Jess, or maybe Tess, and she was trying to think how to convey to them to leave her alone, and someone from the new place arrived and commanded her complete attention and put an end to the division.

"Bonjour Solange!"

It was the man from across the other side of the land owned by her family. Instantly the annoying pests from *roundabout* seemed to disappear.

*   *   *   *

"Will she be like this for long?" Richie asked them. "She seems to be less responsive now than yesterday!"

The doctor stared at him and Richie was unsure if it was because he had asked a stupid question or because the doctor didn't know the answer.

"Hard to know!" said the medic at length.

"Oh! . . ." Richie paused. "Will she make a full recovery if she lives?"

The doctor drew a long breath and then shrugged. "It's impossible to say at the moment!"

"Can she feel me when I touch her hand?" Richie persevered.

"It's difficult to tell . . . sometimes maybe!"

Richie was not an aggressive person but he felt an anger and a frustration so huge he could barely contain it.

"Is there anything you do know?" he said.

The doctor was sallow and unhealthy looking—for a doctor—smaller than Richie with a wiry little body and the look of a schoolboy. He was used to sarcasm in these situations and blinked dismissively. "You play it day to day . . . is all I can tell you!"

Richie stood aside to let him pass. He wondered whether he should be touching her hand at all after what had happened in their relationship. Maybe she would not want it. Perhaps she could feel it and did not know how to stop him.

He vowed not to touch her again, even though a part of him suspected that anyone might touch someone in Tess's current state, as an act of kindness.

Still he felt he was violating some ethic by doing so without her permission. He looked around for a female nurse or doctor to consult on the matter, to get their opinion in the lack of his own moral compass, but no such person was around and anyway it was too personal a dilemma.

He left the hospital and decided to come back next day with flowers and leave them next to her in case she could see them from some invisible function, in the way he had once heard about on a television documentary about out of body experiences.

*   *   *   *

Solange followed the man as he went back to the road abutting the house she lived in with her family. He walked to his horse, tethered at the tree to the right of their stable. The horse stood patiently, the grey dappled gelding that Tess felt she knew from somewhere else besides. It was a fine horse, a sturdy and handsome creature.

"Ride with me . . ." the man entreated. "It will be quicker . . ." He helped her mount and then jumped up behind her.

"I am going to show you the damn!" he said.

Solange knew the man as Didier.

"Your brothers will not take in the importance of the crisis . . ." he shouted to her over her shoulder. "They think tomorrow is soon enough . . . you must look and see for yourself how slowly the water flows now and then tell them . . . . they may listen to you!"

When they reached the damn it indeed flowed slowly, as if something had reduced the amount of water in two days. They moved on towards the river, from where the damn originated and saw that it was low but not dry.

Dismounting they walked along the bank until Didier observed across the other side of the river the possible cause of the problem. The river bank was subsiding, the dry earth crumbling and dissolving and the water flow ebbing away beneath the ground.

Quickly they got back on the horse and rode to the nearest bridge and crossed over to the opposite side and went to the point adjacent where they had stood previously to survey the damage.

"This is just one problem . . ." declared Didier, and Solange looked at him ruefully.

"I will guess that that the erosion has been going on for a while and has caused a secondary problem at the damn so that there is a blockage!"

He was leaning down and smelling the water and tasting it as if suspicious of other causes. "But I cannot tackle it alone . . . I need help!"

"Of course!"

Solange hoisted her skirts to venture into the water with him and get a closer inspection. "I'll talk to them at dinner tonight! My brothers and my father!"

They went back to the horse. Solange stroked it and spoke softly to it and the horse nuzzled her and the man smiled. He was not himself French but from French speaking Algiers. He was a gypsy of sorts and sought his living sharpening knives and honing other instruments and sometimes welding at the back of his caravan housed on her father's land. He was older than Solange by ten years or so, unmarried, a loner, but he was accepted by the villagers and thought well of by most people; he could shoe horses, heal animals and knew everything there was to know about farm apparatus.

That evening she spoke to the men of the family about what she had seen.

"He told you yesterday but you would not take it seriously!" she said as they ate the soup her mother always made on a Wednesday which lasted until Friday. Delicious soup with onions and garlic and water cress.

"It's not that we wouldn't listen . . ." Her younger brother was very talkative while the elder one said little. "It was that we'd better things to do . . . wasn't that so, Etienne?"

Etienne nodded in agreement and gulped the soup, stuffing bread into his mouth every few seconds.

"Well whatever it was you had better listen now. I have seen it myself . . . soon the water will dry at the damn and the well will suffer!"

"Yes . . . then the cattle!" said her father and glared at his sons. "You should have told me immediately!"

"You were at the market!" said Solange. "Or I would have done so . . . then I forgot . . . I am ashamed to say!"

They went along right away to the river, collecting Didier on route. Her brothers, their cousin George, her father and Solange. All travelling on separate horses.

Solange greeted Didier and smiled at him with hope and a lightening of her mood. They had caught things in time. Didier smiled back, he saw in Solange's eyes something he had been hoping to see for a long time. Later on, after the crisis with the river, he would make an approach to her and see if she would eventually have him. When his money came in finally next year.

They inspected the river, finding that the bank was quite eroded but that it could be shored. They discussed getting a gang of men and starting tomorrow. It would take some days but it could be done.

The damn was a different matter. They could not see what the real problem was. Certainly the water flow was impaired and not just from the low river, but from some unknown blockage that had been building for a while.

Didier lowered himself down the steep stone wall of the damn on a rope and stood at the bottom so that the water washed over him as far as his knees. Had the damn been at full flow the water would have come to his elbows and he would not have been able to stand.

"What do you see?" called Etienne, leaning right out from the bridge wall above and held by his brother and their father so that he would not fall.

"Nothing!" declared Didier. "Merely that the tunnel is darker than usual. I am going in!"

"Take care!" shouted their father.

But Didier had disappeared.

Solange was bored now. They had been stood around for half an hour talking of building and engineering, deciding what best to do in the morning and who would be better qualified to judge the problem.

They knew someone over in the next village who was an expert on rivers and damns and drainage but then that was half a days ride away and he may anyway not be there.

Solange yawned, it was turning chilly and it was after eight o'clock. She pulled a heavy silk shawl around her shoulders and gazed off at the lowering sun and the hills and stroked Didier's magnificent horse. Her mind and attention drifted.

There was suddenly urgent movement and she realized that they had made significant progress, or Didier had, and she had missed it.

It took her a few moments to ascertain that there was a dead animal blocking the underground tunnel of the damn. Didier was going in again to move it.

Her father was imploring him to wait and Didier was saying it was unnecessary. He was out to prove himself and gain the respect and gratitude of her family—she knew it without him having to say it. It had been the look between them earlier.

Her brothers joined the discussion and all were entreating him to wait and then disagreeing about the method he should use for dislodging the dead animal.

Solange grew even more bored and tired and stiff.

And then, apparently, Didier went back into the tunnel.

An age seemed to pass, which was in truth a quarter hour. The daylight faded sharply and there was a loud male cry. Great torrents of stinking water ensued from the tunnel, followed by cleaner water, but the volume of it was fierce.

Obviously Didier had moved the dead animal.

But as she looked over the wall and peered down she saw that the tidal wave of water was carrying something other than the animal carcass. It was a roiling dark mass with moving parts, tossed and rolled on the flood. Shouts came but were muffled by the water itself.

The waters carried the mass along the river someway and her brothers scrambled down the bank and along the sides, clinging to the grass and the bracken, and then reaching the mass which now had been thrown up against a clump of trees on a mound of prominent earth.

It was Didier's body. He had drowned.

They stared at him, his cut and blooded face, his open and terrified eyes his distorted limbs and his sodden clothes. "Quickly roll him over onto his stomach!" Solange screamed at them along the riverbank. "Quickly before he dies!"

"It's too late!" said her father quietly, next to her. "He is already dead!"

Solange opened her mouth to cry out and no sound came, her eyes welled with unshed tears and her throat felt as if it would explode with emotion.

She had loved this man for five years and not known it. All that time he had lived a half kilometre away and she had loved him and not done anything about it.

Then she awoke. In the lighted room of a strange place, lying on a bed, the people wearing strange cotton tunics and trousers of thin blue material with matching tops and white masks over their mouths.

"Tess!" someone called whilst peering down at her.

There was a high grating sound, like foxes barking, feet were running. Tess could partly recall where she had just been, but the death of Didier seemed more inconsequential now, a part of her history.

The thing she knew was that in this other place, where lived her brothers and her parents, everyone loved her. They treated her with respect, as if she meant something. Whereas in this *roundabout* time and place they did not really do that. She was not cared for, never had been. Parents, relatives, lovers—indifferent, rude, uncaring; they none of them cherished or appreciated her.

Only at the other place, where Didier had resided on their land, did they appreciate and love her.

Now some man with a stethoscope around his neck leaned in to her, felt her wrist.

"Tess, I'm Doctor Riley . . . how do you feel?"

"Kind of you to ask," said Tess in fluent French and closed her eyes, "but I'd be glad if you didn't keep bringing me from the other place! . . . I have important things to do!"

"Which other place?"

Thankfully she sank down and down and down into an ever increasing lightness of being, which was a sensuality all its own, and lost utterly that particular focus in which he was asking her questions.

She passed with consummate ease—swiftly back into the other place.

*   *   *   *

Charlie watched covertly as Heather entered the pub with Dean. He knew vaguely who Dean was: the assistant producer from the programme; he had met him briefly with a party of people she'd brought in at Christmas.

But beyond that he had the distinct feeling that this was also her lover, the person she was having the affair with. Charlie no longer doubted that she was having an affair. With each day that passed he had become more and more certain of the fact.

The marked age difference between Dean and Heather gave him some ease of mind; it would not last long. The guy was either a fortune hunter or star struck, or both.

They had come to open the letter no doubt. The letter that Heather had refused to open this morning with Charlie, on the pretext of not wanting to upset herself without recourse to advice, the letter that lay on the shelf of the marble fireplace in the bungalow.

Heather watched Charlie carefully for a few seconds as he moved his gaze to the customers lingering in the elevated bay at the right hand side of the pub—they were 'runners' if he was not mistaken and they would sneak, bolt or scamper from the eating area leaving the bill for four meals unpaid.

Heather clutched at Dean's arm. "Don't say anything to him . . . I don't want him to suspect!"

"What did you think?" Dean said, huffing in contempt, "that I was going to announce myself as the clandestine lover!!"

"No, but Charlie's very astute . . . he can read people like a book!"

"Can he!" said Dean dully.

"Yes . . . . you might just say something to give us away!"

"Like what?"

Charlie shifted his gaze back to them as someone from the right hand bay party came forward with a credit card.

"I'll just make my presence known . . . and then we'll go to the bungalow!" whispered Heather and she smiled at the room at large where one or two people had already recognized her.

"Why don't we just go straight there?" Dean asked.

"Because people in these parts talk . . . . it's not the town . . . it's a small community and it would look odd!"

"Would it?" said Dean. "Someone entering the house with you!"

"Not just anyone . . . a young man alone . . . with me I mean . . . . Charlie might get to hear!"

"Heather, have you never heard of innocent intent! Or on the other hand, behaving suspiciously in a guilty manner without cause!"

Dean was becoming quite annoyed now, he was not used to sneaking about and being treated like a leper, or even as someone that a woman might not be proud to be seen with.

"And have you never heard of tempting fate?" snapped the actress as she moved with a smiling visage and an open confident stride towards her partner.

"Charlie? . . . you know Dean don't you!"

"No!" said Charlie with a brevity that defied response, looking at the credit card machine after the man had entered his digits. "Should I?"

"Yes . . . you met him on Boxing Day!"

Dean held out his hand rather inanely, caught up in Heather's guilty subterfuge and feeling humiliated.

Charlie ignored Dean's outstretched hand on the pretext of it being out of his line of vision, but the customer looked at them both curiously and then at Heather whom he looked away from immediately—her apparent fame terrifying him.

Dean dropped his hand and glowered at Heather.

Heather felt herself blushing. It was ludicrous.

"Charlie . . . we're going to the bungalow!" she said with terse disapproval.

Charlie fixed her with his blankest stare. "Yes . . . and? . . ."

He could not dissemble, could not go through any charade with this younger man, whose clothes and hairdo spoke of artistic media worlds.

"Well I'm just letting you know!"

"You live there . . ." Charlie said flatly, "so why do I need to know!"

"We're going to look at the letter!"

Heather had dropped her voice as she said this, to a level almost inaudible to anyone not close up to her.

"Oh yes . . . right!" Charlie spoke in a facetious stage whisper. "Don't forget to eat it after you've read it!"

He had still not looked at Dean. Dean was beneath his contempt and dismissed from sight.

Dean knew then, knew that Charlie knew he was up to no good with Heather, apart from sneaking around playing amateur lawyer. Charlie knew they were sleeping together.

Heather was speechless with anger. She clutched at Dean's arm and pulled him around. "Come on . . . let's go!"

Charlie handed the credit card back to the diner and tore off the receipt from the machine, moved on to the next customer at the bar, all without looking at Heather or Dean.

Dean followed Heather's angry walk, which was belied by her charming expression to all and sundry, and he vowed never to set foot in the pub again or to encounter Charlie.

Charlie was formidable in the extreme. At first a very mediocre and nondescript individual with no particular presence, but on closer inspection a man with an inscrutable and rock hard demeanour disguising all kinds of character strengths. Dean had met actors like this, nothing much to behold but everything to show when knowing their lines.

Following Heather to her car and getting in beside her silent and furious personna Dean digested the last few minutes of interchange and discovered it was possible he was actually quite afraid of Charlie. It wasn't his pride he was protecting by his defensive decision, it was his personal security.

*   *   *   *

"She spoke fluent French this morning for a few seconds of consciousness!" the nurse told Tess's parents and Richie. "Is she accustomed to being in France?"

"No, she's never been there as far as I know!" said Tess's mother.

"She once went on a day trip with the school!" added Tess's father to his wife.

Tess's mother looked vacantly back at him, her eyes pendulous with the sort of tears that don't go away and don't exactly flow. Tess's father stared at her, waiting to have his memory confirmed at this crucial time.

"I never knew that she could speak French . . . did you know that?" asked the mother of Richie.

"No!" Richie said.

The father grunted with aggravation. "For God's Sake, it doesn't matter . . . ."

"What, that she spoke French and we never knew she could?" Tess's mother tutted and muttered and turned to gaze off up the corridor.

The nurse watched them patiently. "Maybe she learned at school and you weren't aware!"

"That's doubtful!" said her mother "She was seldom in the place!"

Embarrassed, the nurse checked her fob watch and the father looked at his wife as if he would love to throttle her.

"Maybe it was just gibberish!" said Richie casually, ". . . and someone mistook it for French . . . seeing as she's unconscious!"

The nurse blinked her eyes rapidly in Richie's direction. "Unlikely! . . . Doctor Riley has a house on the Dordogne and goes regularly . . . he's fluent in the language!"

Richie smiled slightly in sardonic patience. *'Good for Dr. Riley!'* he retorted in the silence of his own mind.

"Perhaps you got the patients muddled!" Tess's father offered.

Tess's mother hissed in irritation. "Bernard, you just saw Tess for yourself lying there . . . don't be daft!"

Bernard was cowed but not beaten. "I meant temporarily . . ." His desperation was worse than anything so far; Richie thought that Bernard might cry; he had seen kids at Rookeries display such an emotion prior to bursting into tears.

"I meant this Doctor Riley . . . he may have been looking at the wrong patient . . . these things happen!"

"Not on Intensive Care!" interjected the nurse flatly. "Anyway I didn't mean to upset you . . . I wouldn't have mentioned it if I'd known . . ."

"You were right to mention it!" said Bernard. "It's downright odd!"

"People say all kinds of strange things after head trauma!" the nurse contended and saw a perfect opportunity to break the flow of conversation.

"You didn't have to be so sneering Connie . . ." Bernard looked at his wife's distant face staring off down the corridor as if they were waiting for a bus.

Suddenly she swung round on Richie. "Did you know she could speak French these days?"

"No, I didn't! I told you that a moment ago, and besides . . ." Richie was about to add that Tess had enough trouble speaking English and then stopped abruptly.

"What was you going to say?" asked Connie, suddenly alert to his thoughts through the intensity of the situation . . .

"Nothing . . ."

"Yes you was . . ." she persevered. "I could see it in your face!"

Bernard should have escaped years ago! Richie grinned his sardonic grin and Connie (his erstwhile potential mother-in-law) opened her eyes wide in anger. *There but for the grace of God . . .*

"Leave the lad alone!" ordered Bernard. "He's upset . . . she's his girlfriend don't forget!"

It was the time to come clean, to speak out, to sever the ties; not that there were any now, Tess detested her parents. But it was time to put them straight about the break up. Then again, the break-up was not their business: they were not those kind of parents.

Richie walked away slowly, mulling the dilemma over, before he turned back and held up his hand. "Bye then!"

The surprise on Connie's face at his swift exit was the last memory he thought he'd take with him of the hospital.

He did not think he would return. He did not believe that Tess would survive the ordeal and any notion of comforting her parents and being comforted by them was out of the question.

* * * *

"Why were you not more civil to Dean Waters?" Heather demanded of Charlie later that day.

Charlie ignored her and continued to stare at the rugby on the plasma screen in the upstairs apartment of the Golden Hind. It was his break between shifts.

Heather moved in front of him, blocking his view of the match. "I have a reputation to maintain . . . . and I work with Dean Waters, he's the assistant producer!"

"Not my problem!" said Charlie. "Is there something in your contract that states I have to fawn all over your colleagues!"

"You don't need to fawn over anyone! . . . you only needed to be civil!"

Charlie's mobile rang and he answered it. It was Glen to tell him there was someone selling illegal substances outside in the smoking area. "I'm coming!" he told the barman.

Charlie stood up and levelled his gaze at Heather.

"You made me feel very ill at ease!" she said.

"What a shame!"

"Charlie what exactly is the matter with you?"

"Nothing . . . ."

"Liar!"

"Anyway, what did the letter say?"

Heather smiled. "I wondered how long it would take you to ask . . ."

"I'm asking now!"

"It said that if I didn't show up at the studio by Monday they'll sue me for breach of contract!"

"What a surprise!"

"Dean's on my side!" Heather said, avoiding his eyes. "He's trying to get Wendy's role prolonged for at least another year!"

Charlie turned to regard her, his calm and unreadable gaze a little chilling. It felt like someone had silently opened a window and allowed in a winter draft. "Of course he is! . . . it's the least he can do seeing as you're shagging him!"

Heather sat down quickly before she fell and took off one high heeled shoe, rubbed her foot, refused to look at him. Her ears throbbed with the kind of red hot noise that accompanies sudden shock—he had caught her completely on the back foot and the removal of her shoe spoke volumes in body language: it was the last thing she expected him to say, she didn't even know he had suspected.

"Going down to the Smoking Area . . . there's trouble!" said Charlie, and he left the room quietly; a slightly built man with a surprisingly determined tread.

SIX

The trouble in the outside smoking area was not the kind of trouble which was noisy or obvious. It was in fact the picture of serenity. Two young men—who at first looked to Charlie like the dealers—jumped back when they saw his approach, from a man in his sixties who—it became evident—was actually selling the stuff.

Charlie was straight to the point. "I'm going to have to ask you to leave the premises!" he said.

The two younger men were students and made no protest but the dealer was full of nerve. "What's your problem? . . . . we're having a smoke . . . it's the smoking area isn't it?"

"Yes, but it's for the use of tobacco in cigarettes, cigars and pipes not what you're selling!"

"How do you know what I'm selling?" persisted the elderly trader.

"I'm the landlord of the pub and I'm asking you to leave! . . . or the police will be called! . . ."

Out of the corner of his eye Charlie saw Heather running across the front car park, the unbuttoned jacket of her ultra chic suit flapping in the wind, nothing on her feet.

Charlie turned back to the dealer and the man stared at him in blunt defiance, unshaven, less than sober, thoroughly unsavoury. Charlie pulled his phone from his back pocket and put his finger to the keys.

The man turned and left, swearing loudly and bumping into Heather as she entered the area.

"Listen . . . . Charlie, you've got it wrong . . ." she opined.

She was panting from the exertion of running down the stairs and out over the car park. It was the perfect opportunity to get him alone whilst he was in the outside area.

"I don't want to talk about it Heather!" He put his phone away and turned on his heel.

Heather ran after him and caught his sleeve.

He shook her off. "Don't make a fool of me . . . I'm not stupid!"

"I would never hurt you!" Heather implored. "Charlie you know that don't you? . . . . you know you're the only one!"

"Only one for what?" said Charlie turning full circle and halting and looking at her. "Only one to trust! . . . only one to be there for you at the end? When you're glory days are done! Only one not to have moved on and up! . . ."

"Stop it!" wailed Heather, and then she noticed people coming out of the pub; some were looking over and ambling towards the area on the pretence of smoking, but really just to hear what was said. It was not the raised voices attracting them—it was the energy and the positions they had adopted. Charlie, his arms and hands stretched out to her—when he was always so self-contained—like an actor in a still publicity photo of a production at a climactic point. Heather in her stocking-feet her upper body inclined forwards to accommodate the space of several feet between them.

The tiny audience scarcely knew fact from fiction. Heather was an actress, her life off the telly was bound to be as interesting to witness as her other life on it. That was her role, it was her job to entertain everyone wherever she went.

"Please don't say those things . . ." she said in a quiet and desperate voice, but Charlie was walking away, not heeding the small crowd, heading straight into them and aiming for the side entrance. Now she had the choice between discretion and entreaty.

She shouted. "Charlie . . . let's talk!"

"Go and talk with *him*!" Charlie said. "You prefer to usually . . . you can't even show me the all important letter!"

"No . . . I'll show you! . . . it's just that I didn't want to worry you . . . what with everything else!"

There were a few more of the public now, arriving from their parked cars and more coming out to smoke after a meal. They stood agog, hearing every word clearly.

"Charlie!" yelled Heather as he went back into the pub.

She was terrified suddenly. "I love you, Charlie!" she added in a quieter voice.

Charlie disappeared and went into the kitchen, away from the clientele.

One or two of the small crowd were exchanging comments and gawping at her, waiting for more. Someone actually got out a phone to video her where she stood.

Aware that it was happening and alert to the problem with the studio, Heather put up her hand to block the view any camera might have of her from the side as she fled back to the bungalow to change her clothes.

Ten minutes later she was driving out of the gates. There were people gathered there on the grass verge, waiting for her, watching her with owlish and ghoulish expressions of awed fascination.

She was just driving her car for God's Sake! What was the matter with them? Did they not have domestic arguments and spats with their spouses!

She did not know what she would do but she began to drive out towards Limetrees to think. She lit a cigarette and wished she could have had a vodka cranberry juice before she set off.

*   *   *   *

Scott Brangle pulled up in the interior land of Norrington's farm, some distance to the rear of the farm shop and the out-buildings from which the retail side of the business was run.

He limped over to a young girl carrying cartons. The shop sold local produce and served tea and scones at three or four tables; a kind of makeshift cafe with no pretensions to anything but light refreshments. They were always busy.

"Mr Norrington in?" he asked her.

"Which Mr Norrington?" she smiled at him, revealing crooked teeth in an ingenuous face. "There's several of them!"

"Ged Norrington!"

"No . . . but he might be at the house . . . I'll ring through!"

Scott entered, it was buzzing with a couple of wasp and the conversation of female customers.

Nancy Norrington was behind the counter obliging a customer with crumpets and a pot of tea. Scott knew it was Ged's wife because his own wife had told him she worked in the shop and that she always wore a flowered overall.

Incredible the amount of information he absorbed without knowing it.

"This gentleman's asking for the boss!" said the girl to Nancy.

Nancy appraised Scott with a friendly and skittish kind of air. Scott was disadvantaged—he had expected a battle-axe.

"Sit down my love!" said Nancy to Scott. "We'll ring through and see if he's in the office over there . . . . do you want something to drink while you wait?"

"No thanks!" Scott took the weight of his bad leg, though he knew he would spring up again as soon as Ged showed. You couldn't do a confrontation of this kind sitting with a party of women—if you were honest. So getting back onto his feet again, Scott looked at Nancy. "I'll just go and wait outside for him . . . if it's all the same to you!"

The girl with the teeth swung around from the ancient telephone on the wall. "He's wanting to know who it is!"

"A neighbour!" said Scott evasively and several of the customers and Nancy held him in suspended and silent misgivings for a few seconds. It was an odd way to announce himself—the Norringtons didn't have direct neighbours, living as they did on fifty odd acres.

"He says he's a neighbour! . . ." the girl tried to whisper into the phone but was audible, ". . . . he's got a foreign accent and he walks with a limp! . . ."

Scott was embarrassed by this description, it made him sound like a freakish intruder to the district. Then the booming voice of Ged Norrington could be heard expostulating doubtfully with no clear words definable.

"What neighbour?" relayed the hapless assistant, phone held away from her face.

"Scott Brangle!" said Scott, now ashamed of who he was. "From Rookeries!"

He listened to the girl repeating the information and then some kind of giant roar at the other end. He limped back to the door.

"He's coming directly!" the girl informed everyone.

"I'll be outside!" concluded Scott with muted and wimpish politeness that annoyed him.

Ten minutes elapsed.

On hearing the crunch of Ged Norrington's boots on the shale Scott swung around to face him. "Mr Norrington . . . Scott Brangle . . . from Rookeries!"

"Yes, and what the hell do you want?" Ged said loudly, his hat at the back of his head.

"I came to tell you it was nothing to do with us . . . this business with your turkeys!"

Norrington made the kind of noises of derision not often encountered in every day life: braying, ostentatious sounds of sheer contempt.

And then he spoke. "I suppose you think I'll believe that!"

"Believe what you want . . . . I thought you should know before you go throwing any more accusations about!"

"Don't waste my time!"

"Okay . . . ." Scott waited for Ged's eye contact. It was curious and light and like a kid with a new toy. "And please don't pin any more dead birds to our gates!"

Norrington's hesitation was a fraction too long. "Don't know what you mean!"

"There we go then!" Scott saw that the women had gathered around the opened door to listen. "You're in ignorance just like we are . . . except we didn't go to the Police!"

"Ha!" Ged's roar was once again mighty. "Are you comparing the theft of several thousand pounds worth of poultry to a dead bird on your fence? . . . you must be barking!"

"*Ged! . . .*"

The fierce high voice of Nancy was heard emerging from the shop. "Calm down! . . . let the poor lad speak . . . there's no need to be so aggressive . . . yelling like that! Let's talk about it sensibly!"

"I tell you what Nan! . . ." said Ged, his face red and his neck swollen "you talk about it with him all you want . . . I ain't wasting my breath!"

Concluding the interchange from his end, he marched back to the farmhouse and climbed into his Nissan four by four and drove recklessly through the land adjoining the farm to give himself something to do while his temper subsided.

Meanwhile Nancy had taken Scott in to the shop—a little bit against his wishes—and was pouring him a cup of tea.

"It obviously wasn't your lot! . . ." she told him. "Else I doubt you'd be here!"

Scott looked at her. She couldn't know that for sure, she was assuming from the goodness of her heart. That Mrs Norrington had a good heart must be evident to most people meeting her.

"How's Tess doing?" she asked next. "I heard she's not regained consciousness!"

"Richie said yesterday that she was stable and that's all he knows!"

"Such a shame! . . . more than that, a downright tragedy!" said Nancy and stared for a moment into Scott's eyes and then changed the subject abruptly. "Ged is very set in his ways . . . take no notice! . . . don't take it to heart!" She placed the tea in front of him and pushed the milk and sugar forward on the counter. "You drink this! You've obviously got a nasty leg injury there!"

"I fell off a ladder trying to coax down one of the buzzards . . . from a perch at the top of the enclosure . . ."

Nancy looked at him with interest. She liked birds.

Seeing her fascination Scott continued with the details of his injury, now and then glancing at the tea, into which he poured increasing amounts of milk so that he could drink it quicker. He thought that if Ged returned the situation would be worsened by his conversing with his wife. But Nancy seemed unbothered, so he told her more of the buzzard's awkward ways.

"I 'spect it's because she's laid the eggs you mentioned . . ." said Nancy. "Females don't like to be told whats' what when we're pregnant!" A vaguely distracted look clouded Nancy's eyes for a second—she had never been fortunate enough to get pregnant herself.

Scott gazed at her, completely without a clue as to how to respond. He gulped at the tea and then choked a little and coughed for a few moments . . .

"It's alright . . ." Nancy had begun putting Kit-kits onto a tray on the counter. "Ged won't come back inside of an hour if that's what you're worried about . . . he always has a pint at the Hind around now anyway . . ."

*   *   *   *

Meanwhile Ged was driving around the periphery of his estate, the roads which led in and out of the acreage and to and from the various fields and land areas. He drove at a high speed but frequently had to break because of walkers, cyclists and other vehicles. He swore a lot and turned up his radio. He was too annoyed to stand just yet in the Golden Hind drinking beer.

He turned into a small lane close by the river, abutting the old mill now used by a market gardener, attached to which was a small croft for car parking for those wanting to walk or go into the garden.

Ged thought he'd go and stare at the produce and stroll about until his temper subsided.

Reversing into a space he caught sight of a metallic pink car with distinctive black trim parked a few spaces further up. If he wasn't mistaken it was the car belonging to his niece, Francine. He stared at it for a moment or two and saw that his niece was inside. She was busy kissing someone, her face was turned into a man he couldn't see and the man's hands were in her hair, holding the sides of her head. A passionate kiss obviously!

He alighted and walked towards her. It did not occur to him that he could have just gone about his business and refused to get involved; mostly because he believed that everything which happened hereabouts and on his estate was his business.

Francine had not seen him, she pulled away from the man and sat back in the driving seat and shook her hair and ran her fingers through it. Her back was to Ged and she had not noticed him.

But it was not her that Ged was immediately concerned with, he was looking at the man—Richie Southern from Rookeries.

A few seconds passed during which Richie saw Ged and Ged continued to glare. He was filling up with the kind of rage that inflates balloons and dirigibles, and it added to the excited interchange with the other Rookeries fellow, not half an hour since. He felt his blood beginning to boil.

Richie nudged Francine and she turned.

Ged walked to the window and signalled furiously for her to let it down.

"Hello uncle Ged!" said Francine calmly.

"What are you playing at? Kissing with this bloody idiot for all the world to see!"

Francine and Richie looked at each other. It was the kind of statement to which there was no answer.

"I can't believe what I'm seeing!" Ged said, in what for him was a moderate tone. "You know he's stolen most of our turkey stock?"

"But he hasn't!" Francine turned her gamin features upwards to peer at him. "You think he has, but he hasn't!"

"Then he knows who has!" Ged said. "And that's as bad!"

Francine sighed, making the kind of face that Ged was accustomed to seeing on his female relatives when his opinions got to be in conflict with theirs.

"I give up!" He raised his arms in a gesture more suited to an open air production of King Lear. "You do your best for your family and they throw it back in your face!"

Richie sat watching Ged's outburst and waited to see what Francine chose to do. It was not his call; she was the one with the wealthy family connections who had to be treated with kid gloves—or inheritances suffered and allowances dwindled.

"No-one is throwing anything back in your face uncle! . . . I am entitled to meet with people of my own choosing!"

"Yes but not this clown! . . ." said Ged. "I just this morning had the other buggar in telling me how innocent they are! . . . . and now I run into you making a holy show of yourself and snogging with the business partner . . . or whatever he calls himself . . ."

Richie remained reasonable. "We're having our lunch break in the privacy of Francine's car . . . . and sharing a bit of affection! There's nothing wrong in that"

"Bit of affection!" echoed Ged facetiously. "Do you know who pays for her car? . . . our business pays!" He levelled his acrimony at Francine. "Before you're so quick to defend him think on that young lady!"

"I think we should go!" said Francine graciously. "I'll drive you back to Rookeries! I apologise for my uncle!"

Ged was in the act of vacating the window space but swung down into it with renewed rage. "Don't you apologize for me . . . when I want to apologize I'll do it myself!"

"You're being rude and vindictive . . . and there's no call for it!" hissed Francine so that others wouldn't hear.

"No call for it? No call for it! . . ." Ged's entreaty was a sheer bellow and Francine winced. She'd started the engine when Ged suddenly put his hand through the window and grabbed her arm, possessed of a sudden realization.

"It was you wasn't it!"

"Me what?" she asked.

"You as alibied him for the morning of the theft! . . ."

Richie and Francine looked at each other. Francine was trying to remember whether this was info he could find out if she didn't admit to it.

"He was with me when it happened!" she said in finality, a slight pride in her voice which angered Ged more than anything else previously.

"He's behind it . . . some road or another he knows all about it!" Ged's gaze was locked on Richie.

"Animals have rights too!" said Francine.

A genuine bemusement then widened Ged's eye, giving him an altogether younger appearance than his years, until he got a grip on his immediate values.

"You stupid little cow!"

He stepped away from her car and turned and walked toward the river, his personal hurt apparent even from the back view.

*   *   *   *

Gita looked balefully at Heather as she sailed into the Centre, having been admitted by the volunteer overseeing admissions for the afternoon. The woman was just about to leave, it being well past six o'clock, but the persistent knocking at the outer door would lead anyone to open up and let in whoever was on the outer side.

"I don't know what to do now!" Heather announced plaintively to Gita.

Gita took hold of her arm and began to lead her to the office. She was somewhat annoyed at the intrusion as this was the time she always drank her jasmine tea and then meditated, but as Heather was one of her most prestigious and regular clients she felt less inclined to turning her away or leaving her to sit in the outer hall.

"Why?" Gita enquired, her normal calmness undisturbed.

"Charlie is angry with me and won't forgive me . . . and a letter came from the studio threatening legal proceedings if I don't show up . . . . the pub is under threat from the brewery! . . . and Tess is near death's door and lying unconscious in the hospital! . . . ."

Heather collapsed into floods of tears and fell onto the chair at the opposite side of the desk, wiping her eyes and her nose with the sleeve of what looked to be a very expensive suit.

All the while she was scrutinised by Simba, Gita's ginger cat, who sat on the desk in his customary place next to the angle poised lamp. His translucent yellow eyes observed Heather as if she were a strange and mildly interesting intrusion into the absolute and unchanging serenity of the Centre and its irrefutable routine.

"Please start at the beginning!" chided Gita and sat herself down, pushing the cup of untouched jasmine tea towards her client.

"What beginning? . . . there is no beginning . . ." declared Heather reaching for the handle of the tea cup. "It's all a tangled mess of problematic facts and there is no beginning . . . . and no end in sight either!"

"There is always a beginning to each problem!" Gita pronounced sententiously. "But often we must search for it!"

"Well . . . you know the beginning! When the studio said Wendy was to be killed off . . ."

"Not that surely!" intervened Gita sharply and cocked her head to one side.

Heather slurped the tea, coughed as the scalding heat of it hit her throat, and then warily realized that Gita was in contact with some kind of ancestor again. The signs were clear for all to see.

"Well then, what?" said Heather like a child playing for time in a transparent charade.

"Maybe the fact that you sleep with the conductor . . ." said Gita.

Heather slopped the tea onto the grey skirt of her Jaeger suit.

"No, no . . . not conductor . . . *producer!* . . . the producer! . . ." Gita was amending. "The producer of the series perhaps!"

To say that Heather was amazed was an under-statement, and she did what most people did on first witnessing Gita's other-worldly connection with the ancestors; she gazed upwards and around the ceiling to see if they would physically manifest themselves as the mouth-piece and the font of all knowledge they obviously were.

The room was silent but there was an extra warmth in the atmosphere and an almost electrical buzz, like that of a stationery aeroplane just prior to take-off.

Or was she imagining it?

Gita was staring at her—the ancestors were probably on pause or something.

"Well?" enquired Gita softly, but with consummate authority.

"Well . . . well yes . . . . it's true . . . I am seeing Dean Waters!"

"There we are then!" Gita sat back in the chair and regarded Heather as if this was all that needed to be said.

"Charlie is over-reacting!" Heather blurted. "He is everything to me and he should know it!"

"He has discovered this affair with Dean Waters has he?" Gita enquired next, as if she were somehow separate to the ghastly pronouncements of the ancestors themselves.

"It's hardly an affair . . ." Heather lifted the tea cup. "It's more . . . more . . ."

"What?"

"More of a friendship!"

"But one in which you sleep together and creep about!" said Gita lightly.

"We don't creep about . . ."

"But you do sleep together?"

"Well . . . not actually sleep . . . I mean not at night . . . not for eight hours at a time!"

"So you have conjugal relations only!" Gita said the word 'conjugal' carefully as if it might bite her tongue on the way out of her mouth.

Heather wondered where someone as foreign as Gita would pick up that word, but then it might be a medical expression, she supposed.

"We have a . . . let's just say we have a great deal of affection for each other!" lied Heather, and Gita brought her attention from Simba's lustrous fur to Heather's face once more.

Heather's face was convincingly masking the lie.

Gita closed her eyes and listened. The ancestors were demanding attention for the second time.

"We are hearing that you pick him up, this Dean man, and put him down when you so choose . . . . that you ignored his birthday celebration and refused to spend any time with him at all over Christmas! . . . . this is not a great deal of affection being displayed . . . we don't think so!" concluded Gita loftily. "This appears more like lust!"

Heather was breathing deeply to keep from exploding. She was in this surreal drama against her will, where aliens parading as ancestors pried into people's business while they visited the Centre and Gita became as powerful as President Nixon during Watergate.

Perhaps her mobile phone was being hacked by investigators. Or perhaps Gita really worked for the tabloid newspapers.

"And this person, Tess, is not just unconscious . . . she is busy elsewhere doing things!" Gita added carelessly.

Heather looked up sharply from sniffing and dabbing with a tissue at her nose. "What things?"

Gita hesitated and swerved the question. "You may be assured she is not wasting time!"

Heather stared at her tea. "I don't understand any of this . . . I feel like I've fallen down the rabbit hole and gone straight to the tea party!"

"Rabbit hole! . . . what have rabbit holes to do with it?" queried Gita.

"Nothing! . . . it's from a famous British book for children . . . . 'Alice in Wonderland' . . . no doubt you haven't heard of it!"

"I've heard of it a little!" said Gita.

"Gita I don't know what to do now!"

"We are not able to tell you that . . . !" said Gita. "We can only help you to a space where you make better decisions!"

"Well what do they say . . . . the ancestors? Surely they must think and have opinions!"

"I am not sure they do!" retorted Gita unhelpfully. "The only thing I can offer is a greater relaxation . . . . I can help you relax very deeply for an hour or so and when you awake you may see things differently . . . or at least you will be less upset!"

"Okay . . . yes let's do it!" Heather stood up abruptly and Gita led her to one of the small treatment rooms along the hall, where Heather lay on a bed with a pristine white sheet and blanket and Gita covered her with the blanket before fiddling about with her pendulum. Then she bade Heather close her eyes.

Heather fell almost immediately into a deep and soothing sleep. She heard Gita talking of chakras and slowed breathing and counting and mumbling something else which Heather ceased following after only ten seconds—her eyelids were so heavy and her limbs like lead.

She was falling and falling and floating and flying and she had stopped caring.

She seemed to open her eyes again in a dream world where she immediately saw Tess.

Tess was dressed in odd clothes from a different period and spoke in French.

Seconds passed while Heather digested this fact from the point of view of an English speaking person listening to French, and then she made a seamless transition into the flow of the language itself, so that English was no longer a contrasting factor.

She did not stand outside and observe herself, she just entered into the conversation as easily as a swimmer to the shallow end of a pool and she began to converse with Tess in French.

"What has upset you Solange?" she found herself saying.

Solange made no response and turned away and walked several feet along the path skirting the farmhouse, a large and well designed country mansion typical of the French countryside.

She ran to keep up with her and pulled her to a stand still.

"Solange you must tell me . . . or I cannot help you!"

"No-one can help me Monique . . . . I have made such a dreadful mistake . . ."

"What? . . . how?"

Monique had heard about the incident at the damn and the death of the man but she knew little of what had gone on until her brother had told her on his weekly visit.

"If it is about the death of that gypsy, I am sure you could not have prevented it . . . you had to tell the family of the problem . . . you did right!"

"No . . . no . . . Monique you don't understand . . . I loved him . . . I loved Didier all these years, five years or more . . . and I never told him or gave any indication and he is gone without knowing it . . . I will never forgive myself!" Solange collapsed to the ground.

Monique was transfixed by this information and had no idea what to say. In many ways she was one of the wisest women of the district—but she was for once struck dumb. She could not summon anything sensible to say.

It was a tragedy. It was a true tragedy because it was so stark and sudden, and so without hope. It was not the death that saddened her niece but the omission prior to death that could never be made right, could never be obliterated, could never be changed. It was to remain the truth. Until time tempered it with less sting, gave it that veneer of history—like a varnish protecting a fresh masterpiece which became tainted and misted with time.

"I see!" said Monique hopelessly.

She would not insult the girl with platitudes or false sentiments . . . It was not apt.

"There is nothing . . . . nothing of him left . . . . only this!"

Solange began to walk in her customary sharp stride towards the stable and they entered its gloom, where the hired help was brushing and grooming horses.

One new horse stood to the left—a dappled grey stallion.

"This was Didier's horse!" said Solange and she began stroking the animal.

Monique gazed at it and felt some kind of peculiar division opening within herself. It was a kind of precognition in reverse. She felt she knew the horse from somewhere else, somewhere far away and really not of this time, somewhere of old.

The realisation and observation of the fact absorbed her but was overtaken by a cogent sense of fear or extreme melancholy; she could feel an emotion . . . from the horse and Solange and the now absent Didier. All three were real to her and their energies pervaded and overwhelmed her. It was the weirdest thing she had ever experienced and she expected it to fade with the seconds. But it grew more threatening.

She bent over and coughed and breathed deeply a few times.

"What is it aunt?" enquired Solange from the depth of her morbidity.

"I feel unwell suddenly!" said Monique. "I must must get some air . . ."

They went into the open sunny courtyard and Monique closed her eyes and leaned against the hot stone wall of the outbuilding.

"It's passing now!"

"Good!" Solange's face registered relief. "I am going out to ride his horse! . . . .
I love the horse now as if he holds the spirit of Didier!"

Monique said nothing. It was a very silly sentiment to her thinking, but
she knew that people required sentiments at such times as these and she watched
her brother's daughter cantor off into the distance, thankful to have the recent
interlude pass and return her to normality.

SEVEN

When Heather came to again she was in a near pitch black room. She immediately felt she should panic but did not quite have the energy.

She made to move from the bed and was taken by surprise by the narrowness of it as she fell unexpectedly half way to the floor, stopping herself with her outstretched hands and wrenching her left wrist.

Then she panicked and felt desperately around the room for the door.

The door opened normally and tiny stars in the above domed darkness scattered among greyer patches of square light immediately assailed her vision.

She was in the Soul-Light Centre and the lights were in the converted chapel ceiling, left on presumably by Gita, who obviously knew she was still there. The greyer panels of light were the roof windows, now showing twilight, or maybe moonlight.

Leaving the door to the main hall open she went into the tiny room and found the wall switch which at once illuminated the treatment room whilst she located her bag. She thought she would venture outside and then to her car. But she found the large main doors locked.

Obviously!

It was the middle of the night.

When she took out her mobile phone she discovered it was actually two seventeen a.m. She panicked more. Supposing they had gone off somewhere and left her locked in on her own! At the mercy of the countryside and it's alienating stillness! Or worse—at the mercy of the ancestors and their random appearances delivering classified information on everyone's lives in parts that were really quite private. Like maverick news readers intervening with dire pronouncements at inconvenient times during normal programme transmission.

"Hello . . . can anyone hear me?" Heather called, but her voice was almost a whisper.

She wanted human response and not some sudden ghostly retort from one of them to penetrate the silence.

This couldn't be happening to her!

She was wandering along and looking at things with the aid of the flashlight pen she kept in her bag, adding its thin blue beam to the dim lights cast by the subdued lighting from the ceiling.

"*Helloooo . . .*" she called in a slightly louder tone.

And then she came to a back annexe, presumably once the vestry or passage of the chapel, and there was a door to the right marked PRIVATE and another to the left with no label at all which opened onto a galley kitchen equipped with a sink, a work top, a small fridge, several chairs, a microwave and a kettle.

Heather filled the kettle and searched the work top for beverage other than herbal teas. Eventually she came upon decaffeinated coffee. Naturally it would be decaffeinated. Gita would probably forbid any other kind from entering the building.

She boiled the kettle, realized there was no milk in the fridge and settled for the coffee black.

All the while she debated with herself on whether to shout at the top of her voice or bang on the door marked PRIVATE and try to wake Gita and Tridib.

It was surely a mark of her Britishness that she was terrified and miserable whilst some social nicety kept her from making a fuss or inconveniencing others at this time.

Of course she would have to do so unless she went back to the tiny room and tried to sleep.

Drinking the coffee and wandering around the whole place, her fears began to subside; she had grown accustomed to them perhaps. It was maybe called 'facing them'. Whatever it was it enabled her to get a better perspective and to think.

She went back in her mind to what she had just dreamt. It did not feel like a dream. It felt like an alternative experience in somewhere other than the world she inhabited now. She needed to speak with Gita about it. But Gita was most probably fast asleep, wrapped in the arms of Tridib. Or whatever it was they got up to in the wee small hours of their privacy. Maybe she was convening with spirits, more ancestors and other characters from the beyond. Was it fair to wake her? She had been good enough to let her sleep on.

Heather looked squarely at the whole mess of her existence currently.

Being here was no worse than being anywhere else. In fact, it was some kind of a refuge. A haven away from potential hassle and confrontation.

She found herself back at the door of the small-room and she re-entered and lay down on the bed. She left the door open so that she could stare out towards the square window in the ceiling and its surrounding flotilla of lights. Several minutes later she let the empty cup slide to the floor and she fell asleep.

*   *   *   *

Much later that day Ged Norrington had called his family together for a meeting. Those who were involved in any way with the business, and that included most of them except the children and the feeble minded.

His was a large family and he felt himself to be at the very epicentre of the dynasty. He had brought in an extra table to the dining room so that everyone could sit. And even then some sat at the side table to the left of the window and a couple more stood behind those who were seated. In all eighteen people had gathered. There was only one noticeable absence and that was his niece Francine.

Ged paced around and checked his watch and looked from the windows at the expanse of cars parked in front of his farmhouse—expecting any minute to see her pull up in that bright pink abomination she drove, late and flustered and full of excuses. But the minutes ticked on and his ten-thirty deadline was now sixteen minutes into the past.

All looked at him expectantly, the hum of their various conversational threads growing lower and less defined until there was almost silence, waiting upon his pronouncements as to the meaning of the summons.

No-one had dared not attend. They had dropped what they were doing in their planned schedules and made the time. Ged was a formidable relative for anyone to have, and an even worse boss. He made the rule that family and business were not mutually inclusive: whilst being utterly and inextricably linked they were not to be confused as the same thing; family were a variable unit of dependents looking to make a living, a business was a deadly serious undertaking that had laws and demands all of its own. The needs of the business were superior and could not be interfered with or undermined by the more emotional points of family life. The two had to be kept separate, even whilst lending an unusually intense flavour to any business dealings. Therefore it became, in Ged's words, even more important to succeed in business when the business was a family affair.

No-one could really understand where Ged was coming from on the issue, but they nodded and smiled as he pontificated the finer points. It was like listening to Aristotle talking in his original tongue to sightseers at the Acropolis.

'Pick the bones out of that' many of them said to outsiders whilst trying to explain their relative's autocratic yet intensely loyal (often exceedingly generous) tribal inclinations.

It was apparent now that Francine was not coming and her mother, Ged's younger sister Gwen, looked embarrassed and avoided Ged's eye. She did not know where Francine was or why she hadn't attended.

Gwen was in for a complete shock as Ged launched into his reasons for calling them all together.

"There's treachery afoot in the family . . ." he said quietly and sat in the chair, squeezed between Nancy and his younger brother Jack.

An audible ululation of sound, mimicking a united gasp, escaped into the warm air of the Norrington dining room. No-one trusted things when Ged began softly, it always led to greater bellowing farther down the line, whereas if he was initially enraged he became calmer as he exhausted his opinions and his larynx.

Nancy gazed up at him with something like amusement. "Whatever do you mean, treachery? . . . you're not referring to that turkey theft again are you? because we know all about that already . . . and that's burglary not treachery . . . ."

"Will you let me finish woman!" Ged's tone rose along with his eyebrows as he turned to stare at his wife.

Nobody took much notice of this exchange, Ged and Nancy were often on opposing sides of the fence and it meant nothing; they seemed even to have thrived on it over their forty odd years of marriage.

"Well then get on with it . . ." Nancy cried. "We can't all sit here the day long while you dramatise . . . . we're nearly twenty minutes late starting as it is!"

"We've been waiting on Francine!" Ged said irritably. "She's the reason and the cause of the need to convene at all"

"What?" Gwen cut into the slightly stupefied atmosphere of the room with her sharp demand. "What do you mean Ged?"

"She's not here . . ." declared the family elder with a pointed finger, "because she's most likely out fraternising with the enemy even as we speak . . . that's what I mean Gwen!"

"Enemy! what enemy?" Gwen was pushing back her chair in readiness to rise.

"Sit down!" said Ged in the commanding tone his siblings had been listening to since before they could properly speak themselves. "Don't think you're going awol as well!"

Nancy leaned across her brother-in-law in an attempt to touch Gwen. She failed to do this but waved her hand mildly to catch her eye.

"Don't worry! . . . it'll blow over!" she hissed, and Gwen turned to look at Nancy with a horrified gaze. "Which enemy does he mean though?"

Not wanting to attract the attention of her husband to what she was telling his sister Nancy screwed up her face to intimate the nonsense being proposed.

"I won't tolerate usurpers and traitors in our midst!" Ged said, whilst his more bovine relations became uncomfortable and looked about them for ways of cutting to the gist.

Ged's aunt Miriam, seated next to her only daughter, clasped her ancient handbag to her bosom and said in a piping voice: "Gerard, if you're referring to that bit of land I gave to my neighbour for to build a greenhouse . . . I think you'll find my agreement says that I can tithe or devote by covenant to . . ."

"No aunt Miriam, no! that's not at issue here . . . . now shush!" said Ged and turned his head to those on his other side.

"What did he say?" Miriam asked of her daughter and her daughter whispered in her ear. "He says the greenhouse is not the issue!"

Aunt Miriam was still nervous and in an attempt to pacify she directed more comment to her garrulous nephew. "There'll be lovely tommies come next spring . . . you'll benefit when Carol brings you some over!"

Carol began again to explain to her mother so that Ged's next points were blurred somewhat by the buzzing of her subdued but precise tones.

He raised his voice. "Carol, pipe down!"

Carol seemed crushed and Nancy sighed in exasperation. She performed more facial grimacing, aimed this time at Carol.

At last things had fallen silent.

"It's not about greenhouses . . . I've just told you the nub of the matter! It's about people from this family getting intimate with crooks and villains and wrong-uns . . ."

So saying Ged stared directly at Gwen.

Gwen blanched and some kind of realization dawned. Her daughter was involved—Francie was seeing someone or befriending someone inappropriate.

"What has Francie done?" gasped Gwen, her face stricken.

All eyes now veered between Gwen and Ged Norrington.

"She's seeing yon feller from the Rookeries . . . . Richie Southern! . . . that's what she's done . . . and before you deny it, I saw 'em yesterday, kissing in that car of hers . . . that pink vehicle which no-one not blind could miss from a mile away!"

"Who?" cried aunt Miriam, and she was joined in chorus by several relatives whose lives did not connect at all with that of the bird sanctuary.

"One of the owners of the Rookeries!" Ged yelled for the benefit of the entire assembly. "She's taken to literally sleeping with the enemy!"

Gwen fell back in the chair. Speechlessly she stared into space. Her daughter was nineteen now and not exactly known to be a slut, and it was the twenty first century, but this was the Norrington headquarters. This was the Norrington Farm dynasty empire and its entire crew, presided over by the leader and chief purse-string-puller himself. No-one wanted to laugh in the face of the main shareholder for fear of repercussions. In here the world was back as it might have been in 1612.

Gwen opened and closed her bright pink lips and ran her hand along her sleek black hair and thought of her horses needing exercise over at the east paddock and wondered whether to text Annabelle York to help her out. Her mind veered between the two diverse problems—her daughter and her horses.

Nancy gained her attention and Gwen stared at Nancy's eyes as they conveyed some kind of ameliorating message meant to completely negate her spouse's words.

"She says to take no notice!" whispered Carol to her left and Gwen smiled at her weakly in appreciation. "She says it'll be a storm in a teacup! . . . you know what Ged is!"

"Not if Francie weds the chap it won't!" said Nancy's brother-in-law Jack, adroitly catching the drift.

"Shut up!" snapped Jack's wife and elbowed him painfully in the ribs.

Ged stood and waited for order, he could not follow all the various reactions and comments, covert and otherwise, and make sense of it all. He knew only that Nancy was doing what she always did and attempting to brush things under the carpet before they were dealt with.

"I will not have my niece associating with a poacher and a thief and a known Animal Right's spokesman while she's living off the fat of my land!"

There was dead silence broken only by the rasping breath of an uncle who was ninety three but still sharp as a tack. And the whimpering of one of Ged's dogs lying near the door and sleeping.

"I thought she'd moved to a swanky apartment in Limetrees!" whispered aunt Miriam, her voice a reedy insult to shocked and mutually silent family unity.

No-one commented until Carol said quietly: "That's not what he means!"

"Well she can't be living off the fat of Ged's land if she's in an apartment over yonder!" persisted her mother.

"Shush aunt Miriam!" said Ged again in annoyance. "Carol will explain the metaphor later!"

"The what!" enquired aunt Miriam.

"The point is this . . . ." Ged's voice had risen to epic volume in his need to blot out old and feeble dissenters and others who might want to have an opinion of their own. "I will not be made a mockery of while she . . . or anyone else you care to name cavorts with those idiots from the Rookeries!"

"It's actually called *Rookeries* uncle Ged . . ." supplied Jack's son, Alfie, in brave and steady tones.

"I beg your pardon!" Ged turned on him.

"It's not *the* Rookeries . . . it's just Rookeries! Many people make the mistake but . . ."

"Shut up!" said Ged, his neck tendons stiffening beneath his green and white chequered collar. "Or I'll come over there and knock your block off! . . . I don't give a monkeys what it's called and what it's not called! . . . It's called a damned nuisance as far as I'm concerned . . . . first the rabbits and then the turkeys!"

Jack grabbed Alfie's wrist beneath the table to prevent him from rising and leaving and making some vainglorious juvenile stand for independence and honour. Jack gritted his teeth and made a sound of impatience as Alfie wrenched his wrist from his grasp and succeeded in falling against one of his aunts (squashed in the seat next to him) as he ricocheted to the left and collided with her.

The aunt recoiled and rubbed her shoulder. "What are you doing boy!" she declared angrily.

"Sorry . . . it was my dad, he was . . ." Alfie tailed off—the awareness of how feeble he would sound telling the truth.

"What?" demanded the aunt and peered around to see how her cousin could have caused his son to commit such social clumsiness when he was one chair removed.

Jack groaned and sank back in his seat.

"I never knew . . ." Gwen was muttering vaguely. "I thought she was seeing whatshisname from the garage!"

"They've gone into liquidation apparently!" Francine's first cousin Felicity informed her. "And anyway that one wants to go and live in Spain with a girl he met last summer! . . . he told Francine only last week in a text . . . !"

"Did he?" Gwen was aghast. How did one become so alienated from one's children! How did one become so behind the times and vulnerable to the unknown doings of offspring?

"Yes, Francine was gutted . . . she texted back and told him to get stuffed and that she had someone else anyway . . . but really I think she really liked him . . ."

"Can we get back to the point!" bellowed Ged. "Now we've established that Francine is a whore in the making can we move on!"

"Oh Ged!" Gwen wailed. "Stop it!"

Nancy leapt to her feet. "Gerard if you're going to say things like that I'm refusing to bring in the coffee and cake! . . . you're getting carried away and going too far!"

"Not far enough!" said Ged balefully. "Not far enough at all . . . and let me inform everyone! . . . if they want to put up camp with that lot from the bird place or any other of our known enemies they can leave the business . . . and the family!"

General mutterings and utterances followed, and an almost shared disgust at something which wasn't quite clear—it might have been the independent cheek of Francine and her new lover. But it was probably more to do with the unbelievable arrogance of Ged Norrington as self-appointed keeper of their collective moral code.

"Ged, we're not teenagers out dating. What exactly do you expect us to do about the Francine situation anyway?" enquired brother Jack.

"Send her to Coventry for one thing!" declared Ged. "Have nowt to do with her . . . make sure she knows your disgust on the matter! That's what I expect!" Ged glared at his younger brother. "There's no telling where it'll lead if she has truck with that lot . . . . turkeys will only be the start of it!"

"Young girls her age are all the same!" intervened their aged uncle in a shaky voice. "There's nothing new in it . . . unsuitable boyfriends are all the rage with 'em . . . always was the way, even in my day! . . . she'll take no notice!"

"Then she'll find herself in a caravan next to him!" Ged said in rising annoyance. "Because I won't be supporting her no more!"

There came a clamouring to speak and be heard all at once as the relatives were in several minds.

Amidst the cacophony was the sound of Gwen weeping into a tissue and being comforted by Carol and Nancy.

"Napoleon Bonaparte eat your heart out!" Alfie was heard to say, and his mother leaned behind Jack's chair and clouted him across the back of the head.

*   *   *   *

Now that she had slept, Heather could not get out of the Centre quickly enough. She drank the tea that Gita brought her and righted herself as best she could, dragging the comb through her hair and applying fresh make-up, having dabbed at her face with cold water in the small washroom used by visitors. She was not about to risk using the soap for fear of it having a bad effect on her skin, she couldn't be too careful; the camera was a merciless critic of complexion.

Pulling on her jacket she rushed towards the front doors and handed Gita a cheque which was vastly inflated in proportion to the services she had received but which Gita accepted silently and held behind her back, like a discreet majordomo in a grand hotel bribed for her discretion by grateful guests

She decided she would head for Dean's flat. She had decided to tell him that Charlie knew about their affair. She had also decided to add that Charlie *only thought* he knew; things could still be denied.

It was Saturday and she thanked some unknown deity that at least the day of the week was on her side. Dean would be at home, lounging in bed, or working on his film script which had been a work in progress for as long as she could remember.

She decided that the Limetrees route was too dicey, shoppers and tourists out in force in the ancient town centre streets, the market in full flow. To be stuck in one of their gridlocks was to be almost lost to the outside world.

She slowed the car, checked her rear mirror and reversed onto the verge towards the hedgerow as far as she could without risking scratching the car's paintwork. It was a narrow lane leading directly into the centre of Winifred Mead and people tended to speed along there owing to its remoteness and lack of traffic signs.

Alert to the fact that someone could come any time from around the bend in the opposite direction, she put the vehicle into first gear and moved forward in preparation for the one hundred and eighty degree turn needed.

She was straightening the car when she caught sight of the horse again. Standing passively with its head over the bramble, which on its own side of the hedge was lower than on the roadside.

Heather stalled the car, as she had the last time.

That it was the exact same horse she had no doubt. That it had appeared again from seemingly nowhere she also had no doubt. It was watching her with a gentle and solid gaze. She knew nothing of horses—she was a cat person herself—but it seemed to her that she had been with the horse only minutes ago in another scenario entirely. She pulled the car into the roadside, switched off the engine and closed her eyes. Bits of her dream—or whatever the experience was—came back to her like floating pieces of tapestry in a gossamer material, dancing behind her eyelids.

She remembered someone called Solange, and then a young man called Etienne. Solange seemed to be similar to Tess, or maybe Tess was there too, or maybe she had mistaken the name and Solange was actually Tess. The fact that the pieces were ragged and it was a confusion of detail was secondary to the fact that it had left her with a strong feeling, a lingering sense of emotion, an ambience. It was like returning from a foreign holiday and not being able to get the atmosphere out of one's mind.

She lit a cigarette and waited. The horse was still present, watching and waiting in the patient way of a horse.

She alighted from the car and went around and reached upward and touched the animal's head. It nudged her hand in that way horses have of being friendly, almost knocking her off balance. She snatched her hand away, afraid it would bite her, but then warily proffered it once more. This time the horse seemed to gauge her strength and her stance correctly and he returned her caress less forcefully, warm muzzle and moist lips on her palm.

"You beautiful boy!" she said crooningly. "Where are you from?

Seized by the idea that the horse was her ally she went back to her vehicle and rummaged in the glove compartment and came up with a half eaten bar of dark Belgian chocolate. She ripped off the paper and fed it to the horse in three pieces.

The animal relished it and then licked her in gratitude.

Heartened by this affection and badly in need of comfort she moved closer, straining on tip-toes to be nearer to the horse's face she kissed him gently on the side of his long nose.

He shook his head in equine emotion and the movement was too much for her fragile position on the grass verge. She wobbled backward and landed on her behind.

The ground was relatively soft and dry and she was unhurt. She laughed as the horse looked down on her, tranquil gaze never wavering, as if there was nothing odd about her clumsy human attempts at friendship.

It made her happier than she'd been in days. She scanned the surrounding area to see who had observed her. There was a man in a field some half a mile or so away doing something agricultural, beyond that there was no-one.

The horse had done her so much good. Turning to offer her thanks in some way she discovered it had gone.

Of course it had gone. It had supernatural powers and belonged to another world. She had no doubt of that now.

Five meters along the same road, Jack Norrington's son, Alfie, was walking back to the family business. He was learning the dairy trade from his dad but presently he was texting his cousin Francine to alert her to the fact that she was the subject under discussion in today's meeting with *The Fuhrer*—as they both called him.

Heather pulled her car away from the verge and picked up speed and saw a young lad step momentarily onto the road, grinning down at his mobile phone.

She swerved and narrowly missed him. "You bloody idiot!" she yelled from her open window. "Watch where you're going . . . I might have killed you!"

"Stupid bitch!" said Alfie, following the car with his gaze for several seconds before returning to the absorbing topic of what Francine thought of their uncle Ged.

When Heather reached Dean's apartment she knew as soon as she rang the outer bell that it was a mistake to have come. He always answered within seconds were he in and open to callers.

This time there was no reply

She felt she should write a note—seeing that his phone was turned off along with his messaging service—but on these apartments there was no outside letter box. She rang the flat opposite his, owned by a man whom she knew vaguely from going in and out, and asked him to buzz her in.

She gave no explanations and the man asked no question, as she had expected he would not, and presently she was going up to the second floor on which Dean's apartment was located.

She wrote the note on the wide window ledge at the top of the stair next to the lifts where there was much better daylight. Then she walked to Dean's flat and realized that that the letter boxes were all situated downstairs around the corner from the front doors in a kind of annexe with the numbered doors for the resident storage cubicles.

She bent down to slide the paper beneath the door and this was partially successful but then she wondered whether it were stuck half way, as tiny pieces of paper tended to do—so that the person opening the door easily missed them, or dismissed them as litter and left them for days for the cleaner to dispense of.

Several moments passed in these esoteric musings until she fished out a pair of tweezers and poked about beneath the door to make sure the paper was properly on its way to the carpet on the inside.

Suddenly the door opened and she looked up to see Delia—the actress who played her onscreen daughter—standing there in a knee length silky green shirt.

Heather's reaction was less than organised. She opened her mouth to speak, thought better of it, shut her lips tightly, stood up and almost lost her balance and gripped Delia's arm to steady herself. Finally she shook her head slightly, whereby her right earring dropped out onto the corrugated doormat.

"Heather . . . you okay?" enquired Delia in innocent and genuine entreaty.

Delia could not of course imagine what Heather was doing standing at the door of the assistant producer's flat on a Saturday morning. Of course she could not, for she did not really know of their affair. It was not the kind of thing girls her age had time for amid their own frenzied and demanding love lives.

"Yes, I'm fine and dandy . . . . thank you . . . I don't recall seeing you here before! . . . ." Heather realized she was rambling and sounding pompously idiotic. She picked her earring of the mat and replaced it in her earlobe.

Delia, who was quite fond of Heather as her surrogate and screen-time mother, darted forward and gave her a quick kiss and then stepped aside to let her in.

Dean was in the kitchen scraping the burnt bits off some toast. His boxer shorts were a vivid electric blue in the bright sunshine streaming in at the window. He scratched at his fair hair, grunted incoherently at the window for some reason, then turned and saw Heather and grabbed hold of the sink for support.

"Heather's here!" announced Delia unnecessarily.

Dean made an aborted array of reactions similar to Heather's own moments before and finally settled for. "Isn't this a surprise? . . . like a scene from an episode!"

Heather and Delia stared at him as if he had suddenly lost all charisma and reverted to behaving like his grandfather.

"Are you two? . . . are you two having . . . . ?" Heather couldn't bring herself to finish the question.

"Sex!?" offered Delia. "Yes, we are having a bit of a thing!"

"Bit of a thing!" Dean looked at Delia as if she had phrased an obscenity and Heather read more into this reaction than a thousand words.

"Well that is what we're doing . . . ." said Delia on realising his mortification and sensing the trap into which she could fall if not careful: Heather had appeared as a chaperone/catalyst to their intimate interlude and would prompt the introduction of something more conventional if she did not defend her right to be sexually liberated and keep her options open. Men of Dean's age still did not grasp the concept of 'discovery' in relationships and thought that even though marriage was declined as an option one still had an obligation to fidelity. Delia met it all the time, with her gorgeous looks, from anyone over the age of twenty five. And Dean was definitely in excess of that.

"Don't let me disturb you!" said Heather huffily as Dean and Delia parried glares across the small kitchen floor. "I came to give Dean a note!"

"A note?" said Celia, mystified. "Whatever for? . . . I mean why not just tell him stuff on the phone!"

The dead silence in the kitchen was the most awesome thing Heather had experienced amid the train of events ensuing since rising yesterday.

"I thought he'd be out!" said Heather, her voice unreal in the hush. "And his phone was off . . . along with the message service!"

Then Delia remembered the status quo. "Oh . . . I suppose it's about the situation!"

"Situation?" echoed Heather.

"Wendy's departure from the series and that!"

"Oh yes . . . yes, yes it is !" Heather lied.

Delia began bouncing around arranging her breakfast cereals and orange juice. "I'm mortified Heather, . . . we all are! I certainly don't want to lose my mother!" She let out a peel of laughter, as if she'd made the funniest quip, and smiled at Dean.

Dean smiled back obligingly.

"I just love Mummy Wendy!" Delia bounced forward and hugged Heather, kissing her sloppily on the cheek. "We're doing our best to avert the situation . . . aren't we Dean?"

"Sure!" Dean agreed, with little enthusiasm.

"Roy Preston is livid . . ." Delia took a mouthful of bran flakes and spoke as she chewed. "He's forever coming along and asking if anyone's heard anything about you!"

"For God's Sake don't tell him you saw me here!" Heather implored.

Delia hesitated with the shiny silver oversized spoon to her mouth and gawped at Heather and then Dean. "I think they began shooting some kind of thing in the family without you . . . ."

"What?" Heather stared at Dean who swiped a pair of jeans from a pile of washing and began to pull them on. "I was going to tell you!"

"Really? When?"

"Heather, I don't know how long you thought you would get away with that stupid ploy . . . but the show must go on!"

"Evidently!" Heather marched to the front door and then turned. "What are they saying the deal is now? with Wendy . . . in the script?"

Delia had risen and followed closely on her heels and as Heather turned Delia's pert little face was next to hers. "Oh that thing about going out on a boat . . . but this time it's some kind of wedding excursion or reception . . . . isn't it Dean?"

"Something like that!" Dean was hopping about adjusting the jeans to his legs.

"Wedding excursion?" Heather felt the sickening lack of reality kick in.

"A patient of yours . . . I mean of Wendy's . . . they have a wedding on a canal boat and it sinks!"

"For fuck's sake!" said Heather and collapsed against the wall in the hallway.

"Are you leaving or do you want coffee? . . ." Dean enquired.

Delia spotted the note on the floor then and dodged forward to retrieve it. Heather beat her to it and screwed it into a ball and pocketed it.

"Don't you wanna tell him whatever it is you came round to say?" Delia said, and Heather looked at Dean and Dean summoned his emotional intelligence from somewhere.

"Delia, give me a minute . . . I need to talk with Heather privately!"

Delia looked mutinous but disappeared into the kitchen and Dean led Heather out onto the corridor.

"Charlie knows about us . . . or at least he thinks he does!" she blurted as soon as they were alone. "We should deny it!"

"Yes . . . we should . . . he can't prove it one way or the other!"

"No . . ."

Heather was awash with confusion. Her emotions were being tumble dried. She would have said she had little feeling for Dean beyond sexual inclination, but now she was insecure because of Charlie, and more so with the presence of Delia.

"We'll call it a day then!" she said and smiled at him brightly.

"Well, in theory . . . maybe we don't need to actually go that far!"

"Oh we do! . . . we cannot carry on Dean! I am not that hard faced!"

"Aren't you?"

"I do have some integrity you know! You're better off with the young ones, like Delia!"

"Isn't that a decision I should make for myself? . . . 'H' are you jealous?"

Dean watched her in something akin to fascination.

"Don't flatter yourself!" said Heather and turned and went quickly to the stairs. Moments later he heard her heels clattering against the stair surfaces as she descended out of view.

*   *   *   *

Charlie was feeling quite inwardly frantic as he served at the bar. The only outer sign of his turmoil was that he kept on ringing up wrong prices at the till and twice answered the phone with the name of the last pub he had owned.

Glen picked up on it and asked him if he was okay.

"I'm fine!" Charlie lied. "I just need to go off in a few minutes and do something urgently! So can you stay and do an extra shift?"

"I've already done twice the amount of hours!" Glen opined, his face a mask of self-pity.

Charlie gritted his teeth and adopted a less didactic tone. "Yes, but you know how we're fixed with Tess in hospital.

"She'll not be back!" said Glen, diverting the subject morbidly. "They always tell you to look on the positive side but people in those comas rarely come round!"

"Where'd you pick up that kind of info? . . . watching 'Casualty'?" Charlie became his usual sardonic self, then realising how dependent he was currently on his barman he grinned to lighten his attitude.

"Charlie I'm dead tired . . . I'll do half a shift and that's my best offer!"

"Fine!" said Charlie. "And the next person who walks in about the job, give it them . . . if they've two arms and eyes and can speak English just employ them . . . I'll check them out later!"

He made for the car park and felt his pockets for his wallet and phone as he moved to his vehicle.

He was desperate to locate Heather now. He had made a huge mistake of pride and arrogance and he was ready to admit it, in some off-hand and careless way that Heather would know was his sincerest attempt at humility. His love for her was deep and gut-wrenching—no wonder he seldom dwelt on it.

He made firstly for the hairdressers on the perimeter road between Limetrees and St. Winifred Mead, where Heather often went on a whim if she needed to chill out or fancied some impromptu pampering. It was a small place run by a mother and daughter duo, catering to all comers and annexed to their detached cottage, offering most of the techniques and styles available in the ritzier town salons at a fraction of the cost. Heather sent a lot of business their way.

Neither of the hairdressers had set eyes on Heather for a fortnight. They looked in unison at Charlie (whom they had only seen behind the bar at the pub) with a combined sort of pity, having heard of the potential axing of Wendy Tridmore from the series. They could sense with the instinct derived from years of dealing with clients and their traumas that something was badly wrong; not least from Charlie's sudden personal appearance but also by his subdued air of desperation.

Charlie ran from the shop and went again to his car. The hairdressing salon was situated between St.Winifred Mead and the next village a few miles down the road. He looked from right to left, standing on the verge of the road like a traveller in alien territory and he deliberated long and hard.

Then suddenly he had a brainwave. He turned the vehicle around and headed for St. Winifred Mead and for the Soul Light Centre.

It was gone six in the evening but still bright and sunny, although there was that tinge of autumn among the rustle of trees in the breeze and the shape and movement of the small white clouds in a paler sky.

The Soul Light Centre was open and a stream of people seemed to be entering, chattering and laughing and carrying towels and mats. He guessed they were a yoga group.

He hovered on the top of the steps and felt that essence of the stranger, where people immediately recognize you as not one of them. He knew nothing of the place except the little Heather had conveyed, it was some kind of spiritual centre where they dispensed marvellous wisdom—apparently—and assorted holistic methods of health. Heather paid them exorbitant amounts of money. This he knew because he had caught site of the cheque stubs. She was in reverence to someone called Rita or Nita . . . or something similar.

Then a tiny Oriental woman appeared from behind the throng of visitors and stared at him.

"Do I help you?" she said and Charlie took it to mean that she was willing to assist if he required.

"I was looking for Heather Gilbert!" he said, almost embarrassed; who was he to pursue that well known woman he lived with! who was he to think he was even entitled to be someone in relation to her let alone a man she could love? These were the sort of thoughts he was often assailed by as he faced others regarding himself and Heather.

He seldom these days left his comfort zones—the pub and the golf course and occasionally his daughter's house.

The little woman clad in the tunic and trousers of the yoga fraternity extended her hand. "I am Doctor Gita . . ." she said hospitably. "I am afraid we haven't seen Heather since this morning when she left!"

"Left?" repeated Charlie and hesitated, but no further information was forthcoming. "You mean she stayed here all night?"

Gita compressed her lips and and then did the same with her neat hands as she pulled herself to her full height, which wasn't very tall. "I cannot divulge information!"

She partially turned away before turning back again. "Be assured she was well when she went from here!"

"What time was it?" said Charlie and Gita lifting her previous intent of confidentiality considered for a second or two.

"Probably ten thirty!"

"Thank you!" Charlie replied in his soft spoken voice.

Gita felt a little sorry for him. He was not a pushy kind of man, not a presumptuous soul who would demand of a person more than they wanted to give. She felt inclined to wanting to help him.

She watched him go down the steps and head for the vehicle parked a little to the left on the road facing Limetrees. Then she felt that dizzying and decidedly strong sensation of a change of atmosphere. One of the ancestors had arrived.

"Excuse me! . . . ." she called and went down the steps and towards the departing figure of Charlie.

"I don't wish you to think I am nosey . . . or interfering . . . but you should be aware that your uncle, who also owned a public house and drank himself to death . . . or so we are told . . . ." Gita hesitated and seemed to listen with great respect and patience to whoever this spiritual presence was.

Charlie became edgy. "What about him?" he prompted, as if the information in itself was not unusual.

"He says that you should not let the pub go . . . you should put up more of a fight and believe in yourself more!"

Gita bowed slightly, as if she had delivered a performance which might not be to the liking of her audience. Diffidently and with a little shake of her hands, as if to flick excess water from her fingers, she stepped back.

He stared at her. What an odd occurrence! What an altogether disquieting interlude.

He knew well who the uncle was—the proverbial black sheep of the family—but that Gita should know of him when he never mentioned him to anyone, not even Heather . . .

He wanted to digest and imbibe and consider, not moving until he had an understanding of the more hidden elements of the spiritual communication accessible to certain people. He might stand here forever then . . .

He stared at his shoes, and then at the top of the trees along the lane. Then summoning his wry wit he concluded: "Thanks . . . it's incredible that he managed to say all that and I never saw his lips move!"

Gita's laughter tinkled and floated into the light evening air. She was not without a sense of humour. She bowed her head, as if waiting to be dismissed by either Charlie or his uncle, or both of them.

Charlie cleared his throat. "Does he say anything else?"

This remark threw her momentarily; very few people accepted the presence of the ancestors so calmly, not people who were normally uninvolved with the Spiritual.

And then Gita reprimanded herself for being patronising. It was quite likely that Charlie was a believer and that Heather had enlightened him about the ancestors and the work in general.

She smiled towards Charlie. "No . . . . I am afraid not . . . in fact he has just disappeared. A man of very few words, I think!"

"Yes, very few . . . he would go weeks without speaking to his wife and family . . . . he spoke only to the customers and the draymen!"

And so imparting what was for him very personal information, Charlie made for his car. He turned as he unlocked it, feeling the little woman looking at him. "I suppose you don't know where Heather went after she left here?"

"I do not . . ."

"And none of those . . . those other . . . . the invisible . . . they won't know? . . ."

"No, they will not!" pronounced Gita adamantly. "If they did know they would have informed me by now!"

"Yes, of course!"

"And perhaps you are not to know yet . . . perhaps they would not tell me even if they did know!" Gita added.

"Thanks!" said Charlie softly.

"You are most welcome!" Gita announced finally before running up the steps and closing the doors.

Sitting in the car he tried Heather's mobile again which went immediately to answer phone. He left his third message.

Reversing to head back towards the pub he realized that most people would consider only three messages left at a time like this to be an inappropriate attempt at tracing someone—but then Charlie was not one to bombard people with his needs, not even his partner . . . *maybe that was why she was having an affair.*

The thought struck him forcefully and he slowed his speed as a reflex reaction.

Another compelling thought arrived almost alongside the first revelation: if she was having an affair with Dean, as he suspected, she might also be having an affair with other men simultaneously. Ludicrous though it sounded, he had read some kind of article recently about the psychology of the celebrated and the famous and their need to endlessly give of themselves at the expense of their moral boundaries. It had further elaborated that any promiscuity was often not exclusive and personal but offered to something more generic in the way of human emotion.

He needed to find out more. He did not know where Dean Waters lived, except that it was somewhere in Limetrees, nor where any of the other cast members of the series lived. He did not socialise in their circles. Did not attend their parties or anniversary events; he was not one of their exclusive pack, he wasn't one of anyone's exclusive pack. He was that most secular of beings, a publican, well known by many but actively included by only a few.

He slowed the car to think and the engine purred comfortably as he let down the window and stared at familiar landscape.

To his right he saw a man approaching along the bridle path, emerging from the tree-line into a clearing five hundred yards further along and perhaps two hundred yards inset from the road, carrying a bird of prey on his arm

It was Richie Southern and Charlie made the connection of Richie to Tess and from Tess to Heather. Heather talked to Tess, she had asked him not to sack Tess, she liked the girl. Maybe she even confided in her.

Clutching at straws was not within his nature, but he felt that some kind of next step (any step) would be better than this not knowing and this blind angry sense of loss and the self loathing he was succumbing to.

He sprang from the car the better to be heard and shouted to gain Richie's attention.

Richie had his head down and walked imperturbably towards the short cut for the Rookeries, the bird flexing its wing span every few seconds as if to take off. Charlie put his fingers to his mouth and whistled loudly. He had forgotten he could do that. The bird responded first and seemed to rise from Richie's arm by about two foot and scout the surrounding territory.

Richie stopped and looked up and then saw Charlie. Charlie waved and signalled and went to meet him half way across the expanse of scrubland next to the bridle path.

The bird squawked deafeningly and Richie made a sound of some kind in his teeth to quieten it. He seemed openly suspicious at the appearance of Charlie away from his bar and outside his vehicle on a country road.

"Something up?" he enquired without preamble.

"How's Tess now?"

"She's not really any better . . . to tell the truth I don't really know!" said Richie and Charlie gleaned that Richie was uncomfortable.

"Is she conscious?" said Charlie.

"Now and then . . . she goes in an out of it . . . but they wont tell me what the prognosis is when I ring!"

"You ring and don't go to see her?"

Charlie was saved from the acrimonious reaction Richie wanted to make to this unwarranted intrusion into his sensitive business by the screaming of Titch.

Her wings were splayed again and her beak opened wide as if she was about to swallow Charlie alive

"Looks like a miniature pterodactyl . . ." Charlie commented, summoning his humour. "You sure you fed him today?"

"She's a female!" said Richie truculently.

"She's a nice looking bird!" added Charlie hastily. "Anyway, the reason I ask about Tess is . . ."

"You're wondering when she's coming back!" Richie interjected.

"No, no . . . her job's secure . . .but . . ."

"Really? I heard you fired her!"

"Well yes, because her timekeeping's terrible . . ."

"Tell me about it!" said Richie.

"No, I reinstated her again . . . at Heather's request . . . but what I wanted to ask . . . I want to go and visit her!"

"Well I don't have any contact now . . . we split up you know!"

"No I didn't know . . ."

Charlie and Richie were about to bond, by the sheer revelation of previously unrevealed facts concerning one woman, when the horse appeared.

It trotted out of the tree-line and caused Titch to start squawking. The horse seemed oblivious to the noise and came closer to the two men.

Charlie jumped back in alarm while Richie held onto Titch, covering her eyes with his hand so that she would not see the horse clearly.

"Jesus!" said Charlie. "Where did that come from?"

"Search me . . ." Richie let the animal sniff him. "I think it might be the one appearing randomly around these parts . . ."

"It's got a thing around its neck!" said Charlie.

"A leading rein that's all . . ." Richie supplied. "Means nothing . . . it ain't saddled . . . ."

Charlie was not a horsey man, not a natural country dweller. He was not at ease in the country with the equine set. He knew little of these kind of matters. And then a thought occurred to him so strongly that he was for a moment unsure of what to do next.

"That's the same horse Heather kept seeing. . . . the one she was always discussing with your Tess!"

"She ain't my Tess now!" said Richie. "I told you, we parted!"

"Yes but there's got to be a connection . . ." Charlie's tone was slightly raised; it was noticeable in someone like Charlie who seldom let himself become outwardly ruffled.

Riche stared at him and felt Titch grow more settled and easy on his arm. The horse all the while nuzzled his back and attempted to make connection with Charlie every few seconds, but Charlie circled the animal as if in the presence of imminent danger.

"He'll not harm you!" Riche said.

Charlie sensed a ring of contempt in his tone of voice and ignored it. "There has to be a connection!" he told Richie.

"Connection?"

"Heather was obsessed with the sudden appearances of some horse on the lanes here and she talked of it to Tess and now Tess is ill and Heather's gone missing . . ."

"Missing?" Richie reacted. "Heather's gone missing"

"Don't go telling people!"

"You maybe ought to tell the police!"

"I'll decide that!" snapped Charlie.

"Look Charlie . . . you're upset . . . but if Heather is gone missing you need to act . . . things happen to folk, especially women!"

Charlie blinked as if to change the reality. "This must be that same horse!"

"Not necessarily!" Richie was calmly stroking Titch.

"And how many horses do you see roaming around these parts unaccompanied? . . ." Charlie wiped his hand across his mouth in agitation. "Where do you think we are? . . . the Blue Ridge Mountains of Virginia!" He pulled further back from the horse as it moved to touch his jacket with it's muzzle.

Richie exhaled and spread his legs for ease of stance. "So what if it is the same horse?"

"Well it's trying to tell us something . . . obviously!"

Richie was unsure how to respond. He was used to Tess's imaginative and surreal assumptions into the supposed minds of these animals but not the landlord of the local pub, of whom horse whispering was not known to be among his talents.

"Like what?"

"Well I don't know . . . I'm not a psychic! . . . but there's clearly an omen!"

"I didn't have you down as a superstitious man Charlie!"

"Nothing to do with superstition! . . . it's synchronicity!"

Richie raised his head from inspecting Titch's tail feathers. "What? . . ."

Bells were ringing in his head, he thought of the book he had read—twice over—he was familiar with synchronicity, the favourite language of the wider Universe conversing with soul. "Why do you say that?"

"Take too long to explain!" said Charlie with brevity.

"I read about it . . . I do know what it means!"

"Then you should know that there is nothing random here between Heather's disappearance and perhaps your break up with Tess!"

Richie screwed up his good looking face and wore a mask of frozen complexity.

"Are they both at death's door then?" he asked without thinking.

Charlie's mind went though a scrolling set of scenarios where Heather was lying hurt, or drunk, or both, in the open terrain or at the side of a road, broken by a hit and run accident. Maybe having taken a handful of pills in a mad moment of despair.

"I have to go and see if Tess is conscious!" Charlie announced.

"They won't let you in . . ." Richie stared for a longish time across the meadowland. "Unless I come with you and say you're my father or someone like that . . . maybe her future father-in-law!"

"That'll do it!" Charlie grabbed the offer without pausing. "Let's take your bird home!"

Richie looked towards the retreating form of Charlie as he dashed to his car, and he muttered quietly to his peregrine: "We're going for a little ride in a vehicle now babe, don't worry!" He began to follow Charlie at a steady pace, and when he turned to check the horse it had gone—perhaps back into the tree-line, perhaps not.

*   *   *   *

Tess could feel the hands pulling her, she could sense that there was something other than the road and the sunshine and the meadows sweet with fragrances and bitter with farming smells, on the route she took towards Bordeaux.

Now and then she lapsed out of the concentration she held to ride a horse at high speed through a small village and she almost succumbed to the virulent demands and entreaties from the other place, where she sensed that something not of the recent history or surroundings was taking place. She could not remember what it was. Maybe she had dreamt it the night before.

On and on she rode towards the place she would vaguely recognise from the description Didier had given her of where he had once set up home on arriving in France with his relatives after a four week journey across water and unknown land to escape some kind of minor persecution or war.

She tried hard to remember what he had told her, what the trouble or upheaval had consisted of; it was an arduous process, mentally very draining, but it kept her from giving in and surrendering attention to the other place which seemed to be almost parallel to her and threatening to take over her consciousness.

And then she went pell mell through a tiny lane consisting of one or two cottages and a church and someone haled her as she slowed to jump the fence over the land to the larger road.

"Solange . . . . Solange!"

She slowed and halted and the girl caught her up. It was her second cousin, with whom she swapped frequent letters about the latest processes in lace making and the gossip locally.

"Solange, did you receive the sample of red I sent you last week? . . ."

"I did, thank you!" said Solange and leaned down from the mare and kissed her cousin on the cheek.

"Stop and have coffee . . . where are you going in such a hurry?'

"I cannot stop . . . I am on a mission! . . . you must forgive me Cecile! . . . I will come through again in two weeks and we can talk then!"

Cecile laughed and released her hold on the the mare's bridle.

Solange set her gaze directly in front of her and focused to shut out the calls from the other place—she could hear still the weak and tinny strains of this strange name being called out to her.

"Tess . . . Tess . . . Theresa"

She was Solange Gabon of Aquitaine and she had made a bad error of judgement which threatened to spoil her life forever.

There were small things she could do, and she knew in her heart that they would lead to large amendments, as in sewing and dressmaking: one small detour of a stitch could reshape a whole garment.

She set her face to the cool easterly breeze and the strange voices and echoes of this invisible alternative place receded dramatically, like the ocean waves seen on blustery days from a tall cliff.

*　　*　　*　　*

They had deposited Titch back at Rookeries, having transported her in Charlie's car. Charlie was surprised how steady she was on the short journey but felt a mild tingling at the back of his nose as if he wanted to sneeze, inhaling some feint powdery substance, obviously off her feathers.

Charlie and Richie passed the land where Norrington's turkeys had been housed and Richie's mind went to the break-in and then seemed to reach Charlie's thoughts like an airborne virus.

"So you took Norrington's turkeys!" he said into the deafening silence where only the sound of the car engine was to be heard.

"No!" said Richie. "Who said I did?"

"Relax . . . I don't like the Norringtons . . . I'm not going to blow the whistle on you!"

"I haven't admitted it yet!" said Richie flippantly.

"It wasn't you probably . . . it was whatshisname . . . chap with the pigtail!"

Richie held onto the lower part of his seat belt and did not immediately react.

"What's he called by the way? . . . he's often at the bar drinking . . . don't know his name!"

Charlie drove at a frightening speed and Richie was disconcerted by not being in control at the wheel, and by the directness of the conversation. "Curt Chambers!"

Charlie nodded. "Animal Rights Supremo! . . . I've often thought he was a force to be reckoned with but I never spoke with him beyond serving him drink!"

The car was speeding along the country roads now at a fair old rate of knots and Richie thought it imprudent to tell Charlie to mind his own business.

"So . . . . he's the brains eh? The man who gets the job done! . . ."

Richie refused to comment and several moments passed.

"He stands next to Norrington some days you know at the bar, and Norrington is oblivious!" Charlie grinned broadly as if the notion pleased him.

There was silence for quite a while and then Richie suddenly broke it. "Someone ought to serve him up for dinner Christmas Day . . . he'd feed the whole of the county with some to spare!"

"An unappetising, unwholesome prospect!" Charlie retorted, but his thoughts were now elsewhere.

After a few miles Charlie helped himself to a swig of water from a bottle on the dash. "Anyway, I'd say you were well up in points . . . hefting his valuable turkeys and rogering his niece! . . . I'd have a bolt holt to run to though if I were you!"

Richie looked sidelong at Charlie, his mood now bordering on annoyance. He hated his private life being chewed over, but then he considered that Charlie did not speculate out loud or gossip—he simply observed life from the comfort of his bar.

How had he let himself be harangued into this escapade!

"Obviously I hear a lot . . . as the landlord of the Hind!" Charlie said next, glancing at Richie in the mirror. "I'm right though aren't I?"

Richie deliberated. Although not pleased by the intrusion into his affairs he realized that it wouldn't do to upset the publican of his local.

"No shit Sherlock!" he said with no glimmer of amusement.

Charlie laughed for the first time that day.

*   *   *   *

At the hospital the staff nurse listened to the explanation of Charlie being Richie's father and stood aside to admit them. Charlie shrank down a little into his jacket and followed on, he imagined the nurse wondering how someone as unprepossessing as him had sired someone as physically excellent as Richard Southern. It happened of course, all the time, and maybe the lad had been lucky enough to inherit genes from his mother . . . his supposed mother!

Charlie's focus swerved badly as he thought not for the first time what it might have been like to have children by Heather. The magnetic, classically beautiful Heather in her younger child-bearing days . . . .

He snapped back to the present as the nurse held the door for him.

Unfortunately Connie and Bernard were in the ward ahead of them and Tess's parents looked surprised and stared pointedly at Charlie. His assumed parentage of Richie could not be altered now because the nurse was right behind them.

"This is . . ." Richie hesitated too long so that the nurse stared at him strangely.

"I'm Richie's dad!" Charlie said and held out his hand.

The parents looked again at Richie. No doubt they had the same thoughts as the nurse.

"I'm surprised you bothered turning up at all!" said Connie coldly to Richie, "since you didn't bother returning my calls for four days!"

"I was busy . . . . I can't get reception where I work!" Richie lied.

Bernard accepted Charlie's outstretched hand and shook it, but Connie declined pointedly.

"I don't think you care for Tess as you should!" she accused Richie, and then turned to Charlie. "He doesn't visit her for days, doesn't respond to my calls asking when he's coming so we can arrange some kind of a rota! What sort of fiance does he call himself?"

"This is embarrassing!" Charlie said without further ado. "Perhaps I'll go and wait in the outer ward until you have debated things between yourselves!"

"We're leaving anyway . . . ." Connie said. "We've been here ages and we need a drink! The heat in here's fit to shrivel you!"

"It has to be warm!" supplied Charlie helpfully. "The body temperature drops when you're unconscious!"

He was looking down at the recumbent form of Tess lying in the bed, the oxygen specs at her nose and some kind of drip attached to her arm. She was pale and not like her usual bonny self. He looked away from her. He had been wrong to come. What had he been thinking!

The nurse came back into the room and Richie touched her lightly on the arm. "I thought you people said she was on the better side when I rang yesterday?"

"She's had a slight relapse!" the nurse explained.

"When?"

"Only about an hour ago! . . . . It might be better if two of you left . . . there shouldn't be more than two people in here anyway!"

Ignoring everyone else Charlie stepped nearer to the bed, to the rails which guarded against her falling out. It seemed to him an idiotic precaution for someone in her comatose state. He leaned over and took her hand. "Hi girl . . . how are you doing? . . . can you talk to me?"

"Of course she can't talk to you!" expostulated Connie. "Have you seen the state of her!"

"Sorry if I let you down!" Richie suddenly told them. "I'm finding it difficult!"

"We're all finding it difficult lad!" Bernard said. "And it's not us you're letting down!"

Tess's eyelids seemed to flicker under the scrutiny of Charlie's gaze. Encouraged, he squeezed one of her cool hands, her fingers lying still on the stiff white sheet. She wore a ring on her third finger left hand and he remembered it was something Richie had given her the year before last, an inexpensive sort of ring with a small indiscriminate stone. Personally he would have been ashamed to buy a woman of his any such ring. Better to buy her nothing at all.

The ring caught on his own ring on his little finger. He disengaged his hand from hers and her fingers lingered, as if she sensed him.

Her parents left the room.

"I think she may know we're here!" Charlie said to Richie. "I can sense her touch as being in touch, if you see what I mean!"

Richie joined him at the bed and stared at his ex fiance. He felt bad because Charlie seemed to be more sympathetic and in touch with Tess than he was. Charlie seemed to actually radiate some kind of love or compassion towards her.

Tess's eyelids flickered again.

"Tess? . . . Tess listen to me if you can! . . ." Charlie said quietly. "If you can hear me squeeze my hand a little!"

A second or two of soft minute pressure from Tess's hand and Charlie looked at Richie. "Did you see that?"

"Don't tell me she squoze your hand?"

"Just a bit . . ." Charlie leaned closer to her. "Tess I need your help . . . . Heather is missing. I need you to tell me if she's seeing anyone . . . another man besides me!"

Richie's laughter was like a bark or a growl, a mixture of the two, abrasive in the silent ward. "For Christ's Sake! . . . she's at death's door and you're asking her about your love life!"

Charlie ignored this. An age passed and he heard Richie sigh—a long, exasperated subdued sort of sigh. The sigh of those who tolerate those who are clearly out of their tree. Charlie knew he was out of his tree but sensed there was something Tess knew about things. He was being told by the mighty invisible ones who Gita had summoned . . . or who had summoned her. His life would never be the same after this day, he would not ever look at things in the same way . . . a line would have to be drawn.

An aching silence in the sterile hospital room, with its antiseptic smell and its gleaming lights and its feeling of being in some kind of space craft where time and life were suspended in a vacuum between reality and somewhere else.

And then Tess opened her eyes and looked at Charlie for mere seconds.

"Hello Charlie!"

Her voice so low in her throat as to be mostly discernible by the movement of her lips.

"Did you hear me?" Charlie leaned closer, until his ear was next to Tess's mouth and her warm breath was on his face.

"I need to know where she might have gone!" Charlie said gently, but Tess's eyes were closing again, slowly but surely.

Richie joined him, overcoming his fear and distaste; his guilt at the overwhelming sense of wanting to be anywhere but here.

"What she say?"

"Nothing!" said Charlie. "Only my name!"

They stared down at her and waited. Charlie stroked her cheek lightly and Richie was astonished at his gentleness, at the anxious care written all over his face. Was the anxiety for Tess or was it for Heather? Maybe it was for both!

The nurse came back into the room and Richie told her. "She just spoke to Charlie!"

"Really?"

The nurse sprang forward and looked at Tess. "Are you sure?"

"Positive!" said Charlie. "But she's retreated again now!"

"Why didn't you ring for someone?" said the nurse irritably. "I'll call the doctor on duty!"

Charlie took Tess's hand again in his own and held it. His face seemed softer than Richie had ever seen it, it seemed to take years off his age. Richie wondered why Charlie felt this way towards someone who simply worked for him. Richie was embarrassed by it, not the least because he seemed to feel very little at all. As if the occurrence of Tess lying here was not the tragedy everyone thought but the natural course of events for someone who rode as frequently and as vigorously as Tess often rode.

"She can't help you Charlie!" said Richie in finality. "Let's get out of here!"

Charlie was still looking at the sleeping Tess and it was as if Tess was communicating with him, despite the lack of voice and the silence and the void between them.

"Yes, let's go now!" agreed Charlie eventually.

They walked rapidly towards the exit and passed Connie and Bernard hurrying towards the ward.

"She spoke then! . . . according to the nurse!" said Bernard.

"She did!" Charlie affirmed.

"Why the hell would she speak to you and not to us?" said Connie nastily. "Who are you at the end of the day?"

"She works in my pub!" replied Charlie, forgetful of who he was supposed to be in the charade and not giving Connie the satisfaction of eye contact.

"In your pub!" Bernard was flummoxed and resisted the pull of his wife's arm. "You never told us your family owned a pub!" he said to Richie.

"We could have had a nice dinner with you whilst we were staying!" Connie told them.

Charlie drew breath and set his jaw against verbal reaction—he supposed the cheek of the woman went along with the rest of her personality. He looked at Richie to acknowledge the comment.

"It's a long way from here!" Richie said. "The pub is not near the town or the hospital!"

"I'm sorry about Tess!" Charlie told them as he turned to follow Richie's progress away from the scene. "She's a good girl!"

"Pity the same can't be said of your son!" Connie turned abruptly and linked her arm in Bernard's.

PART TWO

EIGHT

Heather watched her alter-ego Wendy Tridmore on television being talked about by her fellow cast members in an episode referring to her death and the incident in which she had first gone missing three months ago, via the dialogue of the script that the writers had devised and Roy Preston had just sent live on air.

Wendy was now apparently found again, or at least her body was found, washed up on the shoreline of some beach, having floated for weeks in a small motorboat which lifeboats and other regular ocean going vessels had failed to spot.

Preposterous!

She watched two of Wendy's children weeping copiously. Delia, as her on screen self, Polly Tridmore, was prostrate on the sofa while their neighbour told her that someone had to identify Wendy and the police wanted to know who was going to the mortuary and when.

Surely after three months there would not be much left of a body to identify!

But then, just as Heather was having that thought, the busybody neighbour from three doors along who ran the local pet shop entered the scene and began pontificating about the properties of salt water and how a body could be preserved if it did not rise above a certain depth for a certain length of time.

Heather listened to Edward (Bill in the show) and thought how she had always liked him. They had done rep together in their young days. She had once played Ruth to his Charles for six months in a touring version of 'Blithe Spirit' . . .

She hated him now, illogically and unreasonably; she wanted to throw things at the television. She did not understand how viewers could tolerate his smug opinionated take on everything life had to offer. She hated the way he exuded that *still part of the community essence* which she recognized as having valued so well herself, whilst she was here at her new home without a hope of ever being part of that community again. On or off screen.

Her new life was set apart from her old life, like the Berlin Wall had set apart East and West Germany.

Her new home was a tiny but reasonably stylish apartment. It consisted of one bedroom and a lounge/dining area, a small kitchen and an even smaller bathroom. It was all she dared allow herself to afford. But at least it had a view of the sea.

Heather did not know why she felt she couldn't go back. Why she couldn't contact Charlie or anyone from her old life. She just could not.

It was as if when they had robbed her of Wendy they had taken away her soul's purpose, her reason to hold her head up. Her reason to get out of bed in the morning. She had let herself down, she had let Charlie down. She had let her family down. The one thing she had not let down was the Golden Hind—selling some of her highest equity shares she had sent the money to Charlie via her solicitors to pay the arrears to the brewery and all was on track again, as much as it would be in the financially difficult times of the hospitality industry. Without her generous salary keeping them afloat he might not survive. He would have to sell the bungalow.

The tabloids ran stories about Heather Gilbert's own disappearance. She was not dead—the world knew that; Charlie had made statements to that effect.

Her solicitors had told him that she was still alive and did not wish her whereabouts to be known. She had withdrawn from life for the seeable future and was living reclusively. But she was not technically a missing person.

Obviously it was only a matter of time before someone spotted her and leaked her whereabouts. But then it was also only a matter of time before the world forgot about Wendy Tridmore.

Perhaps the world never did forget about these iconic characters. Perhaps they became legendary, like nursery rhyme figures or characters from the the great classics.

Heather lay in bed at night and listened to the sounds of the sea and thought of such things.

She met with her sisters at one of their homes once a week, going straight to her car via the staircase (never using the elevator) and then alighting at the other end, a hat pulled down over her face and her shades in place.

Beyond that she walked along the promenade everyday at the quietest times wearing some kind of headgear to disguise her face.

And she was left in peace.

She shopped online from the supermarkets and had the goods delivered and left in crates outside her apartment door.

There was no problem in these modern times; a person could go for weeks without connecting with the outer world if they so wished. The difficult thing was disappearing from the map altogether.

*   *   *   *

Charlie was devastated by the turn of life events. But he was not able to enjoy the privilege of the reclusive lifestyle. He had to soldier on whether he wished it or not. It was true he spent less time in the bar—he was occupied at present with selling the bungalow, but even without that he would have found some other way of avoiding the pub.

People spoke about him. The regulars never tired of talking about the tragedy that had befallen Heather and him. No-one knew why Heather would take it upon herself to disappear in this way, and so the rumours were many and rife. A lot of people said that she had tried to kill herself and that the television people had paid for her to go into one of the clinics where the rich and famous were treated for depression.

Others said she had gone off to live with her younger lover whose name nobody knew but some testified to seeing her with in various locations.

Some even said she had gone abroad.

One of the main reasons Charlie knew he avoided the bar was that he could not stand their pity. They looked at him with that mingled curiosity and sympathy given to people with obviously sad stories. The fact that he was considered a tragic case was almost too much to be borne.

The alternative would have been to put on some kind of up-beat act, to exude the bravado of somebody madly denying something. It would take some doing to sustain a mask of that nature. It was beyond his ken.

He moved into the rooms over the pub and fixed up a webcam so that he could see the actions of the bar anytime he chose. If he chose.

Glen whispered about him behind his back to customers and it wasn't clear if he knew that his covert gossiping was obvious by his body language to Charlie viewing at a distance but he continued nonetheless.

When they were not asking about Charlie they were asking about Heather, and when that was not being discussed the topic of Tess's death was the subject at the bar. Tess had died about a month after Heather's disappearance—never regaining consciousness following the fall from a horse. There had been an inquest at which Tess's other employer—Annabelle York—had testified to Tess having ridden out one morning on one of their best mares, partly to exercise it after a leg injury and partly to search for a mystery horse with which she had become obsessed that appeared randomly in the surrounding area, frightening people who were not themselves horse-lovers.

One of these people was Heather Gilbert, the partner of Tess's other employer who ran the Golden Hind public house.

The fact that Heather Gilbert was a celebrity actress who was known to have disappeared from public view caused quite a stir in the midst of the inquest and it was adjourned while the coroner deliberated on whether this should form another line of enquiry.

Annabelle York and her husband had paid for Tess's funeral. Their business had declined; they were said to be staving off bankruptcy—people were loath to trust a riding school where the instructors took fatal tumbles from the animals they were paid to know and train. Especially people like Tess who lived and breathed the work.

It was a cursed pub the Golden Hind, or so the pronouncement of some of the locals went.

The old men offered tales of past tragedy . . . . someone had once died while sleeping off the effects of a binge many years ago. But the causes of death did not tie in with alcohol excess, nor with old age, and were more consistent with suspicious circumstances. And then there was the wife of a previous owner who had been found at the bottom of the cellar steps one winter's morning by the cleaning woman. No-one had ever found out what she had been doing there, especially as she was known to have an aversion to mice and insects and never set foot in the cellar.

"It's obvious . . ." Charlie chimed in, coming unexpectedly into the bar to help himself to milk. "Her husband pushed her!"

The assembled group of customers looked at him agog in silence—uncertain how to take the remark.

"What do you mean?" Glen enquired. "Why's it obvious?"

"Because that's what men do when they get exasperated with their wives and there's no escape!" Charlie replied.

"Nothing was proved!" said one of the old gaffers.

"I'm sure it wasn't!" Charlie retreated again as quickly as he had appeared.

The gossip took on a new and enriched note after that: Charlie had injured Heather with the intent of killing her and she had gone away to recuperate, preferring not to press charges. Or maybe he had even succeeded and buried her somewhere remote where she would never be found and was keeping up the pretence of her life by false paperwork . . . .

On a freezing cold morning in late November Dean Waters entered the pub.

It was five minutes after opening time and the barmaid looked at him with hostility: ridiculous that someone should walk in at that respectable hour; she usually had time to text ten of her associates and replenish her nail varnish before the first customer appeared.

"Yes?" she enquired briskly, as if this were not a place of hospitality but some kind of police station or booking office.

Dean paused to glare at her so that her bad attitude would become obvious to her.

It didn't happen. The barmaid believed him to be either deaf or slow and merely raised her voice. "Yes love? What can I get you?"

"Is Charlie about?"

"He doesn't come into the bar much now!"

"Why's that?"

"I dunno . . . I only work here! I expect that's his business. Do you want a drink or what?"

"I'd like to speak with Charlie . . . so perhaps you'd be good enough to have him summoned! . . ." Dean said in an affected tone of voice, the parody meant to deflect from the embarrassment

She punched in a number on the bar phone which obviously connected to Charlie. When there was a response she turned her back and spoke so Dean couldn't hear.

She described to Charlie what had taken place.

"What's he want and what's he like?"

"I dunno . . . . he's talking kind of false and theatrical!"

Charlie sighed. It was one of Heather's erstwhile cronies, he could tell from the description.

"What is it?" Charlie demanded of Dean as soon as he arrived in the bar, and then he followed Dean as he moved into the centre of the room.

"I need to get in contact with Heather!"

Charlie stared at him, his eyes like flints. He was unshaven and looked to be seriously undernourished.

"Better get a psychic then!" he said as he moved away.

"It's important!"

"You've got a nerve coming here!"

"Why?"

"Why?? . . . because I could rip your fucking head off!"

Charlie had lowered his voice to a menacing whisper, not to be intimidating but because he did not want the barmaid to be spreading the conversation all over the county. "Don't think I don't know what was happening between you and her! . . . I'm not stupid."

"That's in the past!" said Dean.

"You'll be in the past if you don't fuck off!"

Charlie was livid, he could hardly hear his own voice for the sound of the blood pounding in his ears.

He watched Dean walk to the door, and then a thought occurred to him.

He rushed after the younger man. "When did you last see her?'

Dean turned around and stared. "Don't you know where she is?"

"Of course I don't fucking know where she is . . . when did you last see her?"

"About three or four months back . . . . she came to the flat!" said Dean.

Charlie snorted his contempt and turned his face away.

"You're wrong in what you're thinking . . . I'd spent the night with Delia!"

"Delia!"

"You know, aka Polly, Wendy's t.v. daughter!"

Charlie didn't know but he was digesting the fact that Dean had been in bed with someone other than Heather.

"Not content with Heather you had to have her daughter as well!"

"She's her on screen pretend daughter!"

Dean was edging to the door. Charlie was following him at a distance of yards.

"So that's when you last saw her?"

"Yes! . . . . look, there was never anything serious between Heather and I!"

"What did you want to talk to me about?" Charlie spoke as if he had not heard the last comment.

"Forget it!" Dean made his exit and sprinted to his car, parked on the road for an easy get away under difficult circumstances.

Re-entering the pub Charlie realized he had been stupid in not finding out what Dean needed with Heather at this late date. He turned around and saw Dean backing his light grey car into the pub gates to reverse and head back to Limetrees. He ran after him waving his arms, his voice raised against the strong wind. "Okay . . . let's talk . . . ."

Aware of Charlie's frantic movements, Dean ignored him and drove off. He had had enough for one morning.

*   *   *   *

Dean was driving too fast and swerved to avoid a Land Rover rounding a bend from the opposite direction and his own car careered onto the verge.

The Land Rover stopped. A good looking and outwardly bound sort of guy walked towards him. A girl had also climbed down from the passenger door and was standing next to their vehicle.

Dean grinned as he approached. If there was a fight he would lose; he was not the athletic type and didn't work out or keep fit.

"Are you okay?" Richie Southern asked Dean Waters as he ambled across the road. "Not that you deserve to be, you stupid twat! Do you know the speed you were doing?"

"I'm sorry! I lost concentration . . ."

"And you could have lost your life . . . and mine! . . . and hers . . ."

Richie indicated the girl standing next to the Land Rover. She was extremely pleasing to the eye. Obviously the beautiful people of the county were out in force this morning. Dean reddened somewhat and looked down at his own feet: perfect body language for contrition.

"Better see if your car's still working!" advised Richie and waited until Dean had started the engine and pulled onto the road again before he returned to his own vehicle.

Richie had borrowed the Land Rover from Scott while he helped Francine move her personal belongings into his caravan.

"I can't believe the way some people drive!" Francine commented as they got underway again.

"I can!" muttered Richie. "Happens all the time round here!"

Francine tore open a piece of gum and put it into her mouth. She was silent for a while, unnerved by the near collision. She was even more unnerved by the prospect of living in Richie's caravan for months.

"This will only be temporary won't it?" she asked for the sixth time.

"Yep . . ." Richie was terse; he had grown sick of reassuring her and explaining the proposals for the near future. That he would acquire one of the tithed cottages from Chester's once one had become vacant and he had squared things with the farm manager.

He did not show his impatience; it was because of him Francine had been disenfranchised by her uncle Ged . . . It was down to her association with him and her refusal to give him up. Her valiant need to 'stand by her man' had caused her to be homeless.

Richie tolerated her girlish need to voice the obvious every few minutes and he reached for her hand and held it in the hand he was not using for steering.

She was very young, and in certain matters it showed.

Francine raised his hand and pressed her lips against the backs of his fingers.

Richie was not cheerful about the prospect of future changes or the widening of his horizons. Whereas Francine was ecstatic. She had gained the sympathy of her second cousin who disliked their uncle Ged and his brother as much as Richie did. The cousin had promised Francine a job promoting his dairy products, his business was growing at a rapid rate. If things worked they could rent one of his small barns newly converted as living accommodation. In time, he may even offer Richie a job too.

Silently, Richie was in a decline since the death of Tess. He felt he might never come to terms with it. Never having experienced death at such close quarters before he was agonised, more so by the suddenness of it and the surrounding problems of their relationship break-up. Deep down he believed her accident could have been his fault.

He suffered in silence. But it was something that went with him all the time, no matter what he did or where he was. It haunted him like a shadow.

He hid it well, and Francine was only a little aware of it. If she tried to speak to him about the past and Tess he shrugged it off or told her it would take time. But it was one of those things that was burying itself deeper into his psyche, simply because he had no release for it.

"Go and see someone!" cajoled Scott. "Go and talk to somebody about Tess's death!"

"Like who? . . . a medium or someone?"

"No . . . a counsellor or a psychotherapist!"

"That's never going to happen!" said Richie.

"Then you're going to regret it . . ." Scott threw his arm with the huge eagle into the open space and watched the bird soar into the winter skies higher and higher over Rookeries.

Richie said nothing. He knew that he could not talk to anyone about Tess. He was not that kind of man.

He had dreams instead.

He had long and vivid dreams in which he was chasing Tess down the hill at Chester's towards the Golden Hind, shouting to her to wait while he spoke to her. He dreamed that he was watching her ride at an event. He dreamed that she was all decked out in a riding habit and looked a wonderful woman, like Annabelle York probably looked twenty years before.

And then he began to dream about the horse.

At first it was fleeting—a mere vision as he woke or turned over in the night. And gradually it became a frequent visitor during sleep. A dappled grey gelding of medium height, a slender face and a slender muzzle. A gentle but frisky disposition.

He would be dreaming of other matters; the birds or display events where clowns entered the proceedings, or people arrived in outlandish costume and heckled him in the middle of his presentations, telling him he did not know what he was talking about. Nightmares! Then the unknown horse would appear and prance and rear and circle him—inviting him to mount or ride.

He would awaken in a sweat, disturbed to his core.

He did not know what the horse portended. He did not even know if it was the same horse that Tess had been looking for, he had no proof. But his heart told him it was.

More and more often he would dream of the horse, more and more often it would lead him in the dreams to Tess's side.

And Tess laughed in her open mouthed girlish way, her cheeks flushed, her eyes that vivid clear blue, expectant and honest eyes, gazing full on him, her warmth reaching him from a small distance away.

He shouted in his sleep and woke, trembling with emotion, sweating.

Francine at first showed alarm and resentment. She was still young, she did not see why people like Richie should have anything bad to dream about. She did not understand why the death of one girlfriend should be so distressing, especially as the relationship had turned sour before her demise. She tried to subdue these thoughts, but they were there.

Before too long she became concerned. She saw that he was deeply troubled. She would leap from the bed, fetch him water, get back in beside him in the cold of the caravans winter interior. She held him, shushed him, allowed his breathing to return to normal, and then she would try and arouse him and initiate sex.

Gradually his sexual performance was affected too. He could not sustain an erection at these times. They relied on odd times in the day . . . when he returned from work between employers, when she was calling in for lunch on purpose to seduce him. She wondered whether all relationships went this way after a few months. Or whether it was a kind of teething problem related to the events surrounding their whirlwind romance. After all, they had extenuating circumstances to battle with.

She decided to be patient and see what happened once they had left this dreadful caravan with its inadequate heating and drab fittings. No wonder he and Tess had come apart! What woman would want to live in these conditions? It was too ridiculously 'sixties' and bohemian for words.

Maybe when they moved to the new cottage—which would happen probably in the New year—maybe then Richie would forget. When he wasn't reminded all the time of his days with Tess his bad memories would fade. He might heal and become the lover he had once been.

Meantime, the dreams kept on and Francine had no idea what they contained. He refused to tell her.

*   *   *   *

Dean let time lapse and then decided to try and talk with Charlie again. He walked into the pub while it was fairly full one lunch time and Charlie responded immediately.

"Come into the back!" he said and led Dean into the kitchen where the chef and the assistant were cooking.

"What is it?" said Charlie in such a reasonable tone that Dean wondered what had happened to change him.

"They are saying they may have her back . . . they may write her in again!"

"What?" Charlie rubbed his unshaven chin and screwed up his face. "They identified her body . . . on screen . . . . I mean they were seen and heard to say that it was her by the viewing public!"

"Yes . . . well . . . this is the world of soap Charlie . . . ." Dean shifted from foot to foot in agitation. "They'll write it so that it was a mistake . . . the wrong body!"

Charlie let out a sound of contempt. "They make me fucking sick!" he said aggressively.

The chef looked up from his endless chopping and watched for a second or two.

Charlie had never sworn so much in his life than since Heather had left, and they had all grown used to it. Charlie who did not tolerate loud bad language in his pub, not even during football matches, was now as foul mouthed as anyone could be.

"I don't write the stuff!" Dean said uncomfortably.

"And what do they think I can do about it?" enquired Charlie more calmly.

"They think you might know where she is!"

"I've told you . . ."

"I remember what you told me! But it doesn't stop Roy Preston from pestering me to pester you! . . . . for all he knows you're probably lying for her!"

"Well I'm not!"

"Okay! . . . . so is there no way you can reach her?"

"One way, yes . . ." Charlie looked cagey. Dean waited.

"So will you do it?"

"I'll think about it . . ." Charlie leaned his arm against the cold steel of the refrigerator. "It's not good for her . . . this emotional roller coaster . . . . they shouldn't be doing it!"

"Agreed!"

"I'll give it some thought!" said Charlie and went out into the pub, leaving Dean to assume the conversation was terminated.

NINE

"Of course she's gone living in his caravan . . . ." Nancy told Ged. "She had to do something since you cut off her funds so quick! What did you expect her to do, put her name down for a council flat?" She placed his lunch (which others might call breakfast) in front of him. "The girl's following her man, is all she's doing!"

Ged inhaled in preparation for a loud retort.

"And don't be yelling at this hour of the day!" intercepted Nancy swiftly. "Or I'll leave the house and not return until midnight!"

Ged paused. "There's no point in talking about it!" he said mournfully. "None of you can see what's happening!"

"Tell us what is happening then . . . but do it quietly!"

There was a peaceful half minute silence in which only the dogs growled at the sound of an overhead plane flying low and Ged buttered toast and prepared his next words.

"He's set to wheedle his way into the family and he thinks he'll be in for a share of the estate!"

Nancy suppressed her amusement into a quick squeak. "He'll be lucky, with you guarding the books!"

Ged laid his calm aside and the air was pierced by his vociferous tones. "You'll be thanking me some day! I'm not having her usurp our heritage with that . . . . that bird fancier . . . that Animal Rights hoodlum!"

Nancy sighed. "He's just a young feller with opinions of the world different to yours, is all he is! You can't expect everyone to see life as you do! Remember when we were courting . . . you were forever at loggerheads with my dad about which way to vote!"

"That's different!"

"I thought it might be!"

"Anyway she can kiss goodbye to any of the estate shares . . . and I've warned Gwen that if she gives her any of her own shares I'll revert hers too!"

"Can you do that?"

"I'll find a way! . . . . Jack'll find a way . . . he's the one with the accountancy degree!"

Nancy thought it noteworthy that at that precise moment Jack's wife, Gloria, was pulling up on the gravel area outside, but she did not say so to Ged. "Francine's her daughter, and who would see their child go without!"

"That's up to Gwen . . . she knows the consequences now!"

"Ged, that's not a very nice thing to do at all! I only hope when you're on your death bed you'll not regret any of this!"

"I'll regret it long before that if I don't it!"

Gloria had entered and was staring balefully at Nancy.

Ged grunted in Gloria's direction and then ignored her in favour of his breakfast and his dire thoughts. Gloria swivelled her eyes towards Ged for Nancy's benefit, frowned, and inclined her brows upwards. Nancy caught the drift and together they glided from the room like ageing nymphs in a Gilbert and Sullivan operetta.

"The turkeys have gone again!" Gloria hissed when they had entered the lounge across the hall and she watched as Nancy recoiled in horror. "No!"

"I can't think why Ged doesn't already know!" said Gloria.

"He's had his phone turned off and I've ignored the landline!" Nancy moved to an armchair.

"No prizes for guessing who it was!" Gloria said. "That little madam's feller and his crew . . . ."

"But it don't mean Francie had anything to do with it!" Nancy said with conviction. "Ged thinks she's in cahoots with him but he's not considered things the other way round!"

"What other way round?" Gloria sat on the couch.

"He's just using her to get back at Ged and the rest of us!"

"I don't see that's very likely . . . . although you may be right about her not knowing anything of the turkeys!" Secretly Gloria felt Francine to be capable of anything. Francine was always up to something and always had been since she was toddling.

Gloria watched Nancy fanning herself with a Christmas courtesy menu from the Golden Hind. "I'd better tell him!" Nancy sighed.

"I wouldn't!" Gloria jumped up as though a siren had sounded. "Let Jack do it . . . it's mens' stuff anyway!"

Thoughts of Ged's towering rage just right now was not to be contemplated.

"You're right!" Nancy agreed.

"Listen Nan . . . let's nip over Polly Sharples . . . . she's having a W.I. Scrabble party . . . funds going to Help the Aged!"

Nancy screwed up her face "A Scrabble party! . . . you know I can't spell for toffee!"

"No but you can lift a glass . . . remember how free she is with her gin and her sherry at these do's!"

Nancy relented. "I suppose it's for a good cause!"

"Absolutely! It's a fiver a game . . . be worth it though . . . you know what a character Joanne is! She'll be there, cracking her jokes!"

Nancy did not speak but watched her sister-in-law adjusting the designer spectacles in the low mirror over the writing bureau. Gloria didn't care about farm business, but then she didn't need to because she didn't live with Ged. She lived with his younger brother, such a different kettle of fish as to be almost from a different gene pool.

At length, as she applied more blusher and lipstick Gloria unveiled more of her thoughts. "Jack'll think Ged's aware of the turkeys by now because he's left him two messages! . . . the shit might not hit the fan until later . . . he thinks Ged might be sorting out the problems in the south meadow where there's no reception . . . he'll drive over there soon . . . but the worst of the storm will have passed by nightfall. So I'll pick you up at two fifteen to get you out of the way shall I?"

Nancy nodded and closed her eyes.

"By the by Gloria . . . . I've made a new will . . ."

"What?" Gloria bounced back into view. "Why you telling me this now?"

"Because I made you executor . . . executrix I think it is!"

Gloria stared. "Do I want that responsibility?"

"Course you do!" said Nancy and smiled. "And even if you don't, I'll not be worried then will I? . . . Ged may go before me any road"

"No doubt of it!" said Gloria. "The way he works himself up over trifles!"

"I trust you, see!" said Nancy. "To play fair!"

Gloria was suitably humbled and remained silent, running her index fingers through her hair, coiffured twice weekly into light brown bouncy layers by the hairdresser just outside of Limetrees.

"I'll pick you up at two fifteen then . . . . pretend you don't know anything about the turkeys!" added Gloria unnecessarily.

There was nothing surer—Nancy was never one to pre-empt an explosion. Personally she could not have cared less about the turkeys and if she dwelt on the subject long enough she felt she might begin to laugh while Ged relayed the episode to her and waited for her mortification—in the same way he looked for her approval when things were going right.

*   *   *   *

Heather was taken up these days almost totally by the dreamlike past life recall she had experienced at Gita's. She relived it each day, until eventually she felt she was adding bits that were not there at the time.

She was haunted by the thought of Tess's death. By the phantom horse and the part it might have played. Could it have been the same horse Tess was riding when she was thrown? It seemed unlikely—preposterous even—but she knew that the grey horse was in the equation somewhere.

Each morning she lay and watched the sun (presuming there was to be any) seep through the narrow crack in the curtains.

She watched the light of the sun as she listened to the shoosh of the waves when the wind was in the right direction. And she thought about the session with Gita the last time she had seen her. She thought about the reality she had entered where Tess had been called Solange and she had been called . . . what was it she was called? She could not remember. If she tried very hard it sent her to sleep, the sheer effort of that kind of mind altering concentration into memory. She hoped that during one of these sleeps she would get back there, to that place wherever it was, where she and Tess had known each other before.

Where reincarnation was concerned she had been neither an advocate nor a sceptic. It was not something that occupied her mind prior to these events. Nowadays it was all she ever thought about . . . the death of Tess, and the same horse in the past life scenario . . . and the stuff that Gita's ancestors had brought forth about drowning.

If she were truthful that was what she feared the most. But surely now she was not involved in the television series Wendy's fate could not be interlaced with her own.

Now and then she thought of Charlie. She loved him, she always had, but she had shamed herself and humiliated him, so the honourable thing to do was to remove herself from the glare of curiosity in the life she had with him.

She found she could disconnect from the memories of life before the move to this apartment as easily almost as she disconnected from episodes of the series once they were filmed.

Maybe there was something wrong with her.

That Charlie would forgive her for past misdemeanours she didn't doubt. But things would never be the same. They would live under a cloud, a shadow had passed their joint sun and although she did not know it, she was a perfectionist. She believed that life should be just as perfect as art, and that when a thing had a tempo and a gloss it should stay that way and when it tarnished it should be deleted or left behind.

*   *   *   *

Alfie looked at his cousin and wondered if she had had a personality transplant.

"You actually want to live in that caravan? . . ." he enquired skittishly. "You'll be selling pots and pans door-to-door next and telling fortunes!"

Francine laughed loudly and Alfie looked at her appreciatively—he was at that age where he was beginning to define his ego through the entertaining effect he had on females.

"You'll be joining one of those gypo sites and moving round the country . . . I mean what do you do when you want to have a party?"

"We don't have parties!" replied Francine. "Richie isn't the partying sort!"

"Oh no! Course not . . . . he's more the striding through the woods type with his eagle on his arm . . . like something from Mordor, his hair blowing in the wind and his three day beard glistening with hoar frost . . ."

"What are you on?" Francine fell back against the upholstered bench in the Golden Hind. Girlish and carefree and more appealing thanever . . . . Alfie could hardly resist her, he wanted her now more than he had wanted her since reaching puberty, ever since then. It was a dull ache in the pit of his stomach, a lurching melancholy that couldn't be erased or dealt with.

"So you're enjoying it then? . . . the simple life!" he grinned stiffly.

"Alfie, it's only temporary . . . . it won't be forever!"

"I bet that's what he tells them all . . . . Merlin the Bird Man!"

Francine burbled her amusement. The attention she had gained from becoming the girlfriend of Richie pleased her right now, it made her unique in some way, it made her interesting to others. Richie was at the very least an interesting character. He cared about nature and birds and animals and got to live that kind of life twenty four-seven. He looked the part, he looked like he could figure in films about the subjects he cared for.

Gradually Francine was beginning to see that it was because he *was* the part. He was the *real deal*. Francine herself had dropped out of college; she was subsidised by Norrington Estates anyway, and she felt increasingly like a fake and a phoney. Worse, she realized that she did not know what she would do with any of the study at the end. She felt like a parody.

So now there was a gap where the parody had been and real life had to begin. It was chilling and frightening. When she awoke each morning, mostly alone in the bed in the caravan, she was seized by the fear that Richie would not come back, that he would leave her there, with nowhere to go but home. And home was not an option. If that ever happened she would be stuck forever, unable to climb above the middle class pit of languid dependence, reliance on habitual convention. It was all too easy and therefore it was a trap; it would sneak and crawl and linger before her everyday of her life. Her life would stretch and yawn and swallow her into the oblivion of rural ways.

"I bet that's what he said to that last one . . . the one that died on the horse ride! . . ." Alfie was saying to her.

Francine's face immediately clouded as she caught his meaning.

"Sorry . . . that was a bit tactless . . . . you must be a bit freaked by that!" added her cousin.

"No, not me, but Richie is!" She gulped the last of her cider and loped across to the bar. She counted her coins onto the counter as Charlie watched. "Two more please Charlie!"

In the old days she had never had to watch every penny, it was a totally new concept. In the old days she would have opened a tab and not cared what she spent, and then paid with her credit card at the end.

"What do you mean, Richie is freaked out by it?" asked Alfie when she handed him his glass.

"I mean he's still freaked out by Tess's death . . . by the suddenness of it!" She was exasperated at having to explain what should be obvious.

Alfie considered matters. "Well, I suppose it's to be expected! . . . if I had a girlfriend die suddenly at that young age I'd be freaked too . . . . even if the relationship had gone sour!"

"Yes but . . . there'd come a time when you'd have to get over it!" said Francine pragmatically. "Everyone does . . . . and if they don't they're incapable of loving again and they . . ."

"They what?"

"Nothing!" she said quickly.

She could not talk about her private sex life with her male cousin.

"What?" Alfie pressed her.

Then the sudden appearance of Curt Chambers at the table broke Alfie's persistence. He stared at Chambers with muted animosity; not only disturbing his intimate moments with Francine the man was known to him vaguely via the agricultural grapevine as a troublemaker.

"Seen Richie anywhere?" the man enquired calmly.

"He's at Rookeries, watching a fledgling bird or something!" Francine replied vaguely.

Curt nodded and wandered over to the bar where Charlie served him immediately. Charlie was quick where customers were concerned and his attention was everywhere. His was one of the best run pubs in the area. Everyone knew it.

He smiled at Curt whom he quite liked, the more so because Curt was almost solely responsible for getting one over on Ged Norrington, whom he secretly loathed.

People like Ged Norrington needed to be bested by the likes of Curt Chambers, or the world would be an unbearable place. The Norringtons of this world had a habit of rising to unstoppable heights unless now and then defeated by the redoubtable and quietly fearless people of integrity.

Too few of those about alas.

Charlie watched surreptitiously as Chambers sipped his beer. He continued cleaning and polishing and he surveyed his pub, until Chambers caught his eye and grinned. "How goes it landlord?" he said in his richly timbered voice, somewhat inimical with the rest of his appearance.

"Up and down!" replied Charlie and he moved along the bar, only to move back again a second later and incline his head towards Chambers. "A word to the wise . . . your colleague Richie Southern! . . ."

Curt Chambers leaned in a little towards him, neither of them looking directly at the other. Chambers refrained from enquiring how Charlie meant the word 'colleague'—it was better not to ask.

"Tell him to watch himself!" said Charlie.

Chambers murmured slightly in confirmation and Charlie hung a wine glass.

"Why so?" said Chambers eventually.

"A conversation I overheard . . . Jack Norrington and another of his relatives!"

"Not Ged then?"

"No, no . . . . although his name cropped up!"

"I'll bet!"

"Just let him know . . . I haven't seen him for a few days or I would myself!"

"No more than that?"

"I'll keep you informed if there's more!" said Charlie, barely moving his lips.

Curt Chambers lifted his beer and said loudly. "It's a poor outlook for investors now . . . without a doubt!"

"Agreed!" said Charlie airily.

They both turned on cue and began talking with other people.

It was in fact only three in the afternoon, though the day was so dark and dreary outside it might well have been twilight.

Charlie saw the arrival of the afternoon barmaid through the side window as she alighted from her car and he immediately rung open the till, checked the float, then grabbed his outdoor coat.

He felt it was time to go back to the Soul Light Centre.

*   *   *   *

It was a Saturday, late afternoon and Charlie arrived at the Centre in his inconspicuous car and headed up the steps, suddenly thinking that the place would be closed and his journey wasted. Hoping also that no-one who frequented the pub would see him and think he had gone all New Age and Hippy . . . what next? they would ask: circle dancing in the main function room! fire-walking in the car park after dark! Or maybe poetry reading and chanting where the darts matches ought to be.

Gita opened the door to him and looked unsurprised.

"Yes . . . Mr . . . um . . . Mr Gilbert!" She was making the fatal mistake that he hated.

"Just Charlie will do . . . . Heather and I never married . . . not yet at least!"

Gita remained sublimely disinterested in the information. "Have a seat please?"

Charlie sat in the chair near the statue of the Buddha, where countless other people had sat before him for their first time in the Centre, and he waited to see what would happen. Half an hour passed in Gita's absence but Charlie was capable of being an extremely patient man.

"I can help you in what way?" enquired Gita on her eventual return, with no apology as to time, her syntax erratic but her accent faultless.

"I thought you might know where Heather is!" said Charlie. "I thought you might be able to tell me!"

"I told you all that last time!"

"Yes but the position has changed now . . . the t.v. people want her back!"

"Back?" echoed Gita.

"They want to have Wendy back in the programme!"

"I see . . . is it going to be similar to a science fiction programme now? . . . where the dead rise again and people who have drowned are taken up from the ocean by an unknown force?"

Charlie laughed politely. "Just what I said!"

He was thinking of his rant the first time Dean had suggested the possibility. He had said nothing of the kind but wished he had been similarly erudite instead of just rude.

"Do you have contact with her?" he enquired lightly.

"Now and then she comes . . . . but she does not say where from or where she returns to and we don't ask!"

"No . . . but . . ."

"All I can do is enquire of the ancestors!" interrupted Gita, and she inclined her small body in a slight bow so that he understood she was going to leave the room for another undefined period of time.

When she returned he had dozed off. He had been up very early because he couldn't sleep for thinking about things, and then he had humped a lot of crates around the cellar. He was weary to the bone.

He jumped as she entered, wondering for a moment where he was.

"I'm sorry . . . . I must have closed my eyes!"

"It is really alright . . . it happens a lot in here!"

"Does it?"

"We specialize in tranquil energy . . ." Gita quipped.

"Yes, of course!" Charlie agreed, but wondered too if this energy was something they conducted like a separate frequency through some kind of air vent.

"And besides . . . they will have been conversing with you at the subconscious level as you dozed!" she added.

"Who will?"

"The ancestors!" snapped Gita.

She was not patient when it came to philistines . . . surely Heather had tried to lift this man from the abyss of ignorance in which he might dwell without the assistance of an enlightened person.

"They inform me they cannot help very much . . . and that you ought to know where she is!"

"Really?"

"I wouldn't otherwise say so!" Gita said.

Charlie felt his face becoming hot, he was being upbraided in the most patronising and annoying of ways. He could not say right for saying wrong.

"She was talking to you of this place often enough! . . ." Gita paused for deliberation. "But if you do not realize it then you are not ready to see her!"

"Is that what they said?" Charlie asked dumfounded.

Gita drew breath impatiently. "Do you imagine I invent these things for fun?"

"I don't imagine anything!" he replied without guile.

She rose and paced around the tiny cubicle recess and then relented a little. "It is a question of the emotional and mental effort you put into it . . . not the desire you have to see her return!"

Charlie was silent.

"If you are to proceed with your life together you must have a bond closer than previously . . . to demonstrate the beginnings of that you must think about what she will want in the future now this happens . . ."

There followed a few moments of loud silence into which there fell the sound of a muted gong somewhere in the building, and then low chanting.

Charlie spoke again: "So they won't tell you where she lives exactly?"

Gita looked at her visitor and perceived that he was under immense strain. Altering her breathing as he stared balefully at the floor she turned to listen to more guidance from the ancestors.

She could give him a clue, they informed her.

Charlie looked as if he might at any moment weep and Gita felt sorry for him. He was an inoffensive person; his essence and his energy were of a lighter rather than a darker hue and he seemed to be capable of a growth spurt spiritually with the right mentoring.

"I think she might be near water!" Gita announced casually, causing Charlie to raise his eyes and stare at her.

Without further warning he jumped from the chair. A eureka moment had dawned. He knew immediately where Heather had gone. This little Oriental woman was right—he should have thought of it before. It was where she always took him when they had their very rare days out and their long walks along the beach.

"I see . . . I see what you mean! I think I know now where she is . . . . thanks!"

Charlie fumbled in his back pocket and threw a couple of notes onto the small table, beneath the statue of the Buddha.

"That isn't necessary!" said Gita majestically, staring confusedly at the money.

But Charlie had sprinted towards the double doors and was fiddling with the locks.

She hurried after him, then seeing he was managing his exit without the need of help she returned to pick up the notes he had so generously contributed.

TEN

Francine peeped cautiously around the gingham curtain of the small window at the front of the caravan and saw her aunt—Nancy Norrington—standing below the step to the door, having knocked and knocked in the hope that she would get a response.

Francine did not open the door to any strangers. Richie had told her not to. They were remote here and sometimes people passing through decided they would enquire the way to places or ask for water to drink; some of them might be okay and others would be sheer nutters.

So Francine always ignored the door unless the visitor happened to call out their identity, like Scott Brangle or the Chester's farm people, or someone from Rookeries.

Francine was flabbergasted to see the likes of her aunt, wearing her pink anorak with the hood pulled over her curls, a basket of some kind in her hands. Like a pink version of Red Riding Hood.

Francine let her in, kissed her briefly and then became flummoxed and embarrassed.

Nancy made herself at home in the one armchair near the tiny cooking range.

"Francie love . . . I don't like to see you living this way!"

"Aunt Nan, what is it you want?"

"To know you didn't have nothing to do with the theft of the turkeys!" blurted Nancy unwisely. She had never been capable of subtle conversational intros.

Francine stared at her. "Of course I didn't"

Nancy exhaled visibly. "I said as much to your uncle . . . I said you'd know nothing . . . but I suppose your feller knows!"

Francine turned away and fiddled with the curtain she had twitched out of place.

"I brought you some eggs . . . and some scones!" said Nancy, embarrassed in her turn. "Just to tide you over!"

"We're not charity cases you know, just because we live in a caravan!"

"Oh no! . . . I didn't mean that . . . I meant . . . well I know what young folks are . . . they live on the fruits of love!" said Nancy in a throw away manner.

"I'll make you some tea, shall I?" asked Francine generously of her relative.

"If you like . . . but I can't stop . . . I don't want Ged knowing I came . . . if I don't get back directly he'll likely see me coming over the field at Chester's from the top field and he'll guess where I was . . . I'm never able to lie to him! . . ."

Francine nodded. "It was good of you to come over aunt Nan! . . . I hope you don't think I betrayed you on purpose . . . I know that's what the family all think . . ."

"Not all of us!" said Nancy.

"No, but uncle Ged wants them to think that . . . ."

"Well . . . . he's set in his ways! . . . ." Nancy paused, watched Francine reaching for mugs.

"Francie . . . . do you know what you're getting into?"

"How do you mean?"

"Well, these Animal Rights and so on . . ."

"Doesn't concern me!" said Francine. "Richard feels strongly about it . . . but that's his choice . . . he doesn't try to convert me . . . or involve me!"

"No, no . . . . he seems a nice enough feller to me . . . so does the other one . . . Scott!"

"Yes, they both are nice . . . they're all nice people at Rookeries"

Nancy took a moment to deliberate on the 'all' and how many of them Francine was referring to.

"You know he's disinherited you?" Nancy declared suddenly.

"I don't care! . . ."

"You might! . . . one of these days! . . . your mum's afraid to go against him of course!"

"She always was weak . . ."

"Francine you're very young . . ." Nancy paused to summon courage—talking to people Francine's generation on these kind of matters definitely took courage. "The world is black and white at your age . . . but when you get older . . ."

Francine came across to Nancy and put her arms around her. "Look, aunt Nan . . . don't worry . . . don't jeopardise yourself or compromise yourself for me . . . I'll be fine!"

Nancy stared at the walls of the caravan, covered in posters of various kinds, and there was silence until Francine handed her a cup filled with milky tea.

Nancy hated milky tea but knew that Francine had made it like that so she could drink it and make a quick get away.

Francine was rinsing the mugs and deep in thought after Nancy's departure when minutes later there was a second knock. This time she opened the door without thinking and found Nancy back there again.

"I had to tell you . . . I was going to do it before but then lost my nerve . . . I got some way back and I knew I had to tell you . . .|"

"What?" Francine assumed a look of fear and horror and prepared for what her aunt had to say.

"They're planning to steal one of them birds! . . . one of the expensive ones!"

"Who is?"

"Your uncle Ged, Jack and Jack's brother-in-law! . . . they're putting Alfie up to it!"

"What? . . . . I drink with Alfie . . . we're mates!" Francine was edging backwards to distance herself from the message.

"That's why I didn't want to say nothing! . . . nevertheless, they're making him do it!"

"Bastards!" Francine dropped onto the armchair and slumped like a rag doll. There was no-one left in her family who was trustworthy!

"Best tell him!" said Nancy. "Best tell your man . . . . but don't for the love of Christ tell anyone it was me who told you . . . please don't Francine!"

"I won't!" Francine looked at Nancy with huge eyes. "I give you my word aunt Nan . . . I won't say anything to anyone about you!"

Naturally Francine knew that if she told Richie she would need to reveal the source. It may get back and spread through the family that Nancy had turned traitor. She could not do the right thing by her man and by her relative. It was an unholy dilemma of the sort she hadn't encountered before. But then Alfie had betrayed her, albeit in an involuntary sense and he was a relative, but it amounted to much the same thing.

If she said nothing and one of Richard's beloved birds was stolen and killed he would be in a worse decline. Tess! And then his birds! What if it was Titch! He loved Titch—probably more than he loved her or Tess!

Interspersed between these agonising thoughts and pondering on them, she was filled with the most hideous loathing and anger towards Alfie. She fantasised briefly about getting a gun and shooting him. Killing him stone dead without a word, one shot in the head at close quarters, his eyes registering the horror of realization and remorse before he died!

She rang Alfie's mobile but then stopped the call—if she told him she knew he would ask her how?

Unable to stay conscious and alert in this sea of betrayal and poisonous intrigue she crept beneath the duvet on the bed she shared with Richie and swigged the best part of a bottle of cheap vodka until she slept.

When Richie came in he found her dead drunk and gently snoring, the bottle beside her on the duvet, and he shook her awake.

"What in Christ's name were you doing?" He pulled her to a sitting position. "Trying to top yourself? . . . ."

The look on his face was too much for her, she sank back against the pillows and groaned. Inexperienced and sheltered from life, she could not bear this kind of turmoil. She told him everything, quickly to get it out of the way.

The roar Richie made on hearing the information was enough to shake the caravan. It echoed in the aluminium structure like a top note from a bassoon in an orchestra.

It was not until she had woken from her second long sleep that she realized Richie had shown some healthy emotion for the first time in months.

*   *   *   *

Richie found Scott in the pub—they were going on to a restaurant in Limetrees, he and Julie; it was their wedding anniversary. He weaved his way around the evening drinkers at the bar and found the table at which they both sat. Julie was admiring some kind of bracelet on her wrist that Scott had given her for the occasion and Scott was leaning into her and fingering something silvery dangling from it. Julie saw Richie first.

"If you've come with bad news you can just go away again!" she said.

"What now?" Scott asked.

"Apparently they've plans to take one of the birds!" said Richie briefly. "I'm going over there and I'll set up watch tonight . . . you'll need to relieve me at first light if you can!"

"What? . . . who has these plans?" said Scott bemused.

Charlie was waving at Scott and Scott was distracted—their taxi had arrived.

"Who do you think? . . . . the Norrington clan!"

"Who told you?"

"Never mind . . . I'm between a rock and a hard place and I can't reveal that . . . but just trust me . . . I know exactly what to look out for and I'm going to see to it they don't steal anything else for a few years!"

Julie got to her feet and pulled Scott by the hand. "Let's go before there's a reason not to ! . . . it's our wedding anniversary!" she said into Scott's face as if Richie wasn't there.

"I know!" Scott turned to Richie. "Just don't do anything you can go to prison for!"

"Trust me!" Richie was heading to the bar. "I'll be fine! But relieve me as soon as you can after dawn! . . . If you can't then get one of the lads to do it!"

"I'll be there before that!"

"No you won't!" Julie was pulling Scott behind her. "I'm not allowing it!"

"I'll be there . . . just safeguard Eddy!" Scott called. "It'll be him they target if they target any!"

"Well naturally . . . ." Julie was signalling to the taxi driver at the pub doorway, "as long as Eddy's okay we'll all be laughing!"

Curt Chambers had seen Richie and was heading over. "Wanted a word with you Rich!"

"Follow me out to the car then . . . I have no time to spare!"

Curt was running to keep up with Richie's sprint to the Land Rover. He was shouting against the November wind to warn Richie as Charlie had asked him to.

"It's Eddy they're going for right now . . ." yelled Richie over his shoulder. "I have it on good authority!"

"Eddy who?"

"Eddy the Eagle!"

Curt was not familiar with the Rookeries inmates and he put two and two together only as the Land Rover roared off in the direction of the bird sanctuary. It was lashing rain and his hair gleamed against his head, water dripping from his pigtail.

Retrieving the mobile phone from the pocket of his coat and sheltered by the open porch of the pub Curt made the various phone calls designed to ensure help if necessary.

*   *   *   *

Alfie knew the attempt to steal the eagle would go wrong—that was if he even got close to the bird. He had only agreed to do it because it was better than the aggression and derision he would be forced to tolerate from his male relations in standing against the proposal.

He knew that if Francine discovered she would be hurt, she might even never speak to him again. But what choice did he have!

To accomplish this feat of daring and nerve he thought himself into a state of mind whereby it was a lark, a bit if fun, and not a serious offence in which the law might be broken. Just an in-family caper, so to speak.

He was very wrong.

On the actual night he met with one of his cousins, loosely connected to the farm but not interested in the ins and outs and the money and the politics. Just very interested in the thought of a free drinking binge later that week funded by Alfie, in return for assistance. Kevin was the best kind of ally money could buy.

"What are we doing this for again? . . . . remind me!"

Kevin was Alfie's senior by three or four years. They jogged along the deserted road at three in the morning and headed over the fields to the side area of Rookeries.

"Dunno really! . . . because Ged has decreed it? . . . . he who rules supreme!"

They had reached the fencing and Kevin turned his flashlight onto Alfie's features in the darkness. "You dunno! . . . you're up for pinching an expensive animal and you dunno!"

"Well I know roughly! . . . something to do with this lot nicking his turkeys! . . . incidentally Kev, these ain't animals, they're birds!"

Kevin ignored the reference to his ignorance. "And did they nick his turkeys?"

"I dunno . . ."

"You dunno a lot, Alf, for someone about to commit a felony!"

Kevin was nicely oiled, after much dutch courage consumed in the pub near his own home, but not oiled enough to be incapable of running with the weight of the bird when they pulled it off.

"Okay . . . there's the question of a few thousand quid's worth of livestock which is part of our family business! . . . . then there's the other thing of one of them taking Francine off to live in a caravan!"

"What? Against her will?"

"No, course not against her will . . . . can you picture Francie doing anything against her will! . . . she reckons she's in love with him!"

"She probably is! It does happen! So then it occurs to me . . ." said Kevin importantly, "that Ged should keep his nose out of things don't concern him . . . . turkeys apart!"

The flashlight swerved about the countryside vista in a drunken manner and Alfie became businesslike.

"Will you watch what you're doing with that!"

Kevin shrugged Alfie's arm away from his own impatiently and the flashlight careered giddily—a strong light used in Kevin's trade as an electrician.

"Where's this hole in the fence then?"

"I'll know by the marker I left!" Alfie said in a hushed voice.

"You left a marker? . . . when d'you leave a marker?"

"This afternoon, just before it went pitch black! . . . I paid last week to go in and look at the exhibits and find where we needed to gain entrance and then I came back today and marked the outside of the fencing with a trowel in the ground!"

Alfie was creeping along the outer fence again and Kevin was stumbling after him, the flashlight swaying like a distress beacon.

"Turn that fucking thing off or put it under your coat!" admonished Alfie.

"How do you know they've not discovered it . . . this marker?"

"Unlikely . . . . they won't be looking for it!"

"What's it marking anyway?"

"The ground adjacent to the eagle enclosure!"

Kevin fell against Alfie before righting himself and then dropping the flashlight. "Eagle enclosure! You never said it was an eagle we're lifting!"

"So, what difference? . . . it's a bird!"

"Yeah but I thought it was a parrot or something!"

"A parrot! This is a bird of prey place not the bleeding pet shop!"

Kevin was scrabbling around on all fours looking for the flashlight—how could a large torch disappear from grasp in such a small radius? "You realize it's probably insured and worth thousands! . . ." he said frantically.

Alfie felt the flashlight next to his foot. "Er . . . hello? . . .I think that just might be the point of this exercise!"

"Yeah, well there'd better be a good point because if we get caught we could go down for it!"

"Kev, don't be so fucking dramatic!" Alfie was growing nervous and his planning seemed less flawless than it had three hours ago. "It's not the Great Train Robbery!"

Kevin suddenly stopped dead in his tracks—the hole in the fence had appeared in the beam of the light. "Alf, it's trespass, theft and probably animal cruelty or something! . . . it isn't some kind of jolly schoolboy caper in the tuck shop!"

Alfie bridled. Kevin never lost a chance to jibe at Alfie's education, posher than his own comprehensive schooling. "That's right, it's big grown up business . . . but sometimes, Kev, it's necessary in life to do dangerous things!"

He was searching for the wire clippers and grabbing Kevin's hand holding the flash and directing it at the ragged tear in the fence.

"What? Just because Ged Almighty Norrington wants one up on some feller! . . . the turkeys were probably pinched because of something Ged had done to someone else!"

"They were pinched by Animal Rights!" announced Alfie finally and then he forced and squoze his way trough the hole in the fencing. "You coming or not?"

Kevin followed in some reluctance—they found themselves between the Eagle enclosure and a smaller pen in which an unknown species of birds were housed.

The birds in the smaller pen began to make noises immediately and Kevin froze, his flashlight trained on them.

"Turn it off. . . . you're alarming them!" Alfie got out his own flashlight which was half the size of Kevin's and cautiously directed it at Eddy's enclosure.

Eddy was sleeping, or so it seemed, and Alfie began to trim another hole with his wire cutters to gain admittance to Eddy's abode.

Kevin was wishing he had never agreed to any of this. It was hair-raisingly terrifying. Pitch black and macabre. Strange loud noises emitted by winged creatures, some of which were too large and weird looking to be contemplated.

"Jesus . . . !"

Kevin's yell blasted the black velvet winter night—a buzzard had landed on the side of it's enclosure, parallel to his face, it was peering at him with cold eyes. "What do people see in these repulsive bastards? . . . . they'd be better on a plate surrounded by some kind of vegetable!"

"Shut up!" warned Alfie angrily.

"They won't understand what I'm saying!" replied Kevin airily.

"There could be surveillance cameras with sound!"

Foul language came from Kevin and then some kind of keening guttural shriek from a pen several feet along. "Hurry up Alf, for Christ's Sake!"

"I'm there! . . .'

Alfie carefully lifted the ring of wire he'd cut in a radius and entered the eagle's pen.

He knew nothing of eagles, or large birds, but had taken a cursory look on the internet to see if there was anything he should be appraised of. Eagles, it said, did not usually attack humans unless threatened, or unless their young were being threatened.

He was confident that he could get the bag over Eddy and they could haul him between them back through the hole in the outer fencing and then along the perimeter to where they were parked.

Piece of cake!

Hindsight being that wonderful thing, he knew later that it had been a ridiculously over-confident sort of plan. In fact no plan at all really, just a bit of an intention to break and enter.

Apart from the terrible cacophony of big bird noise, things were reasonably in control, until they tried to pull Eddy from his perch with the hessian bag over him. His talons were lethal and they could not get the bag to cover them because of his grip on the broad perch. So they pulled the mouth of the sack under the perch as best they could and held it together with their joint grip and debated whether to try cutting the perch either side of Eddy's feet and taking it with them. Trouble was they had not got the right tools for the job.

Kevin had a hacksaw, carried for professional purposes, and he retrieved it from the depth of his working jacket.

"Hurry up!" urged Alfie. "I can't hold this sack by myself much longer!"

It was then that another bird, completely unknown to them, landed on Kevin's back and went for his earlobe. Some kind of companion eagle, or Eddy's Mrs perhaps.

This creature lunged its beak at his lobe and then his neck and pulled at chunks of his skin and drew blood.

Kevin yelled in agony while Alfie tried to fight off the interloping bird and hold the sack at the same time.

"Get it the fuck off me . . ." Kevin was screaming.

The avenging bird also screeched—with a deafening and hideous sound.

Alfie let go of the sack and Eddy rose vertically and dropped onto his head countless times, the weight of him threatening to break Alfie's neck, his talons scuffling to penetrate his woollen hat.

Kevin now had his his arms over his head to protect himself from the companion bird. He had dropped the flashlight.

"Let's get out . . ." Alfie yelled. He had just enough presence of mind to stop and pick up the flashlight before they fled the enclosure.

*   *   *   *

Several yards away in the cabin reception area through which visitors entered the Rookeries, Richie was surfacing from an unnaturally deep and uncomfortable sleep on the camp bed he'd brought for the purpose of night surveillance.

He rolled off the bed in a startled and haphazard fashion and listened to the din from the birds and the distant sounds of male voices. He pulled on his coat and unlocked the side door onto the grounds of the sanctuary.

The pre-dawn morning was freezing. He ran, bleary and unfocused, towards the noise of the buzzards and the lone voice of Eddy.

By the time he had squeezed through the hole in the fencing wire leading to the road he realized that whoever it was had gone the other way. They had got in and out through the side fence.

Then there was the sound of a van engine starting up in the distance. He turned around and squinted into the murky light and began pursuing a grey, indistinct shape that was obviously their get away vehicle. He could not even distinguish the make of it let alone anything on the number plate. He watched it gain speed and round the bend of the lane but still he ran pell-mell in a futile chase along the road.

Eventually he petered to a stop, arms swinging, his breath ragged and his chest hurting. He stopped to remedy his heart and lung function and felt his legs weak beneath him. Too much work and not enough sleep, too much booze and not enough exercise, too much stress and exertion, emotional and physical, taking it toll.

He felt he might be dying, right there on the road. Dying at the tender age of twenty nine.

Crawling to where the verge met the fencing of the sanctuary and where the trees gave shelter from the sky, he realized with great sadness that he had not secured the iron gates of Rookeries but merely pulled them after himself in his haste; he could hear them swinging to and fro. He remembered that he had left his phone next to the makeshift bed and that he could not summon help.

He could not be dying surely!

Was this what Tess had felt as she lay fallen from the horse, hours passing as she grew weaker! Was this how she had ended her conscious time? afraid that no-one would find her, remote from help and human-kind! His face was wet with rain and he cursed himself for a loser. He closed his eyes and he seemed to sleep.

When he woke again it was at the foot of a hill where he was standing looking up at someone approaching him, the sun in her hair.

It was Tess, and it was not Tess. It was a facsimile of Tess, without the distinctive features that made her Tess in his recent known memory.

He watched her grow larger in outline as she descended. Her hair was the colour of fresh straw but it was braided in a strange quaint sort of style.

She spoke to him in foreign tongue although he understood she was asking him how long he'd been waiting.

He did not reply, but even so it seemed she knew what his answer was. He began to feel he was between two places. He scrabbled about in his mind for earlier thought, previous memory.

He tried to get back to being just Richie. And it was then he knew he was having some kind of out of body experience.

He looked at Tess, at who Tess had become, at this strange female he knew intimately, and he waited for her to explain. He was filled with sublime love for her, pleasure at just resting his eyes on her.

She was accompanied in the background by a horse. He seemed to recognized the horse from somewhere else. The animal grazed casually and was peaceful in Tess's vicinity. He stared at the horse for a while and tried to remember, and the exertion of this was so tiring he had to stop.

He looked back to Tess who smiled, extended her hand, and he took it. Her hand was real, but it was a different sensation. It was fused with an energy he had never felt before.

When he opened his mouth to speak he knew he had nothing to say, he knew also that when he did say anything it would be in this strange tongue.

He was certainly dying then.

He conveyed this to Tess with one glance. He felt certain he was losing her and the surroundings.

He did not want to lose her, he had only just found her again. The sadness he experienced at the possibility was almost life threatening. His eyes flickered

to the periphery, right and left, to the grass and the trees and the sky-line and
the distant buildings in varying hues of brick and wood and milky grey slate.
He could feel the colours and the textures of the scenery, he could perceive them
with some sense that was a mixture of vision and hearing and taste and smell.
It was superbly heightened and almost unbearable. Too much for his limited
senses. He closed his eyes against the blinding light of the scene and held onto
the gladness and the relief and the love he felt for this woman who might or
might not be Tess.

"*Please don't let me go!*" *he said to her.*

She touched him again, put her hand on his cheek, and he felt himself
retreating, almost dissolving, becoming defused within the whole scenario.

"*Please hold onto me!*" *he shouted to her, like someone in the middle of a*
storm at sea.

"*I will!*" *she said.* "*Don't fear . . . I will!*"

He came to again on the cold damp ground near to Rookeries and
recalled events prior to this strange interlude.

He tried to retain the vision of Tess. It was so vivid. And even as he
realized it he also knew it would fade.

He relived it over again and watched it and sensed it grow less real inside
him, like a film on driving from the cinema. The bleak solitude descending,
the harsh world of reality as he knew it prior to this experience.

He opened his eyes and he saw that the same horse had joined him. It
had spanned two worlds in some way. Sniffing the grass, trying vainly to
graze on the winter verge.

"Who the hell are you?" he asked of the animal.

But it seemed no more strange to him than the experience he had just
undergone in another place. It was just as inexplicable but also just as personal
to his immediate life. He knew it was stupid to have voiced the question to
an animal but he also knew that in some way the animal understood him.
Just as it had understood Charlie and he that night last year.

Staggering and half running back to Rookeries he was consumed by
the events, by a sense of not being properly back in his body but somehow
accompanying it.

Ineptly he closed the torn wiring in Eddy's enclosure, though Eddy had
gone flying, and he was watched only by Queenie—the aged crowned eagle
who was Eddy's female companion.

Eddy would return by morning and be crouched on the roof,
awaiting entry like a brazen fugitive: Eddy knew which side his bread was
buttered.

Richie fell onto the makeshift bed so heavily it rocked and creaked as if it would break. He had left one world to enter another on the verge of death, and then he had left that world and re-emerged to the first world. He had thought he was dying, was sure he had died. But then he had surfaced again. Maybe he was dead, to all intents and purposes, and maybe this was the afterlife, or not so much 'after' as 'parallel'. Maybe there was no death!

Clearly there was a large question mark over what it was. It was not as most people thought it would be. That he knew. Although he did not know much else.

He let himself fall into oblivion.

Scott shook him awake when he entered at five thirty and Richie stared at him as if he might not be real.

"Eddy's on the roof!" Scott said.

"They came . . . they tried to get into Eddy's enclosure . . . . they got away . . . I couldn't catch them!"

"But they didn't steal Eddy!" said Scott, triumphant . . .

"No, they didn't succeed!"

Scott watched Richie moving around the cabin and picking up his clothes.

"You were supposed to be keeping watch!"

"I did, until two or so, and then I was dead to the world!"

"Told you it would all get too much—this vigilance after a hard days work!"

Richie plugged in the kettle and then realized it was without water. He was silent for a few minutes, going about routinely as if it were the start of a normal day.

"You're very calm!" Scott said. "Considering someone just tried to pinch our most prized possession! You okay?"

"We knew it was coming didn't we!"

"You knew . . . I had doubts!"

"Yeah well . . . . there we go!"

Scott accepted a mug of tea and waited.

"Something you're not telling me?"

"No!"

"I think so . . . come on Richie . . . what is it?"

Richie sank onto the visitor bench. "I had a strange experience when I gave chase!"

"What?"

"I'd rather not go into it!"

"Don't you think you can trust me!"

"It's nothing you can do anything about! . . . you'll probably laugh!"

"Poor opinion you have of me there boy!"

"It's personal! . . . . and don't call me 'boy' . . ."

Scott drank the tea with deliberation and then laughed.

"Told you!" said Richie "You're at it already!"

"Maybe you'll tell me later then?"

"Maybe, maybe not."

"Richie, I think you should tell me!"

"It's personal, like I said . . ."

"How can it be personal when we had a break in and you were chasing the people responsible? . . . . how can anything personal have arisen? Unless you killed one of them!"

"Nothing as heroic! . . . I just passed out that's all!"

Scott turned in the midst of pacing the front area and stared. "You passed out? Was that it . . . this personal thing? What happened, when you passed out?"

"Well there's the rub . . ." Richie hesitated but the beckoning relief of getting it off his chest and sharing it was too much. "I entered a place . . ."

"A place . . . what place?"

"I saw Tess!" said Richie in great embarrassment. "And I spoke with her!"

Scott was silent for the longest time. He knew more than to comment without thought. Eventually he cleared his throat and made a noise, a prelude to speech. "Well . . . see . . . I ain't laughing . . . . I told you way back that you need to speak to someone about all this?"

"What? You're saying I'm barmy?"

"Never said that Richie! . . . . there's a lot to these things . . . death and the likes! . . . there's a lot to the mind and what it can do . . . . there's things that can never be explained . . . possibilities and so on . . . . knew an old timer once . . . over in Australia . . . always claimed his dead wife spoke to him and helped with the planning of the farm and so on . . . no-one believed him . . . . until one day she walked amid a whole lot of folk and took them out of the way of a bushfire! . . . ."

Richie digested this for several moments. "Who can I speak to about it?" he said finally.

"Not sure . . . . Julie may know! . . . she talks about some woman over near the ancient church . . . a medium or somesuch . . . great reputation . . . . gets in touch with ancestors and that kind of stuff . . . . heals folk too . . . she'll see you right! . . . . Ill get her phone number from the little woman!"

Richie was dumb-struck and stared at Scott.

"What?" said Scott. "What are you staring at me for?"

"I was thinking . . . . if Julie hears you calling her the '*little woman*' there'll be hell to pay!"

"Better keep your mouth shut about that then!" Scott drank his tea calmly as Richie picked up his belongings and headed for home.

ELEVEN

Ged Norrington stalked around the length of his farmhouse where the walls of the two main rooms had been taken out to provide a space which Nancy was keen on calling the main lounge. It was a long and spacious area and someone at one end had to raise their voice to be heard at the other. This was the case currently as Ged addressed Alfie.

"So where's Kevin now?" Ged called from somewhere near the grandmother clock.

"Resting in bed!" mumbled Alfie from the opposite end.

"Resting in bed? What's the matter with him? . . . the soft sod!"

"Funnily enough, he had a massive chunk of his earlobe bitten off by a huge wild bird!" Alfie was staring truculently at the window, out of the eye-line of his relation. "I think it might just have hurt a bit! . . ."

A sticking plaster covered one side of Alfie's forehead, to protect the laceration made by the eagle's claws, but this was nowhere near as nasty as the wounds sustained by his cousin.

"I hope you didn't say anything at the hospital about the reason for his injury!"

"What do you think? . . . we're stupid?"

"You're stupid enough to bungle the attempt . . . that I do know!"

"Do it yourself then!" retorted Alfie, uncaring.

"You know Alfie, your attitude to your elders is not good!" pronounced Ged in a quiet menacing tone.

"You ask too much of people!" said Alfie, unafraid now this calamitous thing had happened.

"Did they ask you at the hospital what had attacked Kevin?" Ged felt it best to ignore his nephew's effrontery in this quest for important facts.

"Yep . . . we said it was the family budgie!"

"Are you serious? What did they say?"

"Not much . . . they looked sceptical and disbelieving then said they were supposed to report savage animal attacks to the appropriate authorities!"

Ged paced the huge room, tugging his side hair sticking out from under his hat, tutting to himself at intervals.

"Better not go back and try again then!"

"Too right!" said his nephew loudly, adding under his breath. "You moronic twat!"

There was a vacuous pause and then Ged turned. "What did you say?"

"I said: *'that'll have to be that!'* . . ."

Ged turned away and gazed at the expanse of his land beyond the picture window.

"What's your dad have to say?"

"What can he say? . . . much the same as you! . . . he seems to think it was our fault, Kev's and mine!"

"Well son, you were the only two there!"

Alfie drew breath impatiently and sucked his teeth. However did he get to incarnate with this load of wankers passing for a family!

Nancy came in then and Ged moved towards her, anxious not to let her hear anything about the botched bird theft—she was massively disapproving of capers of this kind.

"Hello flower! . . . . I thought you'd gone to the hairdressers!"

"Back half an hour since!" said Nancy and looked suspiciously at Alfie lounging in the chair with the bleak and malefic expression beloved of young men severely out of sorts.

"So it looks like we'll need to wait for the rain to stop!" Ged said innocuously to no-one in particular.

There was a silence whilst Nancy hesitated to see what she might glean from the statement. Nothing more was forthcoming from either of them and she left, thankful not to have to absorb unwanted responsibility.

Ged watched the door shut on her before saying: "So we need someone else for the job!"

"Guess so! . . . if you can find somebody daft enough to risk a jail stretch!" Alfie replied.

His uncle emitted a derisive laugh; comment was quite beneath his contempt.

*   *   *   *

When Richie drew up outside the old church, St. Winifred Mead, he was unsure where the Soul Light Centre was. He thought they would know—they were open for business as usual, being some kind of celebrated ecclesiastical museum or something similar.

An old woman with a marvellously immaculate black hairdo came out of the church doors carrying a mop and bucket and began swabbing a marble tomb.

It was a very cold day and Richie was surprised to see this task taking place. He watched for several moments and then alighted the Land Rover and waved at the elderly lady in a friendly manner.

Promptly she turned and went back into the ancient church. Richie stood for a moment, offended.

Maybe she was shortsighted.

He looked up and down the lane—it was a quiet and somnambulant place, it reeked of years of history and secrets. He had heard that it was renowned for its odd goings on and that it had quite recently boasted a particularly colourful ghost; a female who apparently carried an umbrella.

Richie smiled and thought that by now she was possibly accompanied on and off by Tess. The thought not only amused him but made him feel warm inside. How little we understood of ourselves until we have experience to measure by.

Lighting a cigarette he screwed up his eyes against the harsh winter sun and wondered about following the woman with the bucket and seeking information rather than wandering around and being scanned on umpteen cctv's. It was the kind of ultra affluent district where those would be in abundance.

He was joined suddenly by a man in vicar's attire.

"Can I help you?" said this official body, a tall imposing sort of man with a commanding air.

Richie smiled whilst Reverend Mawl did not.

Reverend Mawl had been informed by one of his wardens, the lady with the mop and bucket, that a youngish fellow was loitering suspiciously outside the gate.

Mawl was ever vigilant about robbery. His ancient church carried the kind of artefacts much prized and highly priced on the international antiquities market. There had been an attempt to rob such an item only last month—but they had fled and dropped the item at the lychgate, pursued by a zealous German visitor who had become alert to the theft as it was happening.

"Looking for the Soul Light Centre! . . ." Richie said. ". . . thought it might be in your grounds!"

"It certainly is not!" said the Reverend Mawl. "It's five hundred yards or so around the bend . . . . like a lot of the people involved in it!"

Richie was astonished at this irreverent comment but surmised that there was some kind of rivalry or commercial envy at work.

"Got you!" he said, and the vicar curled his lip disdainfully and then nodded grandly in the manner of someone from a Dickensian adaptation.

"Thanks . . . appreciate it!" Richie added.

Reverend Mawl watched whilst Richie got back into his vehicle, and on his way back into the church was met by Mrs Oats who said: "Was he another suspect, vicar?"

"No, I doubt it . . . . merely an unsuspecting victim of the Queen of Sheba along the lane!"

*   *   *   *

Gita greeted Richie with a small smile and led him into the main hall of the Centre.

She gazed up at him and took his measure in a few seconds. Her eyes held that slightly whimsical, amused look which in intelligent women told him something to the effect . . . *'I am aware of your masculine attractions, not in a predatory way but in a respectably flirtatious kind of way as behoves my age and position . . . .'*

Richie was used to such visual implications from the fair sex and took it in his stride. Indeed he barely registered it, accepting it as part and parcel of what he evoked. Were he famous or wealthy or otherwise celebrated it may by now have been his ruin or his greatest set-back.

He looked down on Gita and smiled his half smile that had grown out of his more wider and winsome grin in days of old before Tess had perished.

Gita led him to a small treatment room which contained only a couch. She watched him relax his tall and toned frame onto the narrow plinth, pulling out the band which held back his dark blonde hair so that it hung lose around his smooth bare neck. She rarely saw such attractive males of his age in the Centre in her treatment rooms, if they came at all they were nearly always on the yoga mats or sharing meditations with others.

"What is it again I may do?" she asked as she took his pulse and dangled her pendulum.

"I'm having these feelings . . . and these strange moods . . . and then the other day I blacked out and had some kind of NDE . . ." said Richie in a great rush—he did not want to have to name his condition and wanted someone like Gita to heal him, fix him or generally diagnose him without his direct intervention.

"What?" enquired Gita calmly. "You had what?"

"Well maybe it was just an OBE?" he added quickly. "I don't know . . . but I was with Tess! . . . my former girlfriend . . . I found myself with her before I came round!"

"An OBE in the form of a knighthood from the queen do you mean?" enquired Gita and Richie looked at her sharply to see if she were serious.

"No, an OBE in the form of an *out-of-body-experience!*"

There was a total silence but he could see that Gita now had his drift, roughly. He became confused and unconfident. "It may be more accurate to say it was an NDE . . ."

"What do you mean by all these letters?" asked Gita.

He sat up on the couch. He had been duped, the woman was not genuine; if she were she would know these things. "NDE is a *near death experience* . . ." Richie informed her, embarrassed and reluctant to say more. "I recently began reading about things like that . . . and watching documentaries!"

"Is that so?"

Gita walked around the plinth and opened a small lacquered cupboard of Oriental origin. Richie stared and wondered if it were genuine or fake . . . much like he wondered about her!

"Did you not know that? I thought . . . I thought you knew about these kind of things?"

"I might know about these kind of things . . . but I'm not in the habit of using that sort of jargon!" Gita said proudly.

"Jargon!" Richie lay back down.

"Yes, jargon!" repeated Gita.

"What do you call it then?"

"What do I call what?"

"An NDE?"

"I do not call it anything." Gita spoke in such tranquility that Richie was calmed immediately. "I accept the Universe as one mass of consciousness . . . death is not an event like climbing over a style . . . it is a transition along a stream of seamless energy . . . life and death . . . before and after . . . it is all one momentum!"

"And OBE's . . . out of body experiences?" enquired Richie, relaxing into some welcoming cocoon-like state.

"If you are out of body then you are out of gravity . . . . it is one and the same . . . there is no distinction . . . it is merely a question of time!"

"Oh . . . so you do understand what I mean when say I passed out and found myself in a field with my girlfriend"

"Naturally I understand . . ." Gita was dangling the pendulum along the front of his body at varying heights. "I speak English with you don't I?"

"Yes but . . . ."

He felt the effort of speech was beyond him; his eyes were closing and he was going backwards at a rate of knots. He had once had such a sensation on a friend's speedboat in the Canary Isles while facing away from the direction in which they were travelling, lying in the prow of the boat and watching the lowering sun in the skies as they fired along, way beyond the statutory speed limit . . . .

*　　　*　　　*　　　*

It was not until Charlie's fifth visit to the seaside resort that he had any luck at all.

He had been in the habit of returning every few days and walking about the parade of smart shops and up and down the promenade and sitting in draughty shelters staring out at the ocean, drinking tepid tea from the one and only stall still vending hot drinks for three hours a day for the sake of winter seaside enthusiasts.

Each visit he tried not to grow disheartened; he reminded himself that by the law of averages he would one day bump into her: he knew without doubt that this would be where she had fled to, like he knew that she would walk every day, she would come here to look at the sea and to walk. She might by now even have a dog to accompany her.

It was thanks to the clumsiness of another pedestrian that he got his break.

The man bumped into her while moving backwards from the rail dividing the promenade from the stoop leading down to the beach.

Charlie saw this from several hundred yards away. He saw the collision, he saw a woman in jeans and a long heavy blue coat, he saw her hat fly off and her hair, dark and much longer than he remembered it, fall out from beneath it.

He saw her laugh and he saw the man run after her hat to catch it before the wind took it. He was up and off the bench he had been sat on for half an hour before he even had time to register properly that it was her.

She had taken her hat and rammed it back on her head, pushing her hair beneath it, but when she saw Charlie she began to run the other way.

He ran after her. She was quicker than him, but still he ran and he knew that her knowledge of the smaller streets and alleyways at the back of the promenade gave her an advantage. She dodged and darted and evaded him. He ran this way and that and then gauged the buildings, changing direction a few times, so that people stared at him.

He thought that she had disappeared in the vicinity of a long block of commercial buildings to which the back entrances could only be one long alleyway, judging by the landscape of the properties either side.

He was correct. He came upon her after a few hundred yards and a sharp right angle turn into a small car park forming a square behind a restaurant and an adjacent pharmacy. His head for ergonomics had triumphed and he felt immensely relieved.

"Heather . . . don't run again . . . . let me talk to you . . . . please?"

She stared at him, like someone who would never be able to make a sensible choice if she lingered. She kept moving almost drunkenly to one side, as if to lurch off in that direction, and then changing her mind and dithering until she had run out of steam or fright or whatever was compelling her to keep on moving.

"Let's go and get a meal or a drink?" Charlie said.

Heather felt that her love, their love, was the strongest force between their joint wills. It seemed to commandeer her whether she acknowledged it or not.

"What harm can half an hour do?" he said.

"That is what everyone says in these situations . . ." Heather commented pragmatically, but she let him take her arm and move her in the direction of some venue he had already in his view.

*　　*　　*　　*

Richie was back in the strange time and place with Tess. There were other people there whom he knew. There was Scott for one, but Scott was not the man he was nowadays. Richie knew him only by his essence, by his energy. There was also Norrington-in-chief . . . still overweight and still larger than life, but better groomed.

He saw them all in a setting which resembled a courtyard to a more historic and grander place than any of them inhabited in the lifetime from which he had just emerged. It was a mansion perhaps!

Eventually he began to realize it was a chateau and that it was French. He was in France.

They were all ambling around on the lawn in front of the chateau entrance and talking loudly in an animated way and taking leave of each other. Then Tess drew her arm through his own and pulled him along the driveway towards this impressive place. He asked her questions she seemed not to understand. He repeatedly asked her why Ged Norrington was a French landowner and Scott some sort of military officer. "Because that is what they are!" she replied, laughing. "How else should they present themselves?"

He stood flabbergasted for long moments before he understood that he had stepped into something that was established to her but not to himself. She was an insider. He was an outsider—visiting briefly—whilst she was entrenched.

"Do you remember me?" he asked.

"Of course!" she said. "It was only last week when we met!"

Her speech and her movements were far more delicate and refined than he remembered. She was more sophisticated; she was confident and ladylike. Her clothes were good, her hair was perfumed, her manner was polished.

He stared at her, speechless. He recognized her open mouthed laughter better than anything else about her.

"What is wrong with you?"

"With me?" he echoed. "Nothing is wrong with me! . . . I was wondering the same about you?"

"Will you stay this time?" she asked. "Will you stay?"

They heard her name being called then by the man he knew as Scott. "Solange!" cried this man. "Solange . . . . who is that?"

"Say nothing!" she muttered to him under her breath. "Pretend you are come to seek out my cousin!"

"Your cousin? . . . I don't know your cousin!"

"Of course you do not . . ."

The Scott character was coming along the gravel path at a higher speed, frowning; he had about him that carefully controlled and tight anger that one man has for another man who is a stranger and a threat.

"How could you know her . . ." Solange was continuing in a low voice for fear of being heard. "But he won't realize that . . . do not tell him of the other week or the time before in the church . . . and definitely not about the money I lent you! . . . tell him nothing"

"Why? who is he?"

"He's my brother, you clown! You must remember that!"

"Then what is it to do with him?"

"*Everything . . .*" *Birds sang in a sweet melodic refrain and he stared at the dark eyes of the girl before him.* "*My brother will tell my parents! . . . stop behaving like a dolt . . . as if you don't know the proprieties and the taboos . . . . why would my brother take an interest indeed! . . .*" *She made a sound in her throat, half way between a hiss and a shriek. It was very French to his ears, very non-English.*

As if reading his mind she added: "*You are English and that is enough to upset him . . . to upset all of them . . .*"

He stared at her as she walked a little towards her brother, towards Scott, and he was transfixed, rooted to the spot. The man carried on his arm a falcon and he stared at the bird in wonderment.

An unknown breed of dogs trailed behind randomly, barking, maybe four of them.

He waited for the other man to recognize him, to show signs of the familiarity they shared via their work. But the other's eyes told him it was not there, this familiarity, his eyes were hard like flint. He was hurt in a way he did not comprehend, in a way his emotions were not equipped to deal with.

"*If I catch you around her inappropriately I will see to it that you are shot . . . or killed by the dogs!*" *said her brother menacingly, up close to him, breath smelling of strange spices, speaking quietly so that no-one else could hear.*

He made a slight clicking sound with his tongue which was reminiscent of Scott in working hours, and the falcon immediately spread its wing and opened it beak. Viscous and tensed, it raised itself for attack but the man restrained it with a further sound.

"*Go now! . . . run . . . I will say you are collecting gambling debts and I will give you a head-start . . . run now or the dogs will savage you!*"

Richie looked about for clarity, he was rigid with shock and fear. He began to jog away but his limbs were those of an old person, tired and weak, he could not gain speed. He heard the dogs barking behind him and the man's voice exhorting him to run, as if he were purposely not doing so.

He darted and zig-zagged in this pathetic attempt at speed and he seemed to cover very little ground.

Around the shimmering green bushes of the splendid garden there was a lake, and the dogs were almost upon him. He allowed himself to fall into the lake and felt that he had no more strength. He gleaned that he was not who he was in the life he had just left; he was in fact some kind of a cripple, he walked with a limp, a bad one: running was not within his command. Swimming was worse.

He began to panic as the water rose over his head. He was having trouble holding his breath. He was passing out. He saw the water translucent and colourless and the atmosphere fading and he heard the voice of the little woman in the Soul Light Centre saying things to him . . . .

"Come back now . . . . Richard? . . . move your fingers and toes please! . . . clear your throat and open your eyes!"

Gradually he opened his eyes as he moved his limbs, but his throat was locked solid in terror. He wanted to cry. He felt the overwhelming deadening sense of betrayal going straight to the vulnerable inner man, and there was no instantaneous shield. Tears filled his eyes and rolled down his face. "My best mate just tried to kill me!" he said hopelessly. "Why would he do that?"

There was a moment or two of comforting silence, reverent and ominous and filled with knowledge which was indiscernible.

"I will get you water . . ." replied Gita calmly. "Do not move yet . . . please remain lying there!"

She left him alone in the small room to contemplate everything he had just seen.

*   *   *   *

Francine rounded on Alfie as he left the pub nearest his own home and to which she had followed him, using the last bit of petrol she could afford that week.

"You bastard!" she shrieked and then rushed at him.

He fell back against the wall, caught off guard. She saw that a bandage covered one side of his head.

"How could you do it? . . . how could you betray me like that!"

"Francie, it had nothing to do with you. It wasn't personal. Ged made me do it! . . . . you know what he's like!"

She came at him again, arms flailing, hitting him with the flat of her hands and then pushing him in that way females used to attack.

"We failed anyway! . . ."

"Oh what a shame . . . . better luck next time eh?"

She lunged at him with one last thrust and shoved her hip into his groin. He moved quickly to one side to avoid her and scraped his face on the angle of the wall.

She stood watching, panting and crying.

Alfie rubbed his face with the side of his hand and saw the fresh watery blood coming from the graze. "How did you find out?"

"Kevin was blabbing about it of course and the landlord of his local told Charlie . . . it got back to Curt Chambers and he told Richie!" Francine said, leaving out her aunt Nancy.

There was nothing Alfie could say, he looked bleakly at the skyline and felt sick. His life recently was going from bad to worse.

"You didn't have to do it!" Francine said more quietly, her anger diffusing. "You should grow a fucking spine Alfie!"

"And you should try working with my dad and the rest of the family . . . you've no idea, you're a girl!"

He heard Francine emit a sound which might have passed for contempt.

"You know Alfie, you were the one person in the family I thought I could trust . . ."

"Francie I realize that . . . I just didn't think you'd find out!"

"And that makes it alright does it?"

"No, but it makes it less personal!"

"You going to have another go?"

"No . . . and I told Ged and dad that!"

"So who is?"

"Dunno . . . someone they pay well enough I suppose . . . someone Ged trusts, or someone who's desperate enough to do it for money!"

"It's pathetic and low . . . going for a defenceless bird!"

"Defenceless! . . ." Alfie hooted with sharp laughter. "You wouldn't say that if you'd seen Kev's ear after the thing had mangled it!"

"Is that what happened to your head?" She was pulling cigarettes from her bag.

"We weren't going to hurt the bird!" Alfie was blotting his face with the sleeve of his shirt where the blood showed redder and thicker. "Fucking things hurt us more than we hurt them!"

"Serves you right! They are birds of prey you know! . . . not meant to be messed with!"

Alfie stared at the ground and shuffled. He felt like Judas. She was right—he was spineless. "What's your feller said?"

"Not much . . . . he's silent and sulking! He was bad before but now he's withdrawn from me . . . I'm losing him!"

"You're not . . . . he'll get over it!"

Francine considered the end of her cigarette as the night sky fell around them. Something had happened to Richie beyond the attempted theft of the bird, but she couldn't figure out what. She said nothing of it to Alfie and looked instead at his grazed head, bleeding on the opposite side from the bird wound.

"Look, I'm sorry, I shouldn't have attacked you . . . I'm sorry!"

"No, it's okay . . . you had good reason, I understand!"

"You better get that fixed . . . it could turn nasty!" she said, her cool concern sounding to him like endearment.

"Nah . . . it'll be fine . . . I'll go in the toilet here and dab it with soap."

"It may need those special gauze things they have at hospitals! . . . I'll run you to A & E and they can look at it if you like! . . . you can say you fell coming out of the pub!"

"They'll think I'm an alcoholic! . . . wounds and scars all over my face!"

He allowed himself to go with her to the car—it was a way of getting back in her good books. Letting her injure him and then nurse him better. There was actually something very appealing about it. It made him feel manly and cared for simultaneously. He got into the passenger seat and lit his own cigarette.

"I've had an idea anyway . . . ." he paused while she reversed from the tricky little car park adjoining the pub. Her eyes were on the road behind, her head twisted to see to the right.

"What next then?"

"A way of fixing things with Ged and safeguarding your man! . . . . I'll tell you when we're out of here . . ."

*   *   *   *

Above the screeching and keening of the various birds, Scott and Richie chatted. The winter sky was low over the meadowlands and fields surrounding the sanctuary. It seemed a world away from the summer landscape, though Richie could remember clearly the spring when Tess had met him outside the caravan and told him Charlie had fired her. That was when the break-up really started. He pulled his mind away from the memory and rested his eyes on Scott.

"You were my enemy in that life . . ."

"Oh?" Scott straightened his back. He heaved his weight to the other leg. His ligaments had healed but the accident had left him with a limp which might never go. Richie took a moment to digest this. It seemed a diluted reversal of what he had suffered in the lifetime he'd regressed to with Gita.

"I was at a severe disadvantage in that other life . . ." Richie added.

"What?" Scott stared.

"I was handicapped or something!"

"Oh no change there then!" said the New Zealander and Richie threw a damp cloth across the buzzard enclosure which hit Scott on the arm.

They worked in companionable silence for some minutes and then Richie was compelled to say more.

"Thing is . . . . the thing is . . ." He was unable to continue with his sentence.

"Thing is what?" asked Scott.

"Nothing . . . it don't matter!"

"Yes it does . . . thing is what?"

"We were enemies . . . . because of Tess . . . . but she was called something else then . . . Solange or something French! . . . . you were her brother and you disliked me . . . I was English and you were French!" Richie paused, feeling stupid. He was aware that he was babbling and that it sounded mad to anyone who hadn't undergone the experience. It sounded like sheer illusion or fantasy. But he had to get it out. "Anyway, turns out we clashed and you won and I died . . . by drowning!"

Scott frowned over at him, trying to comprehend it. "You saying I was responsible for that? . . . you drowning?"

"Forget it . . . I shouldn't have told you!"

"Why not? If it's what happened!"

"Well only in my mind!"

"So you don't believe it then . . . this reincarnation stuff?"

Richie stroked the head of the senior buzzard of the group, blue-black glossy and coarse, and he weighed his words before speaking.

"As a matter of fact I do believe now . . . but I don't expect others to believe it on my say so!"

Scott heaved a deep breath and turned slowly. "Richie mate, I believe you in everything else so why not this!"

Scott's mobile rang and they were saved from further intense discussion. He spoke to one of the suppliers but barely listened to what was being said. He considered how Richie was much improved since going to the Centre at Winifred Mead. It was hard to pin-point but he was less haggard of face and lighter of mood. It didn't matter how the Chinese woman had effected the healing changes, or what sort of memories she had induced, only that she had brought about a marked improvement.

*   *   *   *

When Heather walked back into the pub she did so through the back door, going straight up to the apartment overhead. She was not ready to see anyone publicly yet. She was not sure whether she would ever want to be a celebrity again. She was uncertain about whether to accept the studio's offer of return. She wanted just to be reunited with Charlie—and so they were, partially.

Charlie carried her cases and went steadily up the stairs behind her, both of them treading quietly, so as not to attract attention.

Lisa appeared at the bottom of the staircase and peered upwards. "Charlie! . . . there's a problem with the electrical circuit on the far wall . . . can you get whatshisname in?"

Charlie ignored her and she peered around him to find out who he was with.

Heather ran and stumbled up the rest of the stairs and disappeared into the door leading to the office.

"You got a woman up there?" said Lisa in cavalier manner.

Charlie's face was mutinous. "Back to the kitchen . . . I'll tell you when you need to know the details of my private life!"

Lisa bridled. "Thought you might like the heads up before your pub goes up in flames!"

Charlie again ignored her. She knew better than to take it further and he waited until she had turned and was out of sight.

"Sorry!" he said to Heather. "She's a nosey bitch at the best of times.!"

Heather smiled her sweetest smile and he knew she had come home.

*   *   *   *

Francine cuddled up to Richie as they watched the small television high up in one corner of the caravan. "Richie, what is going on with you?" she began tentatively.

He instinctively squoze her shoulder, more because he did not want to offend her than because he desired her—he no longer desired her in the way he had only weeks previously. "Nothing at all . . ."

"I don't believe that!" she said and there followed the kind of dead silence into which it is hard to intervene without seeming interrogative or clumsy.

"Why won't you let me in?"

After a long while he said: "Because even if you came in you'd be in the dark!"

"Try me?"

"No!" he said and picked up a glass of lager and drank deeply from it.

Francine watched him sidelong—one of the things she liked about him was that he poured his drinks into glasses and did not swig from the can.

No-one could say she hadn't tried; it was becoming easier to let things lie and to not communicate than to persevere and cause an awkwardness and make herself feel belittled.

"As long as there's nothing I can do . . . . as long as there's nothing wrong between us!"

"There's not . . . in either way!" he said.

His mind leapt to the appointment he had with the little Chinese woman the day after tomorrow. She had rung him earlier to ask if he would mind partaking in an experiment in his next session, with someone he knew, someone who had a vested interest in the past lifetime he had regressed to. He was naturally intrigued, he couldn't keep from thinking about it. He was extremely apprehensive but there was no way he was going to swerve such an opportunity.

"Here . . ." he said to Francine, reaching into his back pocket and leaning away from her.

She watched his movements with her ernest pouting smile, the kind that frowned as it laughed. She was very young and very gorgeous. He felt he had the custody of an exotic and rare female for an undefined period. He felt the same kind of responsibility he felt towards his birds. It was not right, this relationship, but neither was it so wrong . . . for now.

"Here's some money I won on the machine . . . not a lot . . . but it'll get you a nice hairdo or something . . . treat yourself!"

She looked at him and then at the money. She took it gingerly, unsure. He felt himself blushing a little. It was like bribing a child to keep them sweet and off your back.

TWELVE

In the kitchen at the Norrington farm Nancy was entertaining her sisters-in-law and two of her close friends, and there was only one man present—her nephew Alfie.

The wine flowed copiously with the talk.

Alfie eyed them all languidly, his thoughts jaundiced and limited to his inexperience . . . . a gaggle of middle-aged women trying to forget that life was slipping by and they were no longer desirable. Except one; his aunt Irene, destined to be still attractive in her coffin—according to his mother. Irene was one of nature's beauties, apparently, unmarried and fifty five. And that, said his mother, was the reason she had stayed so lovely; no man's hands mauling her every night, and no-one to tell her where she should go and what time she needed to be back.

Alfie's mother, Gloria, occasionally said things like this; irreverent things which his father disapproved of so that there was an atmosphere in the room. She made aunt Irene the object of her own disgruntlement and resentment and gave her dialogue and feelings she probably did not own.

Alfie was watching aunt Irene as she ran her manicured finger nail around the rim of the wine glass, her light golden-grey hair soft around her cheeks which glowed smoothly, better than some girls he knew who were less than half her age.

Irene felt Alfie's gaze and looked at him quickly. Alfie winked in a jokey way as if he were simply passing his glance around the company.

"So what's happening with your cousin Francine?" Nan suddenly asked of him.

Alfie heaved a breath. "Dunno . . ."

"Course you know! . . . . you were seen with her in the Singing Kettle the other night, so you must know!"

"Don't put him on the spot, Nan!" said Francine's mother, Gwen.

"Is she staying put with the gamekeeper or what?" enquired Irene more gently.

Alfie said nothing and did not intend to. They could ask all they liked. Eventually they began filling in their own blanks and he listened.

"He's not a gamekeeper . . . he's a bird-keeper!" said Nan.

"I think you'll find he's a falconer!" said Gloria in her precise fashion, and then added. "She'll be back soon enough! She's just making a statement!"

"A statement!" said Gwen with disgust. "More like a full scale affidavit! What worries me is what she does all day now that she's packed in uni . . . and what she intends doing all day in the future!"

"Perhaps she'll join him in the bird-keeping . . . or the falconry or whatever it is!" Irene offered.

One of Nan's close friends then began to tell the tale of her niece who had gone off with a circus performer from Eastern Europe and returned two months later because he was trying to force her to learn some kind of fire eating skill.

Alfie stopped picking at the scabs left from the bird injuries which were healing nicely and he stood up. He had heard enough nonsense for one evening. He felt his guilt coming over him again. He was only present in the house waiting for his father to pick him up and give him a lift home. "I don't see any of you lot doing anything that useful during the day either!" he muttered as he left the room.

He imagined fleetingly the gaping mouths of the female company and the shocked expressions on their faces as he exited, and he wondered what the repercussions might be from his fall from grace. He stared from the window of the truck at the dark and dreary winter's evening.

"Drop me at the Kettle!" he told his father.

"You may as well move into that place!"

"It's a pub!" said Alfie. "I like a drink after work . . . what's wrong with that?

"You're too bloody lippy for your own good!" said his father.

At the bar in the Singing Kettle, Kevin was waiting for him.

"You got it?" Alfie enquired.

"Yep . . . it's coming in half an hour!"

"Coming from where? I thought you'd have it!"

"What? you think I'm going to transport it in my hatch-back? Are you barmy boy?"

Nearly an hour of companionable drinking went by whilst Alfie swilled Guinness and Kevin stayed sober on Coca-Cola.

Alfie felt his stomach rumbling. The food in the pub was off owing to the the evening chef not turning in and the drink was going straight to his head.

Along the bar Curt Chambers watched them for the first five minutes of their arrival and then sauntered to the toilets, lingering to speak to someone directly behind them for the next ten. By the time the cargo arrived he was smoking in the porch of the pub and watching as the doors of a large white van opened and a sack was lifted out and handed to Kevin and Alfie. Chambers texted casually on his phone, his eyes on the lighted screen. Here was the action beginning; the pair of them were cretins and this time he was sure they would see the cost of it.

Alfie listed to one side as they carried the sack to Kevin's girlfriend's van normally used in her cleaning business and borrowed for the evening.

"Good job you're not driving!" said Kevin as he pulled at his side of the sack to help keep Alfie upright. "You fucking lush!"

"Hark who's talking!"

"Shut it now! . . . and don't draw attention to us!" admonished Kevin.

Curt Chambers wandered back into the Singing Kettle.

Kevin drove studiously and listened to the infrequent squawks from the tranquilized bird in the back of the vehicle.

"Bloody thing's coming round!"

"So . . . ." Alfie himself had trouble keeping awake—he'd been up since dawn gathering runaway cattle and his eyelids would not stay open. He shouldn't have had the four pints of Guinness on an empty stomach.

"Now think on . . . we give Ged and your dad a look at the bird as proof . . . and then we get it back where it came from!"

"Where's that?" asked Alfie blearily.

"Wouldn't you love to know?"

"That's maybe why I'm enquiring!"

Kevin sealed his mouth in an obdurate line in his large fleshy face then took a bend too fast and the little van slid around the road before centring.

"Watch what you're doing . . ." Alfie moaned. "We'll be dead before we reach the house! . . . what sort is it?" he enquired next, having dozed for thirty seconds.

"A bird . . . . some sort of bird!"

"Yes, and? what sort?"

"How should I know? . . . . I'm not interested . . . . it's large and heavy, I know that!"

There was a silence as the journey progressed on it's most hazardous last lap, around the unadopted road and unpaved slope up to Alfie's parents' farmhouse.

Ged Norrington had joined his brother at the house, summoned to witness the theft of one of the large birds from Rookeries, the *'pound of flesh'* he was demanding which would hopefully keep him quiet on the subject of revenge and the feud resurrected over the turkey theft.

Jack was bemoaning the difficult communication between himself and his son: "He couldn't answer me civil when I dropped him off at the Kettle tonight!"

"Well, it's maybe his age!" uttered Ged in a rare moment of tolerance. "He maybe feels he has no choices in life . . . . he's said as much to Nan! He says his life is mapped out for him and we own all the aces . . . or some'at like that"

"He should think himself bloody lucky to be part of this family!" Jack couldn't help the boastful edge to his voice. "I mean look at our heritage!" He slid his gaze neatly towards his elder brother who had assumed the kind of expression which told of doubtful but persuadable pride. Ged could always be won around in this way, the thought of who the family were and what they owned, it lulled him to deep and satisfying contemplation; that far away look of the perusal of things inward. It was times like these when Jack perceived the normally pragmatic Gerard to have an imagination after all, a contemplative side to his nature which he didn't want to own up to.

"True!" Ged concurred at last into the silence of the house and he picked up a copy of the daily paper he'd only skimmed previously that day for lack of time.

At length came a knocking on the back door, and a banging-scraping noise against the heavy wood.

Jack put down his glass of lager and Ged discarded the paper and moved out of the room. "That'll be them!"

"You sure Gloria's not here?" Ged followed him.

"She's enjoying herself over at yours isn't she?" Jack hesitated on his way down the hall, at the end of which lay a side door to the garden. "Was there a change in their plans?"

"Not as I'm aware . . . but you never know!" said Ged.

"She's not here leastways!" Jack hesitated still, pending Ged's next comments.

"Well then! Open up! . . . but we don't want no witnesses . . . you know how women are . . . they get all worked up and then blab to folk!"

Jack stretched an arm up to release the bolt as he pulled the stiff and normally unused door.

Alfie was the first to enter and fell into the hall under the difficult weight of the heaving sack. Ged and Jack stared as the mouth of the sack was loosened for their closer inspection and the partially tranquilized bird struggled to emerge.

"Shut the sack again . . . quick!" said Kevin. "Hurry up before it escapes!"

Alfie tried vainly to pull his side of the sack over the bird's head, but the bird's beak was venomously on the move, it's noise growing more ferocious and it's one exposed eye deadly to behold. He dropped the sack in panic and Kevin, fearing a repeat of the attack at Rookeries, stood back, dropping his side of the sack also.

Kevin touched his ear where the gauze padding still covered the gouged tip of the lobe. The eyes of the older men went automatically to Kevin's injuries.

"That what happened last week?" said Jack.

"Yep!"

"God in Heaven!" muttered Ged contemptuously, but did not elaborate.

The bird had now become free. It was a Griffon Vulture with a wingspan of 235 centimetres. It put the fear of God into them all, except Ged.

"Fancy opening the sack like that . . . you gormless sods!"

"You said you wanted to see it for yourself!" accused Alfie.

"Yes, but not at such close range, you moron! you should have called us outside!" yelled his father. "We could have gone into the garden!"

"And risk its escape?" said Kevin. "Do you know how much it's worth!"

They were frozen to the spot and watching in mortification as the bird began to climb out of the sack as if emerging for the first time ever from its shell.

The vulture began walking in the manner of a ground bird around the hall, still dopey from the tranquilizer but now and then attempting to lift its wings and take off. Its talons skittering around the polished floor and causing it to collide with the hall table and a large china vase holding silk flowers.

"Where's it from?" Jack demanded in the manner of someone for whom the penny had suddenly dropped. And Alfie, whose brain was suffering the confusion of extreme malnourishment and alcohol overload, blurted: "A zoo!"

Ged almost jumped. "What bloody zoo! You were supposed to pinch the thing from the bird place yonder . . . not from a zoo!"

While the attention of the two older men fixed upon the chaotic movement of the bird, Kevin thumped Alfie in the centre of his back with a hard fist and Alfie stumbled and coughed and realized his error.

"No, he means Rookeries!" said Kevin hastily. "He's confused . . . . he's had a few too many . . ."

"Yeah . . . I always refer to that bird place as a zoo . . . by mistake!"

The brothers exchanged looks. Jack knew immediately that they had not taken the bird from Rookeries and that they had somehow arranged with somebody to have it delivered to them, and he wondered whether his brother would also realize.

Ged was staring suspiciously at Alfie. "How can anyone with half a brain think that place is a zoo?"

"Well for lack of the right term . . ." said Alfie. "I never know what to call it! . . . bunch of freaks!" he added for good measure.

The bird was now successfully raising and spanning one massive wing and hopping and lifting itself along the hall. The next thing to get ruined was the Moorcroft bowl from the antique dresser. It rolled to the end and then smashed to the floor. The bird seemed to gaze at it mournfully before managing to raise the other wing and rise as high as the top of the dresser itself. It careered into more china on the narrow shelf along the opposite wall and certain family heirlooms went down and were lost forever.

"For Christ's Sake . . . get it out!" shouted Jack. "Your mother'll have a blue fit!"

Kevin was focusing on the bird but keeping well back, his body pressed into the wall. Alfie was uselessly flapping the sack as if the bird would hop back in of its own volition.

"You'd best say you had a burglary!" Kevin offered.

Ged sprang to the side door and opened it.

"No . . . no . . ." cried Kevin. "What are you doing? . . . we need to return it! . . . I mean we need to keep it as hostage don't we? until Francine returns or they pay for the turkeys or something!"

Ged ignored him and began shooing the bird as if it were a hen. The vulture was panicked now and Ged's experience with foul and other farm animals was wasted. The vulture skittered backwards, dropping its wings adroitly to pass through Ged's legs and then through the opened door to the second living room.

There was a crash as the standard lamp was overturned by the bird in semi flight and then another as the small glass chandelier became an obstacle in its airborne path.

Ged took control and leapt forward and ran into the room and threw open the patio doors as Kevin and Alfie dodged after him to try to close them.

The bird, sensing the cold air, flew for the doors and skidded to a halt on the decking in the garden. The arc lights came on and for a few seconds illuminated the vulture as the men stood powerlessly by. None were brave enough to tackle the bird and they watched as it hopped down from the decking and took to its weakened wings and flew off into nearby trees.

"Shit!" cried Alfie.

"Fucking hell!" Kevin said with a desperation painful to hear.

They sank onto various seating around the room and there was an eerie and ominous silence in the middle of the broken china and glass. Only the overturned Ormolu clock ticked loudly as a reminder of things that could be relied upon in an erratic and unsafe world.

Perhaps a quarter hour went past and the whisky was taken out and poured and drank, and the bird began to make an eerie sound, unfamiliar and not at all reminiscent of any birds known in the English countryside.

Ged went swiftly from the room as they gaped after him and returned in less than two minutes with an air rifle from his car.

Kevin leapt to his feet as Ged made again for the patio doors. "What are you doing with that?"

Ged was out into the darkness and had almost disappeared from view while Kevin could only follow the sound his boots made on the frosty ground.

"We'd better get rid of it . . ." Ged was taking a torch from the depth of his inside coat pocket. "If someone shines the flash for me I'll take aim!" He was moving now from tree to tree at the perimeter of the land forming the garden of Jack's house, trying to trace the location of the peculiar noise the bird was making.

Alfie and Jack were hot on their tail. "You can't just shoot it!" Alfie was shouting "Its worth a lot of money!"

Ged was loading the rifle. "Who says I can't! Its an offence to keep a bird like that without a licence, let alone to pinch one!"

"But no-one knows we got it!" said Kevin.

"They will if it flies all over and makes that bleeding noise! . . . it'll bring the police right to our door! . . . some interfering do-gooder will call in the RSPB . . . !"

The bird appeared suddenly on the lower branches of the oak tree ten yards away. The moon was brighter than it had been minutes ago and the tree was illuminated with the outline of the vulture stark against its winter branches.

"There it is . . . the bastard!" Ged lifted the rifle and fired.

Jack sprang forward and pulled at Ged arm. "Give over! you'll alert the nearest neighbours!"

"So? . . . I could be shooting foxes or rabbits!"

"That's against the law too . . . especially at this time of night!"

Ged let the gun drop to his side. "Listen bonehead . . . if you believe that idle son of yours has stolen the thing from the Rookeries place you're as dim witted as him! . . . they've pinched it from somewhere else. Do you think I was born yesterday?"

"Well you can't just shoot it!" said Jack. "These kind of birds are rare and it's valuable!"

"Give over . . . its gnarled and ancient and past its prime!"

"So are you!" said Kevin. "But we don't propose to put you down in the back garden!"

Dropping the air rifle, Ged took a swing at Kevin's jaw and missed. Staggering slightly to the left and then righting himself, he shoved Kevin hard and picked up the rifle again.

The bird let out one of its shrill squawks and Ged lifted the air rifle and took careful aim and was about to fire a second time when Jack pushed him. The gun went off in the opposite direction from the bird, and at that same moment Alfie dropped to the ground unconscious. The entire scene was frozen and suspended in time for seconds.

"If you've killed him . . ." Jack said desperately. "I'm going to kill you!"

Nonplussed Ged allowed Kevin to take the rifle from him and stash it behind the herbaceous border out of harms way.

Kneeling next to Alfie his father discovered that Alfie still had a pulse. "Has he eaten?" he asked Kevin.

"How should I know!" Kevin was staring down in disgust at Alfie; he was a pathetic loser and he didn't see why he undertook any schemes with him, let alone these kind of capers which could cost him his freedom. "He was moaning about the pub not doing any grub . . . so I suppose not . . . he had a skinful of Guinness though . . . that should have fed him!"

"It's his diabetes!" said Jack. "His blood sugar will have fallen abnormally low! Help me get him in and inject him before his mother comes back!"

The vulture, disturbed by the shouting and the gun shots, took itself up into the night air and disappeared from the Norrington farmstead.

THIRTEEN

Richie entered the Centre and saw Gita talking with Heather Gilbert. He stopped and looked over in bewilderment. He remembered that she had disappeared or gone away or something. The talk of it was all over the Golden Hind, and it had appeared in papers and magazines. He had that odd sinking feeling of having missed a piece of the plan.

Heather moved towards him. "I'm so sorry for Tess's death!"

Richie took the hand she proffered. "S'okay . . . I'm with someone else now!" he said unthinkingly and then watched as her eyes changed to shock at the cold statement.

"I meant . . . what I meant was that we were not an item towards the end . . . we were not close . . . . I mean we . . ."

"Please!" Heather held up her hand. "I didn't want to put you on the spot! It's not my business. I only meant that it was sad!"

"Yes . . . . very sad!" He cast his eyes downward and the energy seemed to go from him in one fell swoop.

Gita intervened and took Richie's arm and then Heather's arm, so that she was between them and guiding them forwards.

"You both have had experience of former lives in which you have been with Tess. It is important that you pull the threads together now that you have met in present time . . . under such circumstances. And so I have suggested this experiment!" concluded Gita almost gaily.

Richie and Heather exchanged looks.

"Not worrying . . ." Gita said, "let us just see what can be done!"

She led them into the small treatment room where she had placed two treatment plinths side by side with just enough room for her to move between them.

"Lie down please and relax by breathing deeply . . . do not bother thinking or analyzing . . . just relax!"

Heather and Richie removed their shoes and lay on the plinths and the macabre thought struck Richie that it was like lying on a mortuary table. He tried to sooth his anxiety with the breathing but Gita was ahead of him. She laid her hand on his brow and he seemed to float backwards and leave all care behind.

Heather glanced at him sidelong and smiled. "Bizarre isn't the word darling!" she said and giggled. She had on her actressy veneer, it was better for dealing with strange and uncomfortable situations. Richie did not smile back at her and certainly did not laugh but his eyes told her that he was not uncomfortable with what they were doing.

Gita was passing her hand over Heather's eyes and then her throat and heart chakras, and Heather felt the low movement to serene peace as her mind and body dropped to the alpha state.

After what seemed an age of moving and travelling Richie felt earth beneath his feet, and he looked for Heather next to him but she was not there. He was confused; he had retained a vestige of what had been left behind, like a far away echo, the suggestion and explanation Gita had given about going back in time or to past life. But where was Heather?

The answer lay in front of him in terms of some distance along a corridor in a house; it took several seconds to steady the scene—the long passageway—and to allow it to become a firm or solid enclosure. To have it form around him like a room in which someone awakes and find oneself after a sleep.

Heather was sitting on an ornate sofa, talking with the girl who looked like Tess. The girl who for the benefit of this setting was named Solange.

Heather was now referred to by an old woman present as Monique. She largely ignored what the old woman was saying as the woman fussed and fretted around the sofa, arranging little tables and placing drinks and then touching up Solange's hair.

"We are leaving you shortly!" said Monique. "We wanted only to abide by the formalities and see you both settled!"

He began to realize that this scene predated somewhat the scene in which he had met Solange in the garden and been chased to the river death by her brother's dogs.

As the last threads of cognisant memory continued to make more sense from the point of view of a detached observer, he knew that this scene was some kind of illicit place of union for people whose fates were not meant from a cultural perspective to aline. A sort of rented retreat or acquirable love nest run by a

Madam posing as a socialite and offering innocent recreation to the fashionable and the well-to-do . . . or those who could afford it.

It was a high class brothel perhaps in other parts, with the added function of hotel rooms hired by the day, or the week, and supplying the perfect mistress of ceremonies to soften the edges with innocent ministrations and polite sophistications.

The last remnants of connective memory dissolved and when he came around he could not remember anything beyond the polite niceties which had begun his second and last interlude with Solange, whom he was destined to meet two centuries later as Theresa Bailey, known to most people as Tess.

"You remember anything?" Richie asked Heather as they sat quietly in the main hall of the Centre and contemplated the statues and the esoteric artefacts and sipped the jasmine tea Gita had made them.

"Not a thing? . . . . I went out like a light, but I know there was activity! . . . . you?"

"Not much!" said Richie evasively. He might tell her soon what he had seen and heard but not quite yet.

"Fancy a quiet drink?" Heather looked hopefully at the young man. "Talk things through a bit more?"

"Yep . . . that would be good!"

"We'll use my car and drive out somewhere from here!" She stood and he watched as she left a bundle of notes on the little table next to the Buddha. He delved into his back pocket and she caught his arm. "I covered it . . . don't worry! . . . you can buy the drinks!"

Heather turned abruptly so that he would not be embarrassed. Richie followed her out onto the quiet country lane. He checked his phone as he walked and he read two messages from Curt Chambers about the Norrington boys and some matter concerning a large bird; it was uncertain whether or not it was one of their own from Rookeries.

In her car they drove without speaking for several miles while Heather chose a route through Limetrees which would send them south west to a small town one motorway exit along. Richie texted Scott to find out if things were good on Scott's watch and the message came back that they were. He was lightheaded with relief; there was no immediate threat to Rookeries.

Gradually he found he was possessed of the urge to confide in Heather and he began relating what he had heard and seen, and what he had experienced last time on Gita's couch and on the road in the dead of night when there had been an attempt to steal Eddy and he had passed out.

Heather listened without interruption and drove the car slower so that she could concentrate safely.

"The names Solange and Monique, they concur with what I also know of that past life!" she said eventually.

For seconds he had that shivery feeling at the back of his neck. As if a light came on in his brain, flooding backwater memory that might be sorted at his request but would never go away and would be always on show, awaiting inspection. It was a new feeling, a consummate knowing, an epiphany of his life-time journey so far. A turning point in the way his mind would work from now on.

Richie could not speak. Heather touched his wrist gently with the hand that was not steering.

*   *   *   *

Meanwhile Alfie pushed his father's hands off him and sprinted for Kevin's vehicle. "I'm fine dad! . . . don't fret . . . I was just hungry and drunk . . . go back inside and clear up before mum sees!"

Kevin had the vehicle's engine running and was urging Alfie to climb in.

"Stupid fuckers the pair of them!" Kevin angrily reversed and jarred the gears. "The police will be crawling over the place soon. . . . those gun shots could be heard all over the county on a still night like tonight!"

They drove towards Limetrees, around the winding bends of the countryside where the family farmlands were situated, the little van bumping and clattering along the roads and straining as Kevin changed up through the gears too quickly.

"This piddling little effort does my head in!" he said, referring to his girlfriend's van. "What we going to do now? What'll we say to my mate at the zoo about the bird never coming back?"

"We'll have to think about it!" Alfie retorted . . .

"It was a stupid idea anyway . . . I don't know why I went along with it . . ."

"Same reason as always . . . because there was something in it for you!"

"What if my mate reports it to the police!" Kevin demanded.

"What? and tells 'em he agreed to lend it us for a price! . . . I don't think so somehow, do you?"

"No but . . . suppose it flies all over everywhere doing that bloody squawking!"

"Well we don't know anything about it do we! . . . maybe it just escaped!"

"Do they escape a lot?"

"How should I know Kev! I'm not a bird expert. My point is that they can't link it to us!"

"That's why Jack and Ged wanted to shoot it! Because it's a liability!" Kevin added.

"Thank Christ my dad stopped that then!" reasoned Alfie. "Imagine if someone discovered it dead and wanted to investigate! . . . first place they'd go would be to Rookeries and those lot would be bang on the case with them! better it flies around . . . maybe it'll end up back at the zoo!"

"And what if it doesn't?"

"Doesn't what? fly around?"

"Find it's way back to the zoo! Suppose it kills people's pets or their little kids, and eats them!"

Alfie was bent over retrieving a ham sandwich from beneath the seat, made hastily in the kitchen before leaving. "Some imagination you got there son!"

"You hear of it . . . that's what vultures do"

"Not in these parts they don't!"

"Only because there ain't no vultures usually in these parts!" argued Kevin.

Alfie munched on half the sandwich, mumbling with his mouth full. "Button it now, Kev! Your limited knowledge of wildlife is frying my brain!"

They had gone perhaps a mile more when they were intercepted by a grey standard van with some kind of insignia on the side. It looked official so Kevin at once pulled over.

Alfie stuffed the rest of his sandwich in the glove compartment and cleared his mouth with a swig of Lucozade. "Whoever it is let me do the talking!"

A man wearing a uniform approached them, but Alfie could see at once that it was not a police uniform. He became more confident. "Can we help you with something mate?"

"Would you open the van please sir?"

"And who are you again?"

A woman was also alighting from the official vehicle to join him, flashing some kind of official badge while the man was hurrying around to the back of their van.

"We're from the R.S.P.C.A.!" said the female in the smug voice that Alfie associated with all the do-gooding fraternity.

"Just open the van please sir?" repeated the man.

"Why?" said Alfie.

"We had a report that you could be in illegal possession of a large bird that might not actually be yours to transport!"

"Well you're entirely wrong pal!" said Kevin. "Ain't no birds of any kind in this van . . . not even the two legged human kind!"

The female officer looked at Kevin sourly.

"We will still require you to open the van!" said the male.

"I don't think so!" Alfie said.

"I have to tell you that if you don't comply we'll summon police assistance!" said the woman in that unctuous *you can't win with us* tone that Alfie found so irritating in people like her. He weighed her up and down—she was about three or four years older than himself and might even look good scrubbed up and wearing feminine clothes.

The man was taking out his phone and Kevin thought of his girlfriend, a glamorous termagant who prized her van and her business over anything he might have to offer. He leapt out of the van and jingled his keys. "Okay . . . hold your horses!"

The back doors were opened to reveal nothing but tins of floor wax and a large cylinder of toilet bleach amid discarded brushes on long staves.

"Thank you sir!" said the man undaunted. "Close the vehicle please . . . . and perhaps you would tell us where your last call was made tonight!"

"At this point you can piss off!" said Alfie, exasperated. "Like we're going to do that for two jumped up jobsworths . . ."

*   *   *   *

Francine was looking for Richie. It was past eleven o'clock and he'd been gone since before five. She had no petrol in her car so she ran along the road to Rookeries. It was dark and horribly cold, it was the countryside at its most bleak and daunting in the dead of night and she was terrified. She had friends who walked home miles from parties and pubs to where they lived in the country and said they didn't fear it. She knew people who had all their lives dwelt in the middle of nowhere and didn't fear it. She had always lived in a rural spot, except for the last year, but she did fear it. The sounds and the inexplicable rustlings, the feeling of the open dark sky about to descend and swallow her up.

She ran until she panted for breath. It was stupid to run, her father had told her that often before he had gone to live in Africa. If you ran before it was necessary and then you needed desperately to run you'd have no breath left to accomplish any distance. She remembered this advice and tears filled her eyes. She slowed her pace. She had a stitch in her side and her toes were hurting in the inappropriate shoes she wore. Her father's face was clear in her mind as she moved through the darkness, relieved only by the outline of trees and other shapes, her father's voice sounding in her mind as it used to sound to her.

Why did her menfolk always have to disappear or leave her in a quandary!

She met the Rookeries fencing unexpectedly and exhaled a long hard breath, at last there was some civilisation.

Above her, on the lean-to cabin roof which almost touched the high fencing, there was a crouched figure, like a child . . . or a goblin! She believed in goblins, mainly because two of her cousins, one of them Alfie, had told her when she was ten while swearing on a Bible that they had seen goblins in the garden and talked with them. Long lurid descriptions had followed and she had never forgotten. No matter how much rational explanation her parents gave to disclaim the probability of them being real, she had always believed the cousins were telling the truth.

'How could the goblins possibly converse with the boys?' her father had queried, thinking to bring common sense to bear. Francine said she didn't know but that perhaps the goblins had learned to speak English; after all, it was England. Her father's warm and hearty laughter . . . 'At a Further Education college perhaps?'

"No, by listening to humans when they pass by!" Francine had said practically.

She gazed at the creature on the cabin and was terrified, and then suddenly it hopped and moved and seemed to raise a black cloak. She screamed an involuntary blood curdling scream and startled the creature into rising up into the night sky.

She realized it was some kind of large bird.

Falling backwards onto the fencing and sinking to her haunches she was overcome by the memory of her father, the cold of the night, her painful toes, her loss of Richie.

She heard the front gates grinding open and felt she didn't care what happened—she was not up to the continuing effort of worrying about survival.

Scott appeared and shone his flashlight on her crouched form.

"S'truth girl! What's happening?" He pulled her to her feet.

"I thought there was a goblin!" she blurted, before she could prevent her tongue, and saw him look at her searchingly to see if he had heard properly. Or to ascertain whether she was on drugs. He smothered a sound of amusement and straightened his face. "A what?"

"Nothing!" said Francine hurriedly. "I was looking for Richie but there was a bird on the roof there!" Her voice was choked and small and her face was a pitiful mask of tortured fear and restraint.

"Come on in!" Scott held the gate open before darting back to where she had been and trained his flashlight onto the roof. No bird to be seen.

Francine hovered in the enclosure and waited for him. "Where's Richie?"

"I don't know sweetheart! . . . isn't he with you?"

"No . . . he's been gone since five but he said he'd be home by eight thirty!"

"Maybe he's been making sure they're not setting badger traps over in Ravensvale!"

"He'd have told me . . ." Francine looked pathetic, much less than her nineteen years, and Scott felt unreasonable annoyance with Richie for taking up with someone this vulnerable and adding to life's responsibilities. Stripped of her make-up and veneer she looked like a waif and stray. "You tried ringing him?"

Francine tutted. "No . . . what's that then? Has there been some kind of invention I don't know of? . . ." she paused and it was seconds before he realized she was being sarcastic. "Do you think I'm stupid? . . . naturally I rang him . . . I rang all night on and off . . . his answering service is on!"

"He's due on watch here at two thirty! Maybe wait here for him until he turns up?? . . . you can sleep in the trestle bed . . . I have things to do anyway!"

Francine remained unsure. She accepted the hot drink he gave her and pulled a face as she tried it. It was without milk and too sweet.

"What kind of bird did you see on the roof?" he enquired casually.

"I don't know . . . just a big one! enormous actually, which is why I thought . . . ." she tailed off.

Scott was watching her carefully—she wasn't going to make that verbal gaffe twice. He heaved on his thicker coat and checked his pockets. He was sceptical she had seen anything at all, considering she seemed to believe in goblins, but you never knew and with the present tensions he couldn't be too careful.

"I'd better go and check the residents are all present and correct!" he quipped and Francine raised her head from the tea mug. "Which residents?" she asked, her eyes huge.

"The birds! . . . it was a joke!"

He saw that her nervous system was wrecked and her sense of humour completely missing. He became serious. "Francine, don't worry . . . he'll be fine . . . there'll be a reasonable explanation . . . I'll be back in two ticks . . . I just have to go and check!"

He jogged out of the back door of the cabin into the inside region of the sanctuary where the public emerged after paying to see the exhibits and the flying displays. He hurried about the enclosures and found no birds missing that he could discern and no damage to any of the pens or the perimeter wiring. He got out his phone and tried Richie's number, expecting him to have his answering device on, but Richie answered on the third ring.

"Where are you?" Scott demanded, knowing he sounded bossy. "I got Francine with me . . . she's frantic with worry!"

"I'm at the Golden Hind!" lied Richie evasively.

"Have they taken to having 'lock-ins?"

"No, but I had a bit of business to attend to! I'm with Hea . . ." Richie broke off as he recalled Heather saying she didn't like people to know she was back. "I'm talking with Charlie!"

Scott was bemused, he wasn't even aware Richie and Charlie Roberts were friendly. "What shall I do with your girl here!"

"Tell her I'll be around soon to take her home if she doesn't want to go by herself"

"She shouldn't be going by herself at all mate! It's pitch black and gone mid-night!" said Scott shortly. He was beginning to feel one of those dreamlike qualities, little to do with the fact that it was the dead of night and more to do with events taking on a lurid and inexplicable tone.

Making his way back through the reception area of the cabin he planned what he would say to Francine without mentioning the Golden Hind. He would avoid the subject of where exactly Richie was and just reassure her.

When he entered the back room Francine was gone. He rushed to the front gates and found them open. He had not padlocked them after bringing her in and she had pulled back the bolt and taken her leave.

He looked around the lane and across the meadow from right to left. There was no sign of her. There was that lone horse which sometimes appeared, the one Richie went on about and Tess had been interested in, and apart from that there was the usual empty expanse of tranquility.

*   *   *   *

Francine was about to take the short cut to the caravan across the potato field belonging to Chester's when she heard voices coming from a parked car with an opened window. She slowly moved nearer and saw that the driver's side was occupied by a woman, smoking and blowing the fumes into the night air.

The car was pulled right into the verge near the footbridge. She stopped and listened, her curiosity leading her.

It was Richie's voice she heard first, the unmistakable slow and steady phrasing, the inflection on certain words. She was almost paralysed by the realization of her worst fears—he was with another woman!

She heard references to Tess that she couldn't make head or tail of, talk of someone called Solange and Richie's involvement with her, and this unknown woman driver's part in it all. Her mind scrambled to fit pieces that were too diverse; she was ignorant of much of his life details prior to meeting him.

The passenger door of the car was to the inner side of the road and it was impossible to see the identity of the driver, this woman Richie was with who took precedence over her.

She knew for maybe a fleeting second that the woman and Richie were not lovers and not intimate, knew in that part of herself which knows instinctively what is what and what is not. But what else would they be doing out together at this time of night if they were not lovers? In some way they were intimate, they were cosy; their voices denoted the level of warmth and understanding people have after much interaction or depth of acquaintance. So who the hell could she be! Her voice sounded like that of an older woman, she was cultured and articulate. Someone he had met at the sanctuary while doing his displays perhaps, or a private collector of birds, the kind he told her occasionally descended from all over the globe.

Maybe she was married and they had begun an affair! Maybe she was wealthy and he was cultivating her patronage. People her mother knew did that in the horse world, so why not in the bird world too!

She realized that the best way to get to the truth was just to ask. She understood that many women in her position would feel justified in raising hell, in making themselves known and causing a stir, even if it was the dead of night in the middle of nowhere.

But she could not do that.

She began creeping along the outer edge of the field so that she could round the bend of the lane and disappear from view and get in through the hedge without attracting their attention. She saw then that the woman driving the car was an actress from the soap opera her mother always watched. The one who had disappeared and was written out of the series as drowned. She searched her memory for the name . . . Wendy Tridmore! That was the character's name. She tried to recall the name of the actress playing the part. Her attention was completely diverted by it.

Suddenly it came to her—Heather Gilbert! She lived with the guy who ran the Golden Hind, the one who formerly employed Tess. Maybe it was why they were talking about Tess. Although what they were saying didn't make any sense at all.

She had begun to cross the lane when a van came around the bend from nowhere like a bat out of hell and almost hit her. Perhaps it had hit her, she was numb with cold and it was hard to feel any sensation in her body. She screamed for a second time that night like she had never screamed in her life. The van swerved into the side of the lane and stopped.

Richie and Heather heard it. Richie didn't know where to look for it. The scream of a female is a compelling sound and his vision followed his hearing and he saw ahead a girl heading towards the field. He recognized the hair and the way she was moving and quickly reached across Heather and switched on the engine so that the headlights illuminated the lane, making out the identity of Francine.

He sat for several seconds in shock and then saw the van driver and the passenger alight from their vehicle. Richie got out and crossed to Alfie.

"I might have known it was you! You could have killed her!"

"Who?" Alfie was nonplussed.

"Francine!"

Alfie began running towards her as she scrambled through the sparse end of the winter hawthorn protecting the potato yield. But before he had gone much farther Richie caught him and yanked him back. "No you don't . . . just leave her . . . I'll go and get her!"

Resentful of this instruction, Alfie shoved Richie away and Richie turned and lifted his fist and hit him in the face. Alfie went backwards and hit the ground for the second time that night.

Alfie sat up a little and took his own weight on one elbow; he watched as Richie took off after Francine. Meanwhile Heather sat in her car and pulled her soft brimmed hat over her face so as not to be recognized, and then waited to see what turn events would take before doing anything further.

*   *   *   *

Ged was fuming, he stormed about Jack's lounge in the absence of his own and ranted. The R.S.P.C.A. had only just left. How they knew to call there was beyond both Ged and his brother. It must have something to do with their stopping Alfie and Kevin. Or it had to do with Rookeries?

The inspectors were obliged to investigate claims of animals kept unlawfully, especially in view of the fact reports had already been made about the inappropriate housing of poultry in the past on the Norrington Farm Estate, and the recent sighting of a large bird flying around after alleged gun shots.

"I'll throttle your bloody son!" said Ged to Jack as he quaffed the last of the liquor. "He has brought all this on us!"

"Not you then?" said Jack, inebriated after three unaccustomed brandies following the lager. "Not you with your stupid vendetta against the bird sanctuary! Nothing to do with your angry and vengeful nature! All to do with Alfie . . . who was only doing your bidding!"

"Doing my bidding! . . . he can't do anyone's bidding without messing it up!" said Ged and the brothers glared at each other and circled the carpet edgily and unsteadily.

The lounge had been set to rights and the china and glass cleared away and Jack was thinking what to tell Gloria, unbothered by the R.S.P.C.A. call as much as what his wife would make of it all.

"So I should just let those wankers get away with robbing our poultry should I? . . . costing us thousands! I suppose you prefer we let them walk all over us do you? . . . you always were weak . . . which is why your son is out of control!"

Jack was not familiar with the feeling of being incensed and it suddenly came over him like a hot sweat and he saw colours in front of his eyes . . . the mixture of anger and drink and worry about Gloria's reaction was all too much. He lunged at Ged and Ged went down onto the sofa heavily. The sofa went crashing over under his weight and into the sideboard and the more precious china and glassware hit the ground.

"You opinionated loud-mouthed buggar!" Jack yelled as he hit Ged in the shoulder with his elbow to prevent Ged from thumping him. Ged winced with pain and felt his arm go numb.

"I'll kill you yet!" Jack muttered.

"Get off me!" bellowed Ged. "There's more important things at stake here than your pride . . . get off me and let me go and find that bird or we're in trouble!"

"No! . . . . you'll apologize for that remark about me and mine . . . or I'll kill you!"

There was a sudden female voice in their midst. "You wont' kill anyone . . . the pair of you can just get up now . . ." said Gloria, removing her suede boots on the beige carpet. "I don't know what's been going on but it stops here!"

The two men righted themselves and stood up blearily, as if stepping out of a stage production.

"Hello Glo!" said Jack pleasantly.

"Don't 'hello Glo' me!" Gloria countered. "I turn my back for an hour and all hell breaks lose in the house . . . . what have you been doing? . . . and where's the Moorcroft bowl and the Lalique vase from the hall?"

"I'm off . . ." Ged resisted Jack's hold on his sleeve to try to prevent him. He freed his clothing and then moved with the agility—often seen in large people at unexpected times—to the unlocked side door and made a timely exit, picking up the air rifle from its hiding place behind the border and loping off into the night.

*   *   *   *

Charlie answered the phone to Heather from his sleep. He was *'sleeping like the dead'* he informed her. Heather thought that when she told him certain things he would never say that again . . . the dead didn't sleep!

"You're *where?*" Charlie said. "I don't understand you, Heather. Why are you looking for this girl and who is she?"

Heather began explaining about herself and Richie sharing their experiences at the Soul-Light Centre and parking up to talk and then seeing Richie's current girlfriend almost killed by a van owned by one of

the Norrington clan and the girl then disappearing into the night. The fact
that she was helping Richie look for her.

Charlie brought the Francine girl vaguely to mind, along with Curt
Chambers who talked to her sometimes as they drank in the pub. Then he
thought of Richie and Ged Norrington and the animosity. They appeared
in sequence like a set of iconic characters from some classic book everyone
had read and knew the story of. "You'd better call the police!" he mumbled
to Heather.

"No Charlie, not yet . . . . she's not a child and the van incident was less
than an hour ago . . . they'll not act! We're better off searching ourselves."

"Be careful then!" said Charlie, but as he made the statement he knew
that Heather was a changed woman . . . she had told him so. She did things
that made little sense to him at present but would be all revealing later
on . . . or so she told him! And anyway, no longer acting professionally she
probably had a dramatic withdrawal void to fill.

His tiredness engulfed him like a fog; he listened to her reassurances
and let her hang up first, and then he fell back into the bed and entered his
customary coma following a full days work in a busy public house.

FOURTEEN

Alfie was very sober again. He checked his watch and it said 1.35 a.m. He turned to look at the expression on his cousin's face. His own face was swollen on one side and his eye was closing from where Richie had hit him.

"I'm not going back home without knowing she's okay!" he told Kevin.

"Oh right! . . . and how you gunna do that when she's disappeared?" Kevin was getting furious. "Silly tart! what's she want running around in the countryside for at this hour?"

"I dunno . . . something to do with her feller being with the woman in the car I expect?"

"What woman?" asked Kevin sourly.

"How do I know? I only saw her briefly! obviously doesn't want to to be recognized or caught out! . . . dead give away!"

"What of?"

"Furtive behaviour . . . . dodgy doings!"

"Hark who's talking!" Kevin hooted with phoney laughter.

"keep it down! sound travels at night out here!"

"If you know what's good for you you'll leave well alone now!" Kevin cautioned. "Or he's likely to put you in hospital! . . . you saw how mental he was!"

"He just over-reacted!" Alfie said practically and watched Kevin managing his impatience and disgust and trying to form coherent wording on some form of next action—they might be here for hours.

"What are we going to do now then? . . ." Kevin asked eventually. "I ain't staying out here much longer freezing my bollocks off looking for Francie! If she wants to go missing that's her problem . . . . she's got a screw lose to begin with! She goes off with that mad bastard, disinheriting herself and getting on the wrong side of old tight-wad, then she can't keep lover boy happy . . . next thing she's careering about the area at midnight like a maniac and trying to—" Kevin was cut short by Alfie's hand clamping his mouth. He gagged and pulled himself free. "What the fuck is it now?"

He followed Alfie's gaze off into the night.

"It's Ged! I just saw him lumbering down the canal with the air rifle . . . he's unmistakable! . . . that rolling half human gait he has when he tries to run, that stupid antique hat! . . . him and my old feller, they make me sick when they're together . . . they think they're Butch Cassidy and the Sundance Kid!"

Kevin lit a cigarette. "He'll be after the vulture . . . do-gooders'll go straight to your farm . . . Rookeries might even have pointed the finger of suspicion! . . ."

"We can't worry about them just now!" Alfie said.

"I don't know what else you think there is to worry about! . . . taking a bird of that caliber and then losing it and being associated with idiots who try to shoot it . . ."

"We have to find Francie . . . I betrayed her and she's lost the plot!"

"She lost the plot ages ago Alfie my boy! The day she went against the Norrington convention . . . . ain't no turning back for her now! "Kevin stretched his wide mouth into a humourless grin. "I knew you were sweet on her . . . always knew it! that's incest you know! . . . not that she'd look at you in that way!"

"Shut the fuck up! . . . it's not incest . . . we're just first cousins!"

Alfie had alighted from the van and was hiding behind it and keeping track on Ged as he stopped and started and gazed up into tree branches and looked through the rifle sight, morphing gradually into a bulky figure and blurring into the distant hues of darkness on the other side of the canal, going in the opposite direction.

"You'll have deformed kids!" Kevin trailed behind Alfie into the next part of this unwise venture. "That's if she ever consents to put out for you . . . which is doubtful . . . not with her taste for fit blokes and—" Kevin's diatribe broke a second time as the first round of gunshots were fired.

*   *   *   *

"I'll get Titch!" Richie said to Heather outside Rookeries. "My pet falcon!"

"What help will that be?" asked Heather.

"She can fly ahead and look down on things . . ."

"But how will she know what you're looking for? . . . or who you're looking for?"

"You'd be surprised what she knows and how she knows it!"

Heather hesitated to find the logic and sense in these moves and then the wave of energy which had been with her since the past life recall took her up again and she said: "I'll take you where you need to go when you've got the bird! You've had some drink remember!"

Scott said nothing at all to Richie's announcement of Francine's disappearance and the van almost hitting her. Resigning himself to a full night of watch at Rookeries he saw Richie get back into the unknown car with Titch on his wrist, the car driven by a woman he thought he may have seen about somewhere He watched the vehicle out to the higher end of the road and then he rang his wife to tell her he'd be out until morning.

"If ever a man had a doomed love life it's Richie Southern!" Julie said tersely, "If ever a man brought trouble to women! . . . if it's not one drama it's another! When's he going to learn to keep the snake in the box for a while and examine his own short-comings!"

"There's a witty retort to that somewhere!" said Scott, "but I'm too knackered to think of it!"

It was not going to end well, this latest set of developments, Scott could feel it in his water.

*　　*　　*　　*

The first gun shots coincided with the sharp pain in Francine's hip as she fell. At First she thought it was the the shock and then she realized that the van at the footbridge may have actually dealt her a glancing serious blow.

She did not know why she had been running, she was just running. It was futile. It did not make sense anymore. None of it made sense . . . why she'd left home to move into Richie's caravan! Why Richie would be seeing another woman! Why Alfie would have betrayed her by trying to ruin her boyfriend's business!

She remembered driving Alfie to the Minor Injuries at the hospital in Limetrees to have his head seen to when he had fallen against the pub wall after she'd shoved him. He had told her then of some hair-brained scheme, dreamt up by himself and Kevin, to borrow a bird of prey from someone

Kevin knew who worked in a zoo and show it to the elder Norrington men and say it had been pinched from Rookeries and . . . . the rest of the tale escaped her; her mind was fuzzy and light. Too much ketamine and too much vodka in her late afternoon juice . . . . she was sinking into sleep.

A beautiful horse, a dapple grey wearing a leading rein and bridle seemed to be surveying her from some distance away—she was on the opposite side of the canal from where the car was parked and had no way of knowing they had driven off.

The horse was watching her patiently, as if waiting for her to move to it and mount. It was not one of her mother's horses, she knew that. Making noises of entreaty towards it she pulled herself up by the trunk of a tree to a sitting position.

If the horse came close to her she may have a chance to mount it. There were rustlings in the branches above and when she looked up she saw the ghost-like silhouette of the large bird. Her fear now was of dying in this lonely spot.

She wondered if the bird could see her, or was even interested in her. The horse would come no further, it circled the same space on the gentle incline to the road beyond the towpath.

Then the bird made a screeching sound, loud and raucous; it was not native to Britain, it was too big for one thing. Francine thought it had escaped from Rookeries and that Scott had not managed to recapture it.

The raucous cawing continued and then there was the calling of a second bird, a similar but different sound. The tree branches shook and the large bird took to the air.

Francine visually scoured the sky in confusion. Which bird was which? One was smaller, but they were both moving and it was hard to tell. The big goblin-type bird ascended above the newcomer and seemed to tail its movements, keeping a respectable distance.

The sound of more rifle fire. Someone was shooting at the birds. She could hear the ground crunching with a nearing heavy tread and her trepidation of the great outdoors and what and who it contained gave way to common sense. She found her voice and called out.

"Help . . . can someone please help me?"

More gunfire, and both birds disappeared into the depth of the far off trees.

Francine waited. The horse she had seen was perhaps related to the owner of the gun. She looked again but the horse had gone. She recalled the phantom horse she had heard of around the time of Tess's death from people in the pub and she fell into a speculation about whether this could be the same horse, and if so was it a ghost or was it real.

In the midst of the reverie and from the middle of the sparser hedgerow bordering the path, Ged Norrington appeared.

"Good God Francie! . . . what're you doing here?"

Francine looked up at him from beneath her dishevelled hair and weighed the odds. Had he been firing at her and not the birds! Was she such a liability to the family that he would dispose of her in some way so that no-one ever knew? But then why was he displaying amazement at the sight of her!

Her eyelids were drooping with tiredness. She began to tremble but held onto her focus and watched him warily as she thought out her answer.

"I just fell . . ."

Her mother's elder brother surveyed her curiously. The night was turning to one long catalogue of horror. He looked about him as if a taxi or a bus might pass.

"Francine, what are you doing here at this time?"

"What you doing shooting things?" she replied.

"Come on . . . get up!" Ged said, as if he could still give orders under such conditions and expect to be obeyed.

"I can't . . . I'm injured . . . a car hit me!"

"Where? Ain't no cars here . . . . it's the bridle path!"

"I know that!"

Movement in the tree branches nearby alerted him to the bird again. He lifted his rifle as a bird took to the sky and flew east. He fired. The bird let out a massive cry and picked up speed. Maybe he had hit it. Maybe not.

Two seconds later the vulture appeared on the lower branches of the tree. It stared at Ged and the girl with its bleak and ominous eye and Ged was unnerved. How had it done that from so far away?

Then it dawned on him that there were two birds and he panicked. He lifted the rifle and aimed and Francine—against her better self control—screamed.

"Shut up!" roared Ged "You'll fright it!"

The vulture came at Ged without warning. It seemed to simply drop from above. It plucked at Ged's iconic hat with its lethal claws, as if on a planned mission, and the hat fell and lay like a dead creature. The vulture stared at the hat for a second, its head on one side, and then it trained its vision on the hat's owner.

It attacked Ged's head again and again, until Ged dropped the rifle and flayed his arms and crouched and rolled over on the ground, his breath ragged in the quiet night air.

Francine wondered if she were hallucinating. She wondered if she'd died of the cold or gone unconscious or delirious. She had never witnessed anything like this. She cried out in alarm, appealing to someone, to anyone who might be able to help her. She felt sure the bird would attack her next.

But the bird circled, and seeing Ged lying still it made a vertical lift into the night and headed east after the other bird.

Francine closed her eyes and rested. An age seemed to pass and the pain in her leg and hip had been replaced by a dull thudding ache; she knew she couldn't walk.

Ged stirred and rose, clambering to his feet with great effort and then stamping about to restore circulation, gradually getting his wind back.

"You hurt?" Francine enquired.

"No . . . . are you?"

"Not by the bird . . . it's gone!"

Ged moved stiffly to test himself and to see if he was as before. "Stupid bleeding thing . . . I never in all my life . . . ." He did not finish but shook his head to bring back his usual command of life and crossed to where she sat.

"Come on! I'll help you up!"

"I can't walk!" Francine said.

Ged considered matters. A few years ago he might have carried her easily, like a sack of grain over one shoulder. A few years back when he was fitter and slimmer. "I'll go and get help! Stay there . . . I'll get help!"

Francine watched him trundle off into the night towards the farm.

She waited several minutes and then hoisted herself by means of the tree trunk. She could hobble, and she could now move her hip a little more.

She began moving slowly to the road. She would rather drop down dead than get back into the family clutches via Ged. Shamed by circumstance, weakened by trauma and failure she might never get free of them all ever again.

*   *   *   *

Richie trained the binoculars over the general landscape from the top of Chester's meadowland. As near as she could manage, Heather kept the car running for a quick get away.

"Somebody's firing at Titch!" Richie told her, swinging around and shouting to her through the rising wind.

She opened the car door and partially got out, not knowing which way to go. "Why would they do that?"

"No idea . . . unless of course they're after Francine and not the falcon!"

"What? How do you know where Francine is?"

"I don't but Titch does . . . she's hovering nearby so Francie can't be more than a mile down to the west where the canal meets the river . . . and there's another large bird . . . looks like a vulture of some kind! Could be one of ours got free and latched onto Titch for company!"

"Of course!" Heather agreed, although the social niceties of birds defied her.

"I think we'll cross to the other side of the canal and see what we find!" Richie said.

"Are you okay reversing down the incline here?"

"I'm just dandy!" Heather waited for Richie to close the car door on his side.

The horse was at the foot of the incline, a little way into where the meadow met the scrubland which gave way to the road and the towpath. Heather cruised slowly in first gear and shrieked with joy on seeing it, as if she were being met by a close friend at an air terminal.

"Our horse . . . . look Richie . . . do you see her?"

Richie was placid. "I think it's a male gelding!"

"Is it?" Heather said.

"I think Tess told me it was, yes! But she may have been wrong!"

"I doubt she was . . . Tess was never wrong about horses!"

"No!" he agreed and there was that note to his voice alerting her to his sadness and a dip in morale.

"This time I'm going to greet him!" Heather announced. "In light of what we experienced earlier it's an absolutely marvellous sign . . . it's like Paul on the road to Damascus! . . . it's like the famous sightings at Lourdes! It is simply wonderful!"

Richie couldn't disagree but neither could he quite enter into the spirit of enthusiasm for things evangelical in this way. He was having greater problems than Heather in absorbing and making sense of the regressive experience. He needed to step back and take a more philosophical view and relate it to various phenomenon he'd read and heard of. He couldn't take it simply as 'spiritual truth' just yet. Whereas Heather saw it as absolute proof of a wide and subtle realm beyond the physical. She saw it as proof irrefutable of an afterlife. She obviously needed to do so for her own reasons.

'Horses for courses!' Richie thought and the unconscious irony of phrase raised his enthusiasm a little.

She had stopped the car and was out in a shot. Realizing as she moved that she had not actually touched the horse yet, she halted. Supposing she found it to be not solid but some nebulous stream of pure energy, like a phantom or a ghost!

She decided it did not matter and approached the animal carefully. She was overwhelmed with joy when it allowed her to touch its muzzle. It moved its head in that horsey way, as if shaking her off but she knew from what Tess had advised that it was an acknowledgement of the contact and not a rebuff.

She lifted her hand to stroke it more and it moved backward, wheeled around and began to trot, stopping perhaps fifteen yards down the towpath and looking back and then carrying on at a quicker gallop upward amid the tees on the wide and hilly embankment.

"Look Richie, he's asking us to follow! . . . he's showing us something!"

Richie turned from surveying the night skies and watched Heather and then the horse. There was no sign of Titch and he realized that she had met up with another bird; there were low level screeches in the distance. It was unusual for birds of prey to fly this early before dawn (except for owls) but it was not entirely unknown, and Titch now would fly any time if the moon was at all visible. The larger bird was away from its own territory and unsettled, not one of their own, and the gun shots had sent it into defensive flight with no known destination.

"It's heading over the hill to the river . . . we can't drive up that hill without problems. So we'll leave the car and go on foot!" said Richie. "Or do you want to wait in the car?"

"No . . . I'm coming" Heather began pulling on a pair of boots from the car and he marvelled as he marched ahead at the versatility of the female mobile wardrobe.

*   *   *   *

Francine was running/hobbling along the side of the river where it ran at an angle equidistant to the canal. Her lame gait, her hip and leg no longer troubled her, but neither were they serving her body in any efficient way, they were making her lob-sided; her body leaned to the right as if she had suffered a partial collapse. Her fingers, toes and feet were numb, together with her mind. She felt she were losing her senses and she began to hum tunelessly. Into her frozen thoughts suddenly came an image of the Hunchback of Notre Dam. This is what she must look like, she imagined, bowling along the towpath with wild hair and a frantic gait.

Where would all this end! If Richie didn't want her, and she didn't return to her family or let Ged's posse find her, where would she go? There was possibly nowhere to go. Her pride was blinding her to every day sense. The thoughts of home and her mother's cosy kitchen seemed like anathema to that pride which cloaked itself in something else and felt like a hair shirt. Her vanity was an addiction that had to be fed, so that her body might starve but her soul was invincible in the race for conquest over unthinkable falls from grace and set-backs in self respect.

She was on a hiding to nothing, heading over a cliff like a lemming, but she did not know what else she could do and her instinct was to let life take her or to allow fate to overtake her and to hell with the consequences. She had ceased to care.

After a while it was a heady and exhilarating feeling, it felt as if she were leaving herself behind and entering another zone altogether, one in which normal rules did not apply and where there were no signs or warnings or anything resembling usual codes.

Shouts from across the canal permeated her consciousness, but her attention span was limited by low blood pressure and painful movement.

"Francie!"

It was a man's voice. She briefly glanced over her shoulder, her neck was stiff and her peripheral vision less than fifteen percent.

"Francine stop running!" shouted Richie. "Please stop! you're injured!"

Francine did not really hear the words, they made no sense to her now. Suddenly she saw the birds again, the smaller one hovering over her and she held up her head on her painful neck to see whether they were intending aggression or not. She thought she recognised Titch but she couldn't be sure. It was all part of a larger hallucination and she was uncertain. She thought of the many recreational drugs she had done in the past, before she met Richie who frowned on such things. In those days she had had all sorts of weird experiences after taking them, all kinds of imagined sights. Earlier today she had taken only a small amount of ketamine, just enough to blur harsh reality. Her limited budget imposed a greater cautionary note to her indulgences.

Richie followed the direction of the horse, trusting it now as some kind of guide or indicator, and he raced over the bridge from the side of the canal to the inlet leading to the roadway or the river. He was followed by Heather some way behind. The horse stood on the hillside and watched, not wishing or needing to come any further.

"Francie stop!"

Richie came into full view of the river, stopping and doubling over to gain breath. He made whistling sounds and his falcon came swooping in and down onto his bent back, trailed a few feet above by the vulture. Heather came panting alongside. "Francine's obviously ill or off her face on drugs or something . . ."

"She uses very little now!" said Richie. "Anyway . . . she'll run out of steam and collapse any minute . . . and I'll just pick her up and carry her!"

Then from across the bridge appeared Ged and another three of their male clan.

"Get away from her!" roared Ged. "It's you whose done this to her! . . . she was a normal girl before you came along!"

Richie stopped in his tracks, he was taken aback by the Norrington clan. Ged lifted his rifle and aimed it at Titch. "Go back or I'll shoot the bird!"

Richie whispered to the falcon and she lifted into the air and whirled into the trees and Ged tried to shoot her but missed.

When the vulture appeared Ged took further aim. The vulture careened and dropped as if he might have successfully shot it, but then it doubled back and flew into their midst, too close for Ged to take aim. The men scattered and hunched and crouched for safety, having heard about the attack on Ged. The vulture hovered for seconds before it went into a high loop away from them all.

As Alfie appeared some yards behind only Richie noted his arrival. He watched as Alfie sprinted towards Francine and easily outpaced her. She had slowed to a walk and had lifted her head to keep track of the birds and at the same time Alfie tried to catch hold of her. She jerked violently away from him and lost her balance, toppling firstly forwards and then sidewards, her body top heavy as she fell into the river.

It was as if everything froze for a fraction of a second. Then Heather, remembering some kind of life-saving certificate training as a teenager, began removing her thick winter coat in preparation for entering the water. Alfie pushed her to one side roughy as she positioned herself on the river edge and she fell awkwardly into the flowing current still wearing her knee length boots. The current immediately dragged at her and she cried out.

Richie jumped into the water and delayed his trek towards Francie to help Heather, putting his hands under her stomach, supporting her to the edge of the river and urging her to clamber out.

"I'll get to her!" he told Heather calmly. "You stay strong enough to drive . . . don't risk your strength now!"

Hearing the sense in this Heather pulled her heavy coat about her and shivered as she watched on from a sitting position on the bank.

*   *   *   *

Francine was struggling to move her right arm and leg as Richie drew near—with easy strokes at first and then with frantically laboured ones as something pulled him down into the current. Francie wondered through the fog of her mind what was wrong with him. Then she saw through a barrier of cold and searingly freezing water the outline of Alfie beside him. Richie had surfaced with renewed buoyancy but Alfie was yanking his arm as if this were a sport of some kind and he were trying to get ahead.

"Stop it!" Francine called, her voice lost to the wind and the rushing of the water. "Alfie stop it . . . let go of him!"

Heather felt the Norrington men join her at the side of the river and stand next to her as she helplessly watched on.

"What is he doing to him?" she asked. "Why is that stupid boy pulling at Richie in that way!"

"Because he's a bloody cretin!" said Ged listlessly. "Always has been . . . I can't get his pa to see it though!"

The men were shouting to make Alfie see sense while Alfie was sent under again and again as Richie thrust and pushed and spluttered, but he held onto Richie as Richie wriggled out of his shirt to free himself.

Alfie knew it was his one chance to impress Francine, to put right what had gone wrong, maybe even to get her to look at him differently. In the last two minutes he had seen it in a blast of revelation. He turned himself around in the water and put his leg around Richie's leg and anchored him from forward movement.

Francine was trying to steady herself in the lively current of the river, but she was fading; her long distance run and her injury and her fatigue were culminating into a crescendo of disability so great that she knew she was defeated. She tried to care but could not.

To those looking on, she may have seemed to lie back and just float. All eyes were on the struggle between Alfie and Richie, and only Heather saw that Francine had gone supine in the arms of the river. Maybe the current would sustain her, perhaps she would be carried to the edge now on the natural ebb and flow. But maybe not.

"She could be drowning." Heather told the men. But they were busy shouting and commenting and seemed not to hear her as the wind whipped her voice and the general commotion absorbed her concern.

Richie turned his head as his body became suffused with pain which affected his limbs and he saw that Francine was submerging and then reappearing and repeating the motion, and each time she was more lifeless.

"Let me get to her . . . she's drowning!" he yelled to Alfie.

Alfie was not listening. He clung to Richie's leg with his own as he held his breath beneath the surface and fought any movement Richie tried to make.

When Richie finally freed himself it was at the expense of his last bit of strength. He no sooner turned into the current to swim towards Francine than he began to feel the paralysis of his limbs, he began to sink. He could see her face in the watery element into which they were both submerging—firstly as someone who had waited upon him in his 18th century life experience with Tess and then as someone even more beautiful whom he seemed not to know yet, someone older and more worldly who smiled at him, her eyes luminous, the eyes of all people he had loved and followed. He was encapsulated within the warmth of them, the heat, it was the same sensation he had known first on Gita's couch as he ascended into the realm from which all was probable.

His body moved and floated nearer towards Francine and it was Richie they all looked at first when the truth of the tragedy finally began to dawn on them.

Alfie rose in the water and was triumphant, but his moment was lost as his uncles roared with anguish and pointed. One of them took off his own clothes and dived into the river.

"Get an ambulance!" He gripped Richie's body and towed it backwards in the water. "Francine's dead!" he told them flatly as he brought in the body of her lover. "I'll fetch her in next!"

There was only emptiness in the roaring of the wind and the river and the still of the night. It was filled with the bleak despair offered by helpless humans in the grip of mightier and merciless elements. It was eventually broken by Ged Norrington, who all his life had claimed the right to break silences or create them.

"Jesus Holy Christ!" he roared. "Don't say they're both drowned!"

"I was trying to tell you about Francine for the last few minutes!" Heather cried. "I never in my life saw anything so horrendous and so needless . . ."

The shock of the change in circumstance was unbearable. Next to the tragedy itself, it was the most unbearable thing—that life could do this, just as it had given her something so wonderful to understand and cherish. And then in her mind she remembered the words of the ancestors. *'One way or another . . . there'll be a drowning!'* Was it an atonement perhaps! Or was it a natural conclusion to events in physical motion in the service of a greater script!

PART THREE

FIFTEEN

Charlie was sick of the press calling randomly into the pub, on the hunt for Heather, and waiting outside to see if she appeared. She never did appear. She had moved out again to stay with her sister at the seaside resort she was so fond of.

She travelled back to be with Charlie at least twice a month. But she had refused all offers to return to the t.v. soap as Wendy.

She was into some kind of training with Gita now, the likes of which was so mystical that Charlie felt it best not to enquire too closely. She was intending to assist people with past life regression, and even go on tour, using her celebratory status to help swell audience numbers.

Meanwhile the police would not leave alone the incident in which both Richie and Francine had died, Mostly because of Heather's statement. She had told them that she saw Alfie holding onto Richie to purposely stop him from saving either himself or Francine. Certainly in her estimation at least he did not want Richie to save Francine.

The proposed charges against Alfie if proven would be involuntary manslaughter on two counts. But the proving of it was difficult as the Norrington males present that night were vehemently claiming that no such set of events took place. They saw only Francine—who had been in the water longer than they could estimate—and the struggles of Richie Southern to swim efficiently enough having firstly spent time in the freezing water rescuing Heather Gilbert from drowning.

Heather argued that she had not been drowning, merely unable to get out of the river unassisted. But it was always going to be a moot point.

The one facet of the story which gave the police any reason to hang onto credible charges was that Heather testified to being pushed (seemingly accidentally) by Alfie into the river after he had done virtually the same thing to his cousin.

This had been validated by one of the Norrington males who implied the same thing during an unguarded moment in interview and then tried to take it back by over elaboration into Alfie's heated state and lack of balance, which then triggered further suspicion and questioning. *Over egging the pudding* on the part of this Norrington male and having once inferred Alfie's deliberate intent to push Heather, it was hard for him to change the impression given. It did not of course concur with what the rest of the clan said and therein lay the hold-up. The police suspected there was a cover up of some kind, and they were inclined to trust the word of Heather Gilbert who seemed in the situation as a whole to have no axe of any sort to grind.

The vendetta spear-headed by Ged Norrington that had led to alleged attempted bird theft from the sanctuary had been brought to light by Scott Brangle in his statement. Added to this was the fact of Francine deserting to live with one of their number. The onus of motive lay all on the side of the Norringtons, where ill feeling towards Richard Southern became an issue.

It was hearsay evidence that pointed to bad feeling, and that was all, but it laid weight to the conviction that Alfie had it in for Richie and that Richie and Francine had died—both comparatively young and able people—from drowning in an accessible stretch of the river in full view of several others during unexplained and dubious circumstances.

The Coroner's Report was set to be delayed indefinitely whilst a convoluted and long drawn out investigation took place at a not very fast pace, due to more important and pressing police matters intervening.

Heather was quietly mortified. She thought of Richie for long periods of time every day and offered up a sort of new blend of prayer and dialogue she had acquired for her more spiritual questions in the stead of her previous agnostic blank on matters sacred. She blamed herself in part for the tragedy, and had it not been for her stronger beliefs now in the Universal Laws and the rites of passage that seemed to set individual *birth scripts* she might have been desolate.

She had discovered this powerful and interesting young man called Richard Southern and his work and views on nature, plus his associations with her in a past life, but he had gone from her in a matter of seconds because of a self-willed and ignorant youth belonging to a wealthy farming family and believing he had first call on his female cousin's affections . . . . it was always at this point that she began to divert her consideration to what she was understanding these days of past life inheritance and the patterns

carried forward in the cellular memory and how the whole drama here
spun itself forward.

*   *   *   *

"She's not here!" Charlie said curtly to a member of the press. He believed
the word was 'paparazzi' but he balked at using it, lest he become one of
those sad people in the tabloids who needed to go out to the supermarket
disguised as the plumber.

The details of the drownings was of greater interest than the
disappearance of Heather and her storyline drowning on the t.v. series.
Some people could not distinguish fact from fiction. And even to those
who could the irony was so immense you could not have made it up.

Just as interesting was the fact that she was in the company of a younger
man full of unknown and acrimonious issues with his estranged girlfriend
who in her turn had been distraught and running about in the night.

Heather was now free to construct a story which no-one could verify
or deny. She felt it was her duty, as an actress, to everyone involved, both
living and dead, to do this to her utmost ability and honour the privacy
and the integrity of all parties. So she did, and she rehearsed it until it was
perfect in her mind . . . .

Richard Southern and she had known each other from her partner's
pub, but they had also shared the same acupuncturist and often talked
together of their experiences. They had met purely by accident in the pub
on the fateful night when Francine went missing and Heather had offered
to assist Richard in his search of the countryside by driving him in her car,
simply because she had consumed no alcohol and had the vehicle at her
disposal. She then got caught up in the events of the night.

Heather wondered if she were becoming a 'spiritual snob' and
under-estimating the public, a pitfall that many writers and producers
fell into. And so it was at this point of her deliberations that her new
pathway occurred to her. A flash of understanding so profound it couldn't
be dismissed. For the growing numbers of people who were ready for issues
other than the sordid affairs, the petty gossip and other people's gory bits.

*   *   *   *

For the first time in nearly forty five years Nancy did not wish to sleep
with Ged. She stared at the place next to his as she entered the bedroom,

the place where she normally lay by his comfortable and ample frame as they slept or talked or cuddled or fumbled about a bit for fun . . . it was always best to allow men to think that they still might, or would, or should, or could—or one of those prefixes—and Nancy had heard this wisdom not just from the pages of contemporary magazines but from a chat with her maternal grandmother on the eve of her wedding many years previously. Certain things did not change, certain insights pertaining to the natural psychology of men and women.

But everything was different now. She could not bring herself to lie next to him, and it had nothing to do with physical resistance—she might have overcome that for the sake of a quiet life—this was a loathing so deep that she could scarcely bear to look at him.

Except for Ged, Francine might have been alive!

There was no way other to view it. But for him and his prejudices and lingering grudges and fuming rages the lad from Rookeries might also be alive.

Many of her friends and relatives had tried to reason that she could not believe that with definite conviction because she did not know exactly why Francine had been wandering late at night, no-one did. But Nancy knew in her heart of hearts that the reason for Francie's absence from the caravan was not the core of the matter. The core of the matter was Alfie chasing her, the core of the matter lay in a ridiculous plot concerning some large bird Ged had later admitted he'd been trying to shoot. He had burbled as much to her in a fit of remorse, told her of the botched attempt to get rid of the bird which Alfie and Kevin were saying came from Rookeries but he and Jack and the other men knew to be from somewhere else entirely. An informant had watched their exit from the Singing Kettle on the night in question, had watched them receive the bird in a sack from a third party vehicle, traced the registration plate of the vehicle to a large zoo and then had Kevin's small van followed and alerted the R.S.P.C.A. Ged said he believed the informant was part of the *Animal Rights Brigade,* as he liked to call them. She knew then, by bits and pieces, what they had planned. She knew then what the night of Friday the 12th had been about.

This in turn brought her to further considerations, much more abstract but nonetheless real. Which of the two sides had the best moral claim? She had lived off the fat of the land and the blood of animals for her entire life. And she had rarely given it a second thought. It was mankind's given right to kill and eat animals—her father and his father and grandfathers and their offspring believed it, and she had taken it for granted. She was a farmer's daughter so it was useless to believe otherwise, unless she upped sticks and left to lead a different sort of life somewhere else.

But then suddenly had come another moral and query: was it not the duty of the farmer to keep and house the animals in proper and humane conditions prior to taking their lives?

That was another matter entirely. That was the cause that Richie Southern and others like him had taken issue with. If people chose not to consume animal flesh it was their choice. But everyone had a duty to see that animals were cared for as best as possible, whether they ate them or not. She realized this because she had read the pamphlets sent anonymously to the farm after the turkey thefts—before Ged had chance to destroy them.

Her reasoning was far from simple but it was clear to her that Ged had inspired the hatred and the feud to uncontrollable ends where it spiralled a series of events with the direst consequences.

Nancy considered herself to be a an ordinary woman. An averagely decent person. A good wife. An upstanding citizen. A mortal passing through, who did good wherever possible and created no harm.

Nancy Norrington would not say it of herself but others would; she was an extremely moral woman. Now she was unable to get past this massive sequence of events at this point in her life. It was defining her existence, and soon it would be all she had left to dwell upon. She had no kids, no grandchildren, no other achievements beyond the farm and the Norrington Empire.

It was just not enough.

If Francie and Richie had been left alone they would have worked things out. They would either have moved on from the caravan to a house offered by one of the distant Norrington relatives who owned a dairy farm and had expressed an interest in employing Richie. Or they would have grown apart, like so many young people these days who set up home together, and that would have been the end of it.

Of course it would not have been the end of the turkey thefts or the animal rights issue. But at least Alfie would not have been pursuing Francine along the river bank in the early hours and causing her and Heather to fall into the water—according to the gossip being lodged at the Golden Hind.

Alfie's obsession with Francine was yet another factor. It was a thing no-one in the family took seriously, and it was bound to have ended badly one way or another. Francine had never shown him the slightest interest in that way and the infatuation might have been played out somewhere else, under less dangerous circumstances.

Alfie had tried drowning Richie so as to get to Francine first—it was the only likely conclusion to draw in Nancy's estimation. Still a moot point in the whole episode, but a likely conclusion. It was one that the cleverer folk among the gossips postulated. And when they did there was no denying they were probably right; it had grown to become almost legendary. She speculated that several years on the drownings would be part of local legend. There might even be passages written about it in local history books. *The three square mile section of the countryside where a lad thwarted in love had drowned another couple in a fit of unrequited love.*

The episode occupied nearly all of Nancy's waking time. It consumed her thinking and took over the few hours of pleasure she had previously felt in things unrelated to her everyday life. She felt she was dying. She was shrivelling and shrinking inwardly and looking her full age, which she had never before looked . . .

Worst of all, she couldn't talk of how obsessed she'd become by these past events with any friends or neighbours, apart from Carol.

Carol Norrington was the daughter of Ged's paternal uncle. She had never married. She had a good job in a firm of solicitors as a legal executive. She was used to thinking for herself and *thinking outside the box.* Nancy knew this; she observed it often without being able to describe it. Having considered matters for several weeks she contacted Carol and by the time she returned from her first visit to Carol's office she had divested a good amount of her estate shares and personal savings to an easily accessible account and set up standing orders to charities overseeing the change of laws on farm animals and the transportation of livestock.

It was water-tight and could not be undone by any of the grasping greedy manipulations of her husband and his relations.

But that was not all. One early morning in the following March she went to see Scott Brangle at Rookeries.

She had to wait nearly three quarters of an hour because Scott was out in the nearby land flying a new arrival to the sanctuary. The member of staff, a girl who spoke with a heavy accent and few words of English, gave her a cup of tea without sugar. Nancy spent some time trying to explain that she needed sugar but when more water and milk were added she gave up and slurped the insipid cooling tea so as not to seem impolite.

Eventually Scott came in. "Hello Mrs Norrington!" he said cheerfully.

He was a generous hearted man, a good soul, as Richie had been, and Nancy's eyes filled with tears. Her unspoken lamentations were all about her like an invisible cloak and they lately triggered reminders of what had happened all the time.

"Something wrong?" asked Scott.

He limped still, a thing that Nancy noted with care before standing and moving toward him and drawing a deep breath. "I expect you're short of funds now . . . I mean, you and Richard were partners weren't you?"

"Pretty much!" said Scott.

He saw where she was coming from immediately. She was carrying the guilt for her husband's attitudes and actions and she was going to make a donation to salve her conscience. It was often the way with the wives of men like Norrington.

But what Nancy suggested almost blew him away. She offered to become a silent investor in Rookeries, a sleeping partner.

At first he didn't take her seriously, and then she got out a copy of a document from her bank entitling her to funds of up to a quarter of a million for any lawful and viable commercial investment of her choosing.

Scott was hesitant, almost without the power of speech. He needed to speak with his wife.

Nancy was casual. "Take your time! . . . I know these things can't be done in an hour . . . I don't know much about business but I know what you do here is a good thing and it brings a lot of pleasure! It makes up for what we . . . for what our family . . ."

Scott quickly intervened. "I'll call you tomorrow Mrs Norrington . . . . no worries!"

Nancy scurried back to where he stood at the reception area counter. "No I'll call here again . . . . don't whatever you do tell Ged! don't tell anyone what I'm doing! . . . it's our secret . . . until my death, and then you'll have to fight your corner if necessary. But it's my money and I can do what I please with it! . . . my cousin-in-law is an educated woman, a legal executive . . . she looked into it and arranged it for me. It's fine and dandy! No-one will find out about it until after I'm gone!"

Scott almost staggered under the weight of the revelations and leaned forward to support himself on the counter. "Okay . . . it sounds fair . . . let me talk to Julie!"

He wasn't convinced and not secure with the offer; years from now he could have the Norringtons against him in full scale war, if Ged didn't snuff before Nancy. But on the other hand he was struggling financially. Even a two year suspension of overdrafts and limited budgets could evoke a pivotal curve positively. Even a part of what Nancy was offering would mean the difference between commercial survival and eternal struggle, or even bankruptcy.

He stared at Nancy's harrowed face looking up into his, her honest worried eyes pleading with him to reach into her current dimension of understanding. "I'll talk with you tomorrow then!" he said.

"Right you are!"

Nancy went with her wistful smile from his premises, her sad little face beneath her curls etched on his memory for many minutes afterwards.

*   *   *   *

Nancy was due next with her sister-in-law Gwen, mother of Francine. This was the weekly visit she dreaded the most.

Gwen was not getting over the loss of her daughter with any progress. Every visit Nancy was obliged to listen to a glossary of the final two days of events in Francie's young life; she had called to see Gwen two or three times and each time Gwen had been busy, with the horses or with Toby. Gwen believed there was actually a fourth time on the last day of her life, about eight in the evening, when Francie had knocked on the door and shouted her, obviously having seen all the downstairs lights were on. But Gwen was engaged with Toby in the bedroom and had ignored her, at Toby's behest, and Francie had gone away without using her key. Never to be seen alive again.

Gwen was unable to get over this part of things, this was the part where her grieving process got stuck. To the point where she could no longer go to bed with Toby without remembering it all vividly.

Toby was being patient with her, he was not insensitive, but it had been nearly six months now and he was growing weary and frustrated. He was making murmurings about parting from her.

At that stage in the diatribe Nancy always rose to make fresh tea, or pour fresh sherry or whatever it was they were drinking. But of course it was a mere palliative. A salve to Nancy's need to break from the awful gloom arising out of Gwen's mood, the morbidity that engulfed the room like a slow poisonous gas.

Today it was particularly bad. Gwen was without her make-up, and Nancy could not remember seeing her without her make-up since she was a little girl visiting the newly wed Ged and Nancy in their farmhouse.

This lack of eye enhancement made her look bland, as if the real Gwen had left the room and deputised a tepid look-alike to pose as herself.

Nancy at once saw the lack of cosmetics as a bad sign. She followed Gwen into the small room off the kitchen where Gwen appeared to be hiding or taking refuge.

From above came the sounds of things thumping on the floor and Nancy looked upward to the ceiling and Gwen noticed while getting milk from the fridge.

"It's Toby . . ." she paused and Nancy held her breath. "He's packing to leave . . . he's finally leaving me!"

Nothing more was said for a while and Nancy got onto a chair near the kitchen island and put her feet on the staves and remained quiet.

"I think it's for the best . . . . I'll never be able to let him touch me again!" Gwen said eventually.

"Well . . . maybe in time . . ." Nancy ventured.

Gwen swung around. "In time . . . . men like Toby don't understand such sentiment Nan! . . . he's barely thirty five!"

Nancy drew breath and tried to recall how old Gwen herself was. Possibly forty three or four? She was the youngest of the Norrington women so she would not be more than forty six or seven at any rate!

"Best let him be then!" she said the words so quietly they were hardly able to take to the air. She was afraid—exactly of what, she did not know.

She was afraid for herself and for Gwen. And suddenly she saw she was afraid for all women. For all women who had to juggle the demands and the feelings and the angles of complex living. Afraid of their men and of what their men may do, or not do. Afraid of doing the wrong thing themselves. Afraid of not being able to do right for doing wrong. That was what she was afraid of.

"You've got to shake out of this Gwen! . . . . you've got to do something . . . him leaving changes everything! You've got to do something new!"

"Ha!" said Gwen. "Have I now!"

"Yes . . ." Nancy sprung off the chair and ran over to Gwen. "If you don't do something you'll become old overnight . . . you'll wither and shrivel!"

"Cheers Nancy!"

"You know what I mean! You must step back and take a long look at yourself! You can't let Francie's death have been in vain! . . . . I just did something drastic! . . . I just did something I would never have dreamt I could do . . ." she faltered and paused; she might have been carried away by the moment but she was not daft.

"What did you do?" asked Gwen, a spark of curiosity lighting her face from its dreary pallid mask.

"I have an idea! . . . . I'm full of them just recently!"

Nancy outlined a series of steps to a life changing plan and Gwen listened, without enthusiasm, but with a welcome relief from what was going on upstairs and in her usual frame of mind.

"We'll start a business of our own! . . ." Nancy was saying. "We'll use my existing right to land on the estate and my part of the shop investment and we'll begin our own business . . . . that way we'll be free of Ged and Jack and all the Norrington clan who want to control things, and we'll build something good! . . . You with horses, me with my baking and preserves . . . . Gloria with her soft furnishings if she wants it . . . but I want part of the land as an animal sanctuary . . . that's the only thing I am insistent on . . . the rest will take shape and grow!"

"What kind of an animal sanctuary?" Gwen asked dubiously.

"Small animals, domestic animals . . . maybe goats and donkeys too . . . just a few!"

Gwen stared, her naked eyes devoid of the make-up enlarging with an emotion that might have been incredulity or horror.

"I'm not talking about a safari park!" Nancy laughed. "You don't need to look at me like that! . . . it's not a new concept by any means!"

Gwen twitched a smile, or a half-hearted attempt at one. And then Toby emerged into the open room beyond with three cases balanced in his arms. They turned to look at him.

"Hello Toby!" said Nancy.

Toby looked at Nancy pityingly and then shifted his gaze to Gwen.

He was leaving her with her backward relatives and her country cousins. Assigning her to a life of boredom and repetition, but his conscience was clear. He was a man with needs!

"See you later then!" said Gwen, a finality in her tone that urged his exit.

She turned her attention to Nancy and said. "Nan, it's a lot of ideas but will it work?"

"Why not?"

"Because we will need money . . ."

"I have it! . . . I have the money . . . I drew it down!" said Nancy proudly, like a Wall Street broker. "I liquidated funds!"

"You are kidding me?"

"No . . . I am seriously not kidding you!" Nancy grinned widely.

She saw a fleeting look of amusement cross her sister-in-law's features, a flicker of the former smile.

"Can't do any harm to talk . . . can't harm to chew the fat!" Gwen said.

Toby's car doors were banging in a way which betokened his final exit. Gwen seemed not to notice and stared at Nancy like a child waiting to hear the remainder of a good story. For the first time in months Gwen was embracing a new topic other than the death of her daughter.

SIXTEEN

The day Alfie left for the bigger world he said nothing to anyone. He just left.

The morning of his departure he carried on as normal. It was the same morning that his father and Ged discussed Nancy's behaviour.

"She's up to some'at!" said Ged as they drove the tractor.

Ged was along for the ride and the company, whereas this part of the industry was serious responsibility to his father who was a self-appointed expert on agricultural machinery. He bought journals and belonged to some organisation which met twice a month to discuss them. No wonder his mother was always shopping online and swigging wine.

"She's drawn a hell of a lot of money down from the funds! . . . . and she won't say where she's putting it . . ." Ged was explaining. "I got a quick glance at a letter she left lying around . . . before she had chance to hide it!"

"As far as I know she made transfers to her personal account! but she can't be leaving it there!" said Jack distractedly.

Ged looked at his brother while pushing his hat around his head. A silence grew.

Alfie cleared his throat ominously and glared at Ged. "Maybe she's leaving you!" he said laconically.

"Give over!" interjected his father. "Who asked for your opinion!"

"No-one, as usual," muttered Alfie, "and she couldn't be blamed if she did!"

The two men were speechless as Alfie jumped from the tractor turning onto the northern acreage.

"Hold up . . ." Jack said, "We're starting at the far end first off . . . you're too soon!"

"I forgot something!" Alfie improvised.

"You can't go back now, there's work to do!"

"I forgot my phone . . . . I gotta find it . . . it's worth quite a bit of money and its not insured!"

They watched as Alfie ran down towards the main road in the direction of his parents home.

"We'll just have to meet the others and get on without him!" Jack continued to drive the tractor to the other end of the acreage where a gang of men waited. Ged's mind was on his wife. He ran various aspects of her odd behaviour past his younger brother who reserved judgement and nodded in something approaching sympathy. Whereas in reality he felt that Ged had brought it upon himself, whatever Nancy was now doing, for Ged took no interest whatsoever in anything outside of his own immediate concerns and had not the slightest desire to move beyond the rigid agenda of his everyday life in all its ways.

Responsible for the main company accounts, Jack had seen how much money Nancy was bringing down, but what she did with it was anyone's guess; the privacy of her personal bank account was not within his remit.

"She can't be giving it to Francine . . . not now!" he ventured after a moment or so, slowing the tractor and turning it.

Ged groaned, shuffled his bulk about uncomfortably. "It's that business as started all the trouble. She's not been right since!"

"Which of us has?" Jack jarred the gears of the vehicle so that Ged was pitched to one side.

Meanwhile Alfie had reached the farmhouse. He saw his mother talking on the kitchen phone and he by-passed her and went for the stairs. She noticed nothing. Her hair was wrapped in a towelling arrangement, she was putting on colour or highlights or whatever it was women did. He paused and watched her from the middle of the staircase and he felt a passing fondness for her, a mere hint of affection. But he did not feel enough to want to say goodbye. Why was that? Maybe he was unnatural!

There was no longer anyone to make him *natural*. No-one for him to love, no-one to cherish in his thoughts or his heart, now that Francine had gone.

It wasn't that he'd really believed Francie would ever marry him or live with him, or even sleep with him. He just needed to have the possibility there. He liked to have Francine around, to remind him what life could be when you loved someone.

She was gone now and it was his fault.

He could never turn the clock back. He would live with her absence all his life. There was no escape from his own mind. He knew that. He had done a terrible thing. He was marked, in the way of people who had fought wars or gone through terrible acts, and he had taken on the guilt like an indelible tattoo. It was only right that he do so.

If things were ever proven they would think him evil. And perhaps he was. He had limited insight into the totality of what had happened and who it had made him.

It may take him all his life, depending how long he lived, to see the broader picture. He had reacted, he had not planned or thought; he had seized a few moments in time and reacted to them.

He moved up the stairs, his mother's image and voice fading.

Fifteen minutes later he had cleared the farmhouse and the immediate vicinity and hitched a lift from a passing delivery van into the nearest town of Limetrees from where he could catch a train to the airport and leave the country.

The van driver might have given the only clue to what Alfie had decided to do, to where he could have gone. Alfie had accidentally dropped a piece of paper on the van floor showing a road map of Scotland. Someone he had met over the internet had offered him work on a farm more remote than he ever could have imagined. It was perfect. He would stay there a while and then he would use his working experience to go to Australia or New Zealand or Canada. Somewhere at the other end of the earth. And if that didn't work out he would stay put in that small place, the Scottish version of where he had originated from.

The police enquiry had been suspended, but the speculation would go on; the questions people asked would be endless. He would be a legend for all the wrong reasons.

But at the end of his shift the van driver glanced at the scrap of paper and then discarded it with the rest of his litter into a refuse bin on a McDonald's car park. His brief interaction with Alfie Norrington might never have been, it was erased from time as one of those events known only to the two people involved.

*   *   *   *

And then there came the day when Gwen saw the horse in her lower field. It was near to her two chestnut mares, grazing peacefully. She approached it with care, not knowing whether it was schooled.

The horse allowed her to come close, to touch its muzzle, and it turned its gaze upon her. Then it bolted straight for the open gate through which she had just entered and it disappeared.

She stared and stared after it, and looked at her own two horses to see if they could give any clue. Later that day she rang around her friends and associates to ask if anyone had seen it or knew of it, and she learned eventually of the lone horse seen wandering the hinterland over the past year. The horse had become legendary. It was said to be possibly a phantom of some sort. But she had touched it and felt its breath on her!

She thought about it constantly. It took her mind off Francine.

Five days later someone told her of Heather's interest and encouraged her to get in touch with the former actress through the Golden Hind or the Soul Light Centre . . .

It was late in the afternoon when Heather and Gwen met and went into the field where Gwen had sited the horse.

May time, the day lengthening into night and still glorious. They sat on the slope of the pastureland and shared a large bottle of mineral water and talked.

Gwen listened to Heather's account of her experiences and her conversations with Richie and the events on the night that Francine had died. It had come as a shock for her to realize that Heather was the witness to the drowning of her daughter; she had only partially listened to the fact that there was someone beyond the Norrington men present; she had heard vague mention that Richie had met with Heather Gilbert on that terrible evening. But she did not think about the practical details during her darkest hours, she did not envisage anyone else in the scene as being important. Such was her complete absorption with her own despair. And even recently while she was working on the plans Nancy drew for their new business, her dwindling misery was still a narrowed tunnel of light through which any complete fact might be filtered.

Now it all came like a revelation of blinding proportion. *The horse connected her to Francine in some way.*

"Think of the horse as an emissary!" said Heather casually. "A symbol of Francine's continuing energy!"

Gwen felt the layers falling from her previous thinking, over a two hour period, until it was dark and until they were cold in the fall of the chilly night.

"There was Tess and there was Richie . . . and then there was Francine . . . and then the tragedies . . ." said Heather, her voice dropping to the lowest of levels at the last words.

"But all the while there was the horse!"

"Quite!" said Heather. "And there still is the horse!"

"It's like a thread then . . . isn't it?"

"Yes!"

"For whom?"

"For anyone who wishes to see the threads!"

"Or needs to see them!" concluded Gwen.

They rose and returned to their cars. Back to the individual lives they pursued.

And eventually the horse was seen again and again by people of all sorts and ages.

And Nancy and Gwen's commercial venture was injected with a tangential aspect bringing untold and multiple benefit—the financial being perhaps the least important. But significant nonetheless. And as time passed Ged Norrington made occasional appearances to his wife's new concern and told any interested parties that he had always encouraged the development of a place where such a sacred animal might make itself known.